THE MAJESTIC WILDS

Riders of Dark Dragons Book II

C.K. RIEKE

Books by C.K. Rieke

Riders of Dark Dragons I: Mystics on the Mountain

Riders of Dark Dragons II: The Majestic Wilds

Riders of Dark Dragons III: Mages of the Arcane

Riders of Dark Dragons IV: The Fallen and the Flames

Riders of Dark Dragons V: War of the Mystics

The Dragon Sands I: Assassin Born

The Dragon Sands II: Revenge Song

The Dragon Sands III: Serpentine Risen

The Dragon Sands IV: War Dragons

The Dragon Sands V: War's End

The Path of Zaan I: The Road to Light

The Path of Zaan II: The Crooked Knight

The Path of Zaan III: The Devil King

By Sword and Sea: A Novella

This novel was published by Crimson Cro Publishing

Cover by Chris Ricke.

Sign up to join the Reader's Group
CKRicke.com

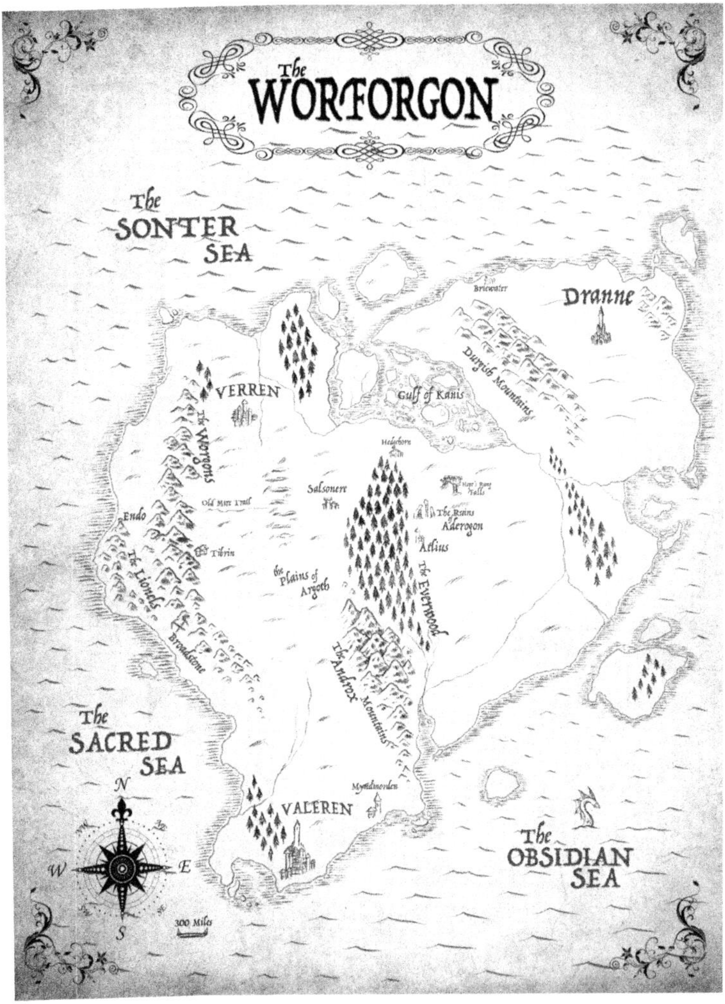

The WORFORGON

The SONTER SEA
Briewater
Dranne
VERREN
Gulf of Kanis
Durgish Mountains
The Worgons
Salsonere
Old Mitt Trail
The Ruins of Aderogon
Atlius
Endo
Tibrin
The Lionels
the Plains of Argoth
The Everwood
Broadstone
The Androx Mountains
The SACRED SEA
VALEREN
The OBSIDIAN SEA
N
S
E
W
300 Miles

PART I
THE LITREONS

Chapter One

Fire rained down from the sky with a thundering intensity, exploding on the ground just south of them with a roaring boom. The ground shook beneath their feet in the rocky plains, crumbling small stones down the broad tan boulder they were hiding behind.

"Damned kings!" Corvaire roared. "Don't they know what is really going on in their own lands?"

Another explosion blasted to the south again, as Stone, Ceres, and Adler each covered the sides of their heads with their cupped hands, even though it did little to stop the already-ringing in their ears. Mud, their canine friend stood out in the field beyond the rock, fearlessly barking.

Since they'd left the mountaintop city of Endo, which the Dark King Arken had burned asunder, they'd been traveling the better part of two weeks on the grassy plains of Argoth. They'd been two long weeks of thirst, struggling to get damp wood aflame at night, and aching blisters on their worn feet.

On the other side of the boulder men screamed out, meshing with the metallic clashing of clanging swords. Stone, with his long black hair pulled back behind his head, leaned out and looked out at the battle with his pale skin glistening in the light of the bright sunlight overhead.

A warm breeze blew past, rustling his hair at his back as he watched the two legions of soldiers colliding into each like a strong, blasting wave onto an immense sharp rock out at sea. Horses neighed and whimpered as they carried armored soldiers with spears and swords throughout the swaths of enemy soldiers.

"What do you see?" Adler asked, with his tan skin—slightly dusted with fresh dirt looking up at Stone with his light blue eyes like sparkling marbles under his thick brown hair. "How many of them are out there?"

"One's outmanned," Stone said. Out in the battlefield, the roars were accompanied with blood-raged screams of pain and agony. "Two thousand, perhaps. They bare the yellow and red banner of Verren."

"And the other army is of Dranne, I would wager every-thin' I own on it," Ceres said, with her emerald-green eyes glaring at Stone. "Fools! What've King Tritus and King Roderix II got to win when we're all dead from the Neferian riders dragonfire incinerating us all?" Her straight blond hair blew past her shoulders as her pale brow furrowed and the freckles on her cheeks were visible in light of the bright sun.

"The army of Dranne perhaps fights with twelve-hundred," Stone said. "They're going to get crushed. The army of Tritus is too many."

Mud continued his relentless barking at the battle out in the valley.

"Get back here, dog," Alder said. "C'mon now. Get over here!" But the dog didn't even glance back at him.

"That mutt never listens," Ceres said.

Drâon Corvaire, the stoic man behind Ceres looked out into the fields to the north, with his shadowy-hazel eyes gazing deeply for a path to take out of sight of the battling armies. His wavy black hair wove down past his shoulders and his strong hand held the dark-brown leather grip of the sheathed sword at his side with the ball of ivory glistening at the tip of its hilt. "We should leave this place. There's too much for us to do to get wrapped up in some bloody civil war that no one is going to win." His black beard covered the disdain he had for the kings as he growled.

Stone looked back at him, as Corvaire's gaze then shot back south. Corvaire rushed over to Stone's side, and Mud stopped barking, running back to the safety behind the tan boulder in the long, rolling fields.

"You hear that?" Corvaire said softly, yet with a low gruff.

"No—" Stone said, listening for anything different down in the bloody battle below.

"Shh," Corvaire said, and it was then Stone saw Corvaire wasn't looking down at the battlefield, but up to the sky.

A wicked fear ripped through Stone's stomach as the shadow appeared out in the distant sky. From that distance it looked like a wide-winged bird—an albatross perhaps—but Stone knew better. It didn't take long for him to see the long neck and tail of the beast as it flew toward them.

The creature finally let out its bone-chilling roar, the intensity and power from it let everything within a thousand miles know what was coming.

"We've got to be moving." Corvaire pushed Stone back past the boulder. "Now!"

He rushed them all out from the safety of the rock out into the northern fields as loud horns blew from both armies in the valley. Stone looked back over his shoulder as soldiers in heavy armor scattered like ants about to be stomped upon by a mighty boot.

The soldiers barked orders at one another: 'retreat,' 'regroup,' 'it's coming…' 'to the forests,' 'find shelter!'

Corvaire's strong fingers gripped Stone's bicep, latching on and pulling him forward. "Come now, you fool, run. Run!"

They ran as fast as they could toward a small wood a mile or so to the north. They had little worry of being spotted by the grizzly soldiers behind, for there was a far more deadly foe swooping in from the sky.

Another roar burst out from the beast, with a trail of black fire coursing out of its maw as the glass-shattered sound echoed throughout the lands. Stone looked back again as the dark dragon glided down upon the army—soaring just overhead as the men screamed and ran as quickly as their legs could carry them.

Upon the dark dragon's back Stone then saw the rider.

"Is it him?" Stone asked as they ran. "Is it King Arken?"

It was only days ago when Stone and his friends were upon the mountain where the Mystics lived. King Arken showed up upon his massive Neferian, killing the three Majestic Wilds, women who'd lived for thousands of years with magical powers that had deemed Stone the one to help kill the Dark King.

"No," Corvaire said. "It's one of his other riders, another one of the Runtue people."

The dragon, with its long arms draped with long, leathery wings glided back up and arced back around to the army. Its long gray, scaly body was lined with dark blue streaks down its back with a dark underside. Its head was angular and wide, with strong jaws and beady, yellow eyes. Its rider sat upon its back like a statuette, fixed to the dragon by a strong magic.

The armies scattered as fast as they could, creating a wide divide between them as horses carried the luckiest of them. The dragon swooped down again. That time however, it didn't turn back. A dark plume of searing, black dragonfire blasted the army of King Roderix. It was a sight Stone wished he'd never have to witness. Dozens were burned in the fire, not even able to let out screams for help, as they were incinerated.

As the grassy plains burned, the Neferian took back to the sky, lowering its left wing, and curving back around to the army of King Tritus.

"It's gonna' kill them all," Ceres said, looking at Corvaire for an answer to help. "Use your magic, can't you cast a spell to help them?"

"All we can do is save ourselves," he yelled. "Now run!"

As the dark dragon and rider decimated the warring armies behind them, Stone thought about the grizzly way King Arken and his massive Neferian burnt the Wild Majestics away to nothing but smoldering flesh and bone. He couldn't help but feel a rage within him, wanting to indeed be the one to help defeat the Dark King and avenge their deaths. And there he was, running away from another one of them. But he knew he had no weapon to defeat such a monster. Stone had no magic, no magical weapons, and no hints as to *how* to defeat them. He didn't even know who he truly was, nor did he know if he'd ever find out.

They reached the woods; rushing in and ducking into the shadows as they stopped to catch their breaths. Corvaire remained calm as he peered out past the trees out at the giant dragon crisscrossing the plains, blasting great plumes of black fire upon the lands.

"Look!" Adler pointed up to the sky as a dark shadow flew overhead, above the trees. The leaves blew over them and strong gusts of wind blasted down upon them as the large, red-scaled head emerged, followed by a long, strong neck. Soon the red dragon with long white horns studded down its back and wings was fully visible, flying out toward the dark dragon, still burning the warring armies.

"It's going to save them," Ceres said with an uplifted voice. "There's a chance some of them will get out alive."

"Some may," Corvaire said gruffly. "But I fear that red dragon won't live to see the light the moon will cast this eve."

"It has a chance!" Stone said. "Grimdore—she lived after her fight with King Arken's dragon."

"Only just by the luck of Crysinthian's golden graces," Corvaire said. "And don't forget she was the first dragon to survive a fight with one of them."

As the red dragon flapped its mighty wings, belted out a raging roar at the dark dragon below, Adler asked, "How long until Grimdore is healed by the seas and will return?"

"There's no telling." Corvaire peered out past the trees as the two dragons collided in a violent snapping of sharp teeth and flapping wings that drowned out every other sound in the lands. "Grimdore's never been injured like that as far as I know. She's going to be needing to take her time to get back to full strength, though. We're going to need her again, and we're going to need every bit of power in that legendary sea dragon."

The red dragon screeched as it blew a blast of bright orange dragonfire upon the dark dragon, as the Neferian flapped its wings, rising higher into the air. Its neck brimmed with a dark glow as smoke smoldered out of the dark dragon's mouth, with its angled head poised at the red dragon who was flying up at it, still blowing its searing dragonfire.

The Neferian let out a devastating plume of its black fire upon the other dragon, pushing it back with an explosion of fire that overwhelmed the smaller dragon.

The red dragon staggered back in the sky, and the rider upon the back of the Neferian whipped its reins, sending the much larger—and stronger—dragon rushing down at the red one. It caught it quickly and tore its strong claws into the other dragon's neck, who roared out, with fire still raging out the sides of its mouth. It fought to break free from the massive dragon's grasp, as the red dragon bit at its neck and throat, but even with its wild thrashing and roars, the long arms of the dark dragon proved far too strong to let go of it.

"Oh no," Ceres sighed. "Not again. Not another one!"

The Neferian pulled its head back, preparing to blast another plume upon the red one, and Stone had seen what it did to the smaller dragons from that distance.

Ceres turned her head away as the Neferian let its black fire rip down onto the red dragon's head, enveloping it in smoldering heat. The red dragon belted out a painful, angry roar that soared into the sky, out into the valley, out to the mountains and deep into the woods, until… like nearly every other dragon that flew in from the other continents to fight off the Neferian, its roar faded to nothing. And as the Neferian's fire extinguished, its giant maw opened, snapping its jaws down around the head and neck of the red dragon, pulling back violently until the smaller dragon's head was ripped from its body.

The dark dragon relaxed its grip upon the red dragon's body, letting it hurtle back to the plains as it gulped its head down its long neck.

Stone and his friends watched in horror as the Neferian flapped its wide wings in victory and the warring armies continued to yell out, scattering as best they could into the plains. It was then the dark dragon flew back down, continuing its deadly blasts of searing black fire upon the armies.

Chapter Two

After a long, dreary night in the forest of scattered cries for help and of long deaths down in the valley, they left the tree line back out onto the plains. They were all weary and hungry—ready to get away from the dying armies of the two kings. Back at their makeshift camp, where none of them went off deep enough into slumber to find good rest, they huddled into their thin blankets remembering the gruesome death of the red dragon.

Stone made sure to look back in the direction of the valley and the skies all around them, searching for the wide wings of death, and luckily saw none. Corvaire didn't seem at all weathered or downtrodden, instead he walked at a steady pace to the north.

"Is this where we're going to start our search?" Ceres asked finally, breaking the long silence.

"In a sense," Corvaire said as he took long strides.

"What do you mean?" Adler asked. "You said you had a secret way of finding them. You know they'll be northward, then?"

"No."

"Then..." Stone said. "Wait... then what are we doing heading north? Is there something we don't know about them?"

"There's a lot you don't know," Corvaire said with keen eyes. "At least not yet."

"Are you going to tell us?" Ceres asked. "I really want to learn how to cast magic spells like you can."

"Not all can learn to cast, but I'll teach you what I can, in what time we have together. And as for where we're heading, do you remember what the Old Mothers told you about what they were going to do for you up in Endo Valair?"

"They said they were going to teach us magic and tell us about the past," Stone said, and then his tone turned somber. "Before... before he killed them..."

"Yes." Corvaire turned to look at them as his tan face was lit in the light of the rising sun and the green grasses swayed at his boots. "But what *else* did they say?"

"We're going to Verren!" Adler said with a wide smile.

Corvaire nodded, turned and walked northward again.

"Verren?" Stone asked. "What's in...?" But that's when it hit him. He remembered the Old Mothers, otherwise known as the Wild Majestics, had told them that they were also to get finely crafted weapons. But at the time he remembered them saying they were *going* to get those crafted in Verren. Now he remembered the three wise women had known they were coming to the mountain and had already sent off someone to get them crafted by a renowned armorer there.

"We're going to get our weapons that they told us about, aren't we?" Adler said excitedly, pulling his sword out and swiping it through the air, thrusting, stabbing and parrying.

"Oh, grow up, will ya?" Ceres said.

"Never!" Adler proclaimed as he swash-buckled with the wind.

"Verren," Stone whispered to himself, looking back at the

hundreds of fallen soldiers back behind them from the same city. "Is it going to be safe there? I don't want to lose any more friends. I'll go alone into the city if I need to."

Corvaire smirked. "We're going to be just fine. Just do yourselves all a favor, and don't get eaten before we get there."

They trudged on for the better part of a half hour before Ceres finally spoke what Stone could tell was lingering on the tip of her tongue.

"Corvaire," she said.

"Magic takes time," he said without hesitation. "It can take years, if you're even able to wield it. In fact…" he turned and gave her a dark glare. "If you try to use it before you're ready, I've even seen some your age burst into a puff of dust."

Ceres scratched her cheek nervously and glanced at Stone, who only shook his head with an entertained smirk. Corvaire turned back around and continued walking. She kicked a patch of dry dirt. Mud ran up to her and panted as she petted his black-furred head with the white spot over one of his eyes.

"Just be a little patient," Stone said. "I'm sure he's got more than a plenty on his mind."

"Sir, is there anything we can do to help find the new Mystics?" Adler asked Corvaire. "You said you had a secret way of finding them, but if there's anything we need to be doing—"

"There's nothing anyone can do, except wait," he said.

"How will ya know?" Ceres asked. "How will anyone know?"

"The way I will know, actually has to do with your other question, Ceres."

They could all tell she was about to burst at the seams from that.

Stone and Adler exchanged amused glances.

"He said he's not going to talk about it now," Adler said. "Just be patient. We've got other things to be concerned with now. Let's get to Verren, so we have at least a good way to protect ourselves."

She didn't seem happy with the mention of that, but they continued on for the better part of the day. That was until Ceres caught a turkey flapping its way out of a tree. She pulled her bow out from behind her back, and with her second arrow —struck it clean through its heart from fifteen yards away. Corvaire turned back with an impressed raise of his eyebrows and an approving nod.

They decided to make camp there for the night, and Adler got to feathering.

THE CRACKLING FIRE warmed their shins and souls as Stone laid heavy, tired eyes upon its entrancing dance. It flickered and popped as he tore another piece of moist, fatty piece of meat from the turkey's thigh. Instead of placing that piece upon his tongue, he tossed it to Mud, who was sitting patiently next to him, but with his dark eyes staring intently on it. His front paws leaped from the ground as he chomped down onto it, swallowing it with one bite—eager for another. Stone then took another piece for himself.

That night upon the plains, they lay—or sat—by the fire, each of them wondering what the quest to find the new Wild Majestics would hold for them.

"What will we do when we find them?" Stone asked Corvaire, who was smoking off his pipe, glaring at the fire with his thick eyebrows lowered. "*If* we find them first."

"We'll protect them. Take them back to Endo Valair," the man said.

"Don't you think we should take them someplace else?" Stone asked with his arms wrapped around his knees. "Arken knows where Endo is."

"Remember," Adler said. "He always knew where Endo was. Him and the Mystics used to be friends."

"That was a very long time ago," Corvaire said. "King Arken is no longer the man he once was. No natural man can live the lives of men that he has. There's something that's changed him. There's something inside of him that made him... *un*natural."

"Corvaire." Ceres shifted her seat on a log. Her eyes reflected the warmth of the fire. "He said that they betrayed him. He said the Mystics lied to him. And you said that he lied to them. Can you tell us about that now?"

He took a deep drag off his wooden pipe and blew a great plume of smoke toward the infinite stars. "Few know that tale. Very few. I'm not quite the one you want to ask about it, for I don't know it that well. Marilyn told me about all that happened only this year, and she was far wiser than I."

"Marilyn," Stone said somberly. "How long has it been since we watched her pass into the Golden Realm? One month? Two months? Every day has been like a dream—or a nightmare—since you dug me up from my grave, Ceres. She gave her life for ours, and I'm not going to let her die in vain. We'll find the new Mystics; I promise her that we will."

"I think about her every day," Ceres said with her head down and golden hair falling in front of her pale face.

"Me too," said Adler.

"Aye," Corvaire said. "I miss my sister. There aren't many left in our lineage."

"There's none in ours," Adler said, looking around at his friends.

"You've no family?" Corvaire wiped his long black hair back. "None at all?"

Adler shook his head. "Armonde took me in when my parents died. Had no siblings. And I was too young to know if I had any cousins out there. He took me in and taught me the ways of bein' in the guild. When he died, I had no one else." He looked around at his friends. "At least I've got something else now."

"We know of your story, Stone," said Corvaire. "And we hope one day to help you unravel the mystery of your past." He looked at Ceres. "What of you, young lass? Any family anywhere to go home to after all of this?"

She shook her head.

"No one?" he asked.

She lowered her head.

"What about you?" Stone asked Corvaire. "You said there aren't many of the Darakon left. Just how many of you are there?"

"Not many at all in these dark times." He took a long puff of his pipe. "And with my sis gone, there's one less star in that sky."

Adler turned the spit of the turkey over the fire.

"Do you want to tell us about the Mystics and the Dark King?" Ceres said, breaking the silence after a long few minutes of listening to the rolling wind and the sounds of the popping embers from the fire.

"Let's save that tale for another eve." He knocked the ash from his pipe into the fire and laying on his side, pulled a blanket up to cover him. "We've got many nights and many days until we reach the city. It'll give you something to look forward to."

Ceres succumbed to sleep soon after, as Adler wrapped the meat in a thin cloth, prepping it for the next day. Mud had fallen asleep ages ago it seemed like.

Stone was about to drift off himself, as he trusted the dog and Corvaire to sense anything out of the ordinary on the vast plains.

"Stone?" Adler said softly so as to not wake the others. "What do you think? What do you think of this all?"

"I—I don't know," Stone said. "We've got to kill King Arken somehow. You heard him. He's not going to stop until I'm dead. We just press forward, figure things out as we go."

Adler nodded, looking to reaffirm himself.

Stone laid his hand on his friend's shoulder. "It's going to be all right. We'll take care of each other. You watch out for me and I'll do the same for you. And we both watch out for her."

"You've seen her fight?" Adler said in an uplifting voice. "Pretty sure she's as ruthless as a hungry snake when given the chance to bite."

Stone smiled. "We'll get through this. Until the end. We'll see it all the way through. The Mystics had their faith in us. So, we won't prove them wrong."

"Actually, Stone… they had their faith in you."

He was taken aback by that statement. He'd never thought about it like that before. He looked at Ceres sleeping soundly by the fire's edge. Mud slept snoring, and Corvaire's shoulders hefted as he took heavy breaths under his blanket.

What if I'm the only one to get to the end of this quest? I can't be the only one. I'll protect them all with every breath I draw. I don't want to be alone again, and I don't want to lose the only family I have left…

"The Wild Majestics met you and were going to teach you their magics," Stone said. "They had weapons made for us that could cut down ogres!"

"I don't want to learn magic still," Adler said. "I really don't."

"I bet you'll be the one to become some grand wizard they sing songs about someday." Stone laughed.

"And Ceres won't learn a single spell," Adler heckled.

"I heard that," Ceres said in a muffled voice.

Adler winced. "I was only jesting."

It was at that second that Stone caught something out in the dark, grassy plains. He leaned in, squinting.

"Adler..."

Adler turned to look where Stone's focus was, and they both heard the low growl of Mud as he stood up with the fur standing up on his back.

"You see it?" Stone whispered. "In the grass. Look. It's not moving. Looks like a stone in the field."

Adler looked around as Stone got to his feet, grabbing Ceres' bow with him.

"I do—I see it now. What is it?"

Ceres was stirred to get up to her feet, and Corvaire awoke, seeing them all looking out into the distance. But before he could stand to look over the grass, Stone was startled by the movement of the dark shadow.

The shadow leaped out of the grass like a quick-leaping frog to the left, to the right, back, and quickly over the distant hill within only a couple of seconds. But it was no frog he knew; it was the size of a man. And those leaps weren't small. They were ten or twenty-feet leaps. *That is no human out there.*

Chapter Three

The remainder of that cool night, they took turns keeping watch—keeping a lookout for the quick-moving creature or anything that it might bring back with it. Corvaire was first to volunteer, but Stone assured him he was wide awake and would be able to stay up for a few more hours. The truth was Stone was so startled by the wild-jumping creature or man, adrenaline was pumping through his veins, and he wanted to be able to keep his friends safe.

Yet when he found his eyelids weighing down like thick curtains, he nudged Adler to take his place.

There was no sign of the creature the remainder of that night.

During their walk along the plains the following afternoon, Stone kept his sight out to the vast grasses and tree line for any sign of the creature—yet he found none. He also knew it wise to keep his gaze to the sky and his ears intent upon what may come flying in at a moment's notice.

Their bellies were satiated with the remaining turkey and moistened with some fresh water from a spring that Corvaire found early in the morning.

A few hours after the high, noon sun, they sat to rest and dry their feet.

"Tell me again." Corvaire rubbed the stubble on his neck. "How did it move?"

"Well," Stone said, scratching the bottom of his foot. "It was dark, and I couldn't make out its body, but it bounced away like an insect, or a frog. It jumped three times in a wide pattern once it knew we were looking at it, and then it went out of sight."

"Was it crouched down?" Corvaire asked. "How long were its legs? Did it have long arms? Was it tall?"

"I—I really don't know. I guess its legs were bent I think—bowed out to the sides as it crouched. It seemed kind of skinny. Maybe as tall as Ceres, but who knows? It could be my height or taller."

"Does that sound like anything you know of?" Ceres asked Corvaire.

He groaned, then shook his head. "No. Very interesting thing, though. And it seemed to be looking at us… We'll have to be careful on our way to the city. Not only is King Arken after you, Stone, but I doubt the kings will want to stay out of the path between him and you. They're bound to be curious why he's after you. And if there's one thing close to being as bad in these lands as the Dark King after you… it's them."

"See, Stone," Adler said with a smile and his arms out. "You're famous! And you're only a couple of months old!"

"Adler," Ceres said. "I swear, I'm gonna smack you upside your dim head one o' these days. When will ya' learn to keep your bloody mouth closed for once?"

"Just trying to lighten the situation," he said.

"Stone's got enough on his mind." She gave a wicked glare. "He doesn't need you mocking him for his past."

"Or lack of past," Adler said slyly with a smirk.

With a *whack* that he didn't see coming, Ceres' open hand found the back side of his head.

Corvaire chuckled over to the side, and Mud's ears perked up at the sound.

"Say one more thing," she said. "Just one more…" Her green eyes were piercing.

"All right, all right." Stone stood up and waved away her aggression. "Thanks for defending my honor, but I can fight my own battles against this hollow head."

"Hollow head?" Adler groaned.

"You're lucky she doesn't have magic," Stone said.

Adler's body tensed at the notion of that.

"Not yet," Corvaire added.

Later, as the sun was setting to the west, and the steep Worgon Mountains were appearing to the east at last, Adler was roasting some purple root vegetables he'd found in the shade of a birch tree. It was no mouth-watering meat, but it would be better than nothing. Mud gave one look at him laying the elongated veggies around the fire and went off to hunt.

"So, what will we do when we get to Verren?" Stone asked, after fixing up a round rock at the base of his back to help him sit.

They sat in a circle as Corvaire lit his pipe and puffed on it. "Let's get there first," he said. "Then I know of a place to go and rest indoors, before and after I go and gather your weapons—when and if they are forged."

"So, we'll just sit inside?" he asked.

"That sound so bad?" Corvaire asked. "Who knows when the next time is we'll be fortunate enough to have a roof over our heads, and I don't have a sack of coins to put us up everywhere we go."

"I'm sure Ceres will take care of that for us," Adler said.

She didn't respond but gave him an icy glare.

"Easy, Adler," said Stone. "She doesn't seem to forget

much, and the first spell she learns may be how to give you bed bugs. Is there a spell for that?"

Corvaire grinned. "I'm sure there is."

There was a dim glow of lightning in the far-off clouds to the east.

Corvaire and Adler gave them a long stare.

"Should be far enough off," Adler said. "Shouldn't reach here."

"You sure about that?" Corvaire asked. "They don't look too friendly."

"We'll wake early," he said. "Find some shelter if we need to."

Once the blackened vegetables were soft and warm, Adler handed them out. They were surprisingly sweet, and Ceres especially seemed to enjoy them.

Then, without warning or indication he was even wanting to talk, Corvaire said, "So… about the Mystics and magic…"

Ceres shifted her seat to point her knees directly at him. Stone even scooted forward. Adler remained where he sat.

"The magics that we know of are based on the four seasons of these lands: Primaver, Sonter, Utumn, and Wendren. The Old Mother's referred to it as The Elessior."

"The Elessior," Ceres mouthed the words with an enchanting tone.

"The Elessior is one whole energy, but its parts are quartered into four. And only a portion of its powers can be summoned by one individual—with one exception to the rule."

"Exception?" Stone asked. *What's he mean an exception? I hope it's one that helps us out.*

"I'll get to that later," Corvaire said, before taking another long draw from his pipe. "Four seasons; four sets of magics. Can any of you guess how you know which set of magic you would get? If you can, that is?"

"Your birthdate?" Ceres asked.

Corvaire nodded. "If you are born on one of the dates of the formal Sonter season, then you'd be able to draw upon the Sonter sets of The Elessior, and so on with the other sets.

"So how do we know if we can wield our set?" Ceres asked.

"She's already saying 'our set.'" Adler snickered.

"Careful," Stone said. "Her slap may come in the form of a fist next time."

"Good question," Corvaire said with dark eyes full of wisdom and the ripping firelight reflected in them. "That's not completely understood. But what the mothers used to say is that instinct is like memory. How a baby elephant knows how to stick to its mother the day it's born, and how we know to suckle upon our own mother's breast is an energy welled deep down within us. And through that energy—or memory—there is a strength or weakness deep down in us too. It doesn't grow with age or diminish. It's either in us at birth, or it isn't. And it takes a long time to develop that into the use of magic. You all are…" He looked around at them. "You're all quite old to just be figuring this out. It may take years longer than it would take a child who could discover their magic within one year and begin to use it."

"Years?" Ceres asked. "We don't have years. Arken is after us now."

"Yes," he said. "That's why I'm telling you this. So that, by some miracle of Crysinthian, you may be able to find a clue as to the value of your Indiema. Your strength to your ancestors. This—if you have it—will determine the strength of your magic, if it is there at all."

Each of them looked harrowingly at Stone.

"Unfortunately, Stone," he said gruffly. "I don't know if you'll have the ability to wield magic."

"I don't even know when and if I was born," Stone said. "So, I understand. Please continue for Ceres, though."

Corvaire nodded. "So, once you know what magic set you

are in, then you can begin to learn how to syncopate with that set. But if you don't know which set you're in; for instance, you study Utumn instead of Primaver, you'll diminish your connection with Primaver—your true set."

"This isn't looking good for you," Adler said to Stone.

"I'm going to knock your hollow head clean off your shoulders," Ceres growled to him.

"It's all right," Stone said shyly. "Please continue..." Their gazes all went back to Corvaire.

"I have the Primaver Set," he said. "At its core, each of the sets are based upon one element loosely, and one animal type. Primaver has its roots in insects and arachnids, as well as in lightning and wind."

"You can call upon lightning?" Ceres asked.

Corvaire nodded. "I'm not the most powerful out there, but yes, I can use lightning. But my magic uses great energy from my own body. And my Indiema needs to regenerate itself. This comes from meditation. So, if you can use magic, use it sparsely, as you need to reconnect with your ancestors to replenish your Indiema."

"I follow," Adler said. "But this is getting sort of confusing."

"Now, I'm about to smack you," Stone said. "Will you just keep your lips sewn together for the rest of the night?"

"I'm going to throw you off the cliffs of Endo," Ceres said. "Just so you know. If we ever get back there."

Adler cleared his throat. "You're only bluffing."

"Try me," she said as her eyes flickered in the firelight. "I'm of the Sonter Set. What's that mean for me, Corvaire?"

"It means, you'll have the same set Marilyn used—if you can wield it. You'll have the magic of the world of plant life and of heat."

"Not really an animal is it?" Adler jested. "Plants aren't animals, are they?"

"You know what spell I will have, though?" she snarled with a wicked glare.

Adler seemed to realize at once what spell she was speaking of.

"Do not say the words," Corvaire said in a loud voice then. "You are referring to the spell of Searing Flesh? Do not ever say the words to that spell unless you've learned many other spells before that. You wouldn't be the first to incinerate yourself by mistake."

"By mistake?" Stone gasped. "That's quite a bad mistake!"

"Magic is dangerous," Corvaire said with a sly smirk. "You still want to learn it, Ceres?"

She nodded with a wide grin full of white teeth.

"I thought so, but we're going to have to take it slow."

She nodded again.

"Adler," he said, "you don't seem interested. But if you are, I'll teach you too. What's your birth date?"

"The twelfth of Novomb," Adler said. "Utumn set, I take it?"

Corvaire nodded. "You'd wield the magic of serpents and the ground itself."

"Snakes?" Adler gasped, shifting around on his bottom.

Stone and Ceres looked at each other and burst into laughter. Stone was soon tearing up at the thought, falling to his side. Ceres clutched onto her stomach at the sheer irony of it.

"I hate snakes," Adler murmured.

"Sounds like you deserve that," Corvaire said in a light tone. "Learn to move past your fears. That's what the mothers would have told you. It's what I'd tell you to do. Utumn is a powerful set, if you can wield it."

"All right, all right," Adler said impatiently to them, turning and waving the thought away with his hand. "Get past it. Ha-ha, it's funny. I know…"

Stone and Ceres wiped the tears away and collected themselves.

"One last one: Wendren," Corvaire said. "Wendren uses fur-covered animals and the cold itself. Those that wield this are often some of the most powerful wizards and sorceresses among us. Seretha was of the Wendren, and her Indiema was of the most powerful even known."

"Pardon my asking," Stone said shyly. "If she had the Wendren Set, why didn't she use it against Arken when he flew in and burnt Endo to the ground?"

"That is a good question, Stone." Corvaire leaned in as he responded as the fire seemed to grow to double its size and a chill wind rushed into their camp. "You see, that leads to a secret of the mothers, and of the Dark King. Do any of you have a guess as to why they ran? As to why they didn't fight against Arken?"

"So, they'd live?" Adler asked. "Figure out how to beat him another time?"

Corvaire didn't respond.

"I assumed it was because they were caught off guard by the attack," Stone said. "They weren't ready for a battle like that."

Corvaire then looked to Ceres.

"I would say…" she said, looking up to the stars. "If I had to guess… there'd have to be a reason their magic wouldn't work…"

Corvaire nodded slightly. "Go on." His long black hair blew in the cool wind.

"Either one magic doesn't work against another," she said. "Or one set doesn't work against itself. So, there were three mothers, each with their own magic. And none of them used them on the Dark King, or his Neferian. And, if you were able to use your magic, then that means… if yours worked, and there's didn't, then that may mean they all had the same magic. They all had the Wendren Set? And would that mean too… that…?"

"Does Arken have the Wendren Set too?" Stone asked.

"You're very clever, Ceres," said Corvaire. "Very clever… Yes, back when he was a man of the Runtue, Arken had the Wendren Set, so their magic wouldn't work against him, and his against them. That's why I had them run off and try to get to safety." He sighed. "But I failed. I failed to protect the mothers. That's why we have to find the new ones. I owe it to them to keep the new mothers safe."

"How?" Stone asked. "How do we find them? What's the secret you spoke of?"

"That goes back to my earlier mention of there is one exception to the rule of each bearer of The Elessior—for each user of it gets one set of its magic based on the season they were born."

"What do you mean?" Stone asked.

"There's another four sets to The Elessior," he said with squinted eyes at each of them. "Far rarer are they and more focused. These are the four that create those that become the mothers, and those that create those are remembered throughout the ages."

Stone, Adler, and Ceres were all anticipating what he was going to tell them next as Stone scratched his pant legs, Ceres twirled her hair, and Adler sat with both hands flat on his cheeks.

"At the corners of the four seasons; at their most concentrated points, the four sets are at their most focused, and create the other four sets."

The fire cascaded hot embers up into the air, blowing away in the cool wind. Lightning struck out in the east, illuminating dark clouds majestically, and the grass whipped all around them. Corvaire's dark eyes lightened as he looked deeply into each of them. Stone felt a nervous, yet warming sensation creep up from the bottom of his spine up to his scalp. *This is knowledge from the old world. These are the things time should have lost, but for some reason, right here, right now, we are hearing about the untold powers of what lies in secret.*

"The four sets are focused with four other sets, like I mentioned," Corvaire said. "The important ones to know now are, at the pinnacle of Wendren is the twenty-eighth of Juenar. That's perhaps the most powerful date known to us. That is the day that every mother was ever born on."

"That's one way to find them," Stone said. "It'll be difficult, but that's a clue."

"There's a much easier way to find them," Corvaire said, as all of their ears perked up. "On the opposite end of the calendar, those that are focused upon the Sonter Set have the ability to search the mothers out. They are called the Litreons, they are the ones who search out for the Majestic Wilds. The Litreons are all born on the eleventh of Augo."

His gaze went to Ceres.

"That's..." she said softly. "That's my birth date."

Chapter Four

"You're a Litreon?" Stone asked Ceres. "You're the one who's going to find the new Mystics?"

"I—I don't know..." she said. "I don't feel anything or feel any different since I've even seen and learned of magic bein' real. How will I know when it happens?"

Corvaire shrugged. "I haven't the faintest idea. You must remember, there hasn't been a new Majestic Wild in generations."

"Do I have to be able to wield magic to use this new set?" she asked him.

"Again, I don't know. But just to be safe, we're going to get you working on spell craft."

"What do I have to do?" she asked.

"So, you're of the Sonter Set. It's best to learn your set in that season, and as we're trailing off into Utumn—we'll do the best we can. First, while you're learning, take your time and touch all of the plants that you can: flowers, trees, vines, shrubs. Touch them softly, let them speak to you, and eventually you should feel their collective power. But for now, lay on the grass, walk barefoot, and also enjoy the heat of the sun and the warmth of this campfire. You're hopefully going to learn how to harness its power."

"So, what am I supposed to do?" Adler asked. "Pet snakes as they bite me and play with rocks?"

"Well," Corvaire said, waving his hand to the side. "Yes, without the biting of course."

The night was still dark, and the lightning continued to the east, flashing and sparking high up in the clouds. That's when they heard the first rumblings of thunder.

"I'm sure it's not gonna get near us," Adler said. "Too far off, and the winds aren't that strong."

Just as he said that, a gust of wind ripped through: chill and brisk.

It took less than an hour for the first heavy raindrops to fall on their heads, and Mud cuddled up into Stone's side. It wasn't long before it was a full downpour—making the fire hiss with each drop.

Ceres shivered next to the fire.

"I'm fine," she said with a serious glare as Stone looked at her, wanting to ask if she needed anything.

Stone himself was quite miserable. He had his hood up over his eyes, but his clothes were soaked through. The rain was cold and sharp, sending a strong shiver up from his spine. Mud even shivered next to him. Yet, Corvaire seemed to remain just as he always was: calm and collected. Yet, he was struggling to get his pipe to light, but eventually he did, covering it with his hand.

"You're not cold?" Stone asked him.

"Who's cold?" he asked. "This is just a nice, summer storm."

"We are," Adler said. "We are cold. I hate being out in the rain like this. I miss a nice warm tavern with plenty to drink and eat!"

"Verren is a little more than a week away," he said. "Then

you'll get some shelter and a warm bed. Just imagine you're lying in it now."

"I'm sopping wet," he replied. "How am I supposed to do that?"

Stone thought he saw something then, looking through the streaking drops of rain to the north. As the grasses blew in the brisk wind, he spotted what looked like a boulder. He thought he saw the reflection of two eyes on it, glowing a dim orange from the reflection of their fire.

"What is it, Stone?" Ceres asked.

"There," Stone said. "I think it's back..."

Corvaire slid his sword out slowly, turning to look north. Ceres gathered her bow.

"You see it?" Stone asked softly.

"Yeah," Corvaire said in a low voice, like a hunter seeking out his prey. "I see it."

"Should we go for it?" Adler bounced his sword in his hand.

"No," Corvaire said. "Let's see how it reacts to this..."

The three of them watched, and Mud got to his feet, growling at the shadowy beast fifty yards out—as it stared back at them. Corvaire stood then with his arms out wide, and Stone saw what he felt was best described as a flare in his eyes.

"Illietomus Creschiendo!" Corvaire said in a commanding, vibrant voice.

The clouds overhead circled, flickering with a humming glow. Then, as if he'd spoken to the thunder itself, a blinding bolt of lightning fell from the heavens down to the ground—off where the shadowy figure was.

Stone had to shut his eyes from the searing blast that shook the dirt at their feet, and roared with a booming thunder, but just after it lit the sky, he was able to open his eyes enough to see the creature as it leaped off to the side. The lightning landed twenty feet to the right, and it jumped left. He inspected it as if time had slowed.

The creature's arms were longer—far longer than a man's—they seemed to reach almost down to its ankles as it jumped through the air. But its legs were short and stout, powerful like a frog's. It wasn't heavy; it looked slender but wore clothing on its torso and legs. It had scraggly hair that flew back as it flew through the air.

What sort of beast wears clothing, but moves like that?"

"What is it?" Ceres asked.

They all watched as it scampered away back past the hill behind it.

As the thunder rolled away and the sharp lightning faded, Mud continued to bark, and as Stone told him it was all right, Mud ran off through the grass toward where it had been.

"Fearless, ain't he?" Adler asked.

"Yes, yes, he is," Stone said. "Glad he's on our side."

"I don't know what that thing was," Corvaire said. "Unfortunately, though, I have the feeling we're going to figure it out in the wrong manner eventually."

"What do you mean?" asked Adler, sheathing his sword, as the others did too, and Ceres laid down her bow.

"I don't think it's hunting us," he said. "But if he is, he's not going to get too close. He'd wait for us to all fall asleep before he approached. I think he's just looking. He's watching and waiting. And the fact he's come twice—that we know of—signals that he may just be spying on us. For how quickly it moves, it could most likely travel at a great speed to whoever was pulling its strings. If we do get the chance though—best to put an arrow through its heart. I don't care to be lurked upon like that..."

"But we don't know if it has ill intentions or not," Stone said. "It may just be curious."

"How curious is too curious?" Corvaire asked. "When you

wake up bound and being carried off by enemy soldiers; was that perhaps a little too 'curious' of the mangy spy?"

"Better safe than sorry, is what you're saying?" asked Adler.

"I swore to the mothers I'd keep you safe until the prophecy is fulfilled," he said. "I'm not taking chances with some weaselly rat like that sulking in the shadows."

"With your spell," Ceres asked. "Were you trying to strike it with the lightning?"

"Young lass, if I were trying to strike it, it would be dead on the plains now. I just wanted a good look at it now."

"Corvaire," Stone asked. "So, just to understand more about The Elessior… since you used a spell, and quite a powerful one, you would need to meditate to draw strength from your ancestors through your Indiema?"

Corvaire nodded. "I'll do it just before the sun comes up, for when the first light of the rising sun hits you when you're connecting to your lost kin, it's at that moment when the connection is the strongest. It's like reforging a broken sword when its rays hit your face."

"Any chance you can stop these incessant rains?" Adler asked him. "I feel like my shoulders are going to shake free off my body."

"Throw some more logs on the fire." Corvaire sat back down. "I don't see them slowing anytime soon."

Adler threw two more logs on the fire. "They're soaked, they're never going to catch."

Stone looked at Ceres, whose eyes were darting around toward the fire. He knew there was something on her mind.

"Ask it, Ceres," Stone said. "The worst thing is that's he's just going to say no."

Still, she seemed unsure as she wrapped her arms around herself in the dim light of the dying fire.

"You want to ask me something, child?" Corvaire asked.

"If I can use the Sonter Set of magic someday, is it possible that I'd be able to use it now?"

"Almost anything is possible," he said. "But it's near impossible."

"Can… can I try?"

His brow furrowed, and then he raised an eyebrow scanning her demeanor. "Don't know if it's a good idea. Bad things can happen from those who don't know what they're doing."

"Please?" she asked in a sweet voice.

Corvaire grimaced. "I don't like the thought of you harming yourself or anyone else."

"I'll be careful. I'll take it slow and easy."

He sighed. "Fine. But it's not going to work. It doesn't just come like this."

"What do I do?"

"Well, first off," he said. "You even notice it's difficult to get burned?"

"What do you mean? I can't be burned? That's not possible." Her wide eyes scanned her bare arms.

"While your friends would get burned by too much sun, and you didn't? Even though your skin is fair? While others would burn their hands on hot skillets, you maybe never had a scar to show of those little accidents?"

"Well… no… I never thought about it."

"Reach down, and touch the fire," he said in a strong voice.

She looked around nervously at her friends.

"It will feel hot," he said. "But you'll not get any burns. Go ahead. Try it."

"What if my Indiema isn't strong?" Ceres reached toward the fire, but looked back at him.

"Then you will get burned," he said. "But if there's any truth to my words about you being burn-less and scar-free then I believe you're going to be just fine. Now remember, it's going to feel hot, but not nearly as much as if I or they did it."

"Go on," Stone said. "Try it. Trust him. Trust yourself."

They all watched anxiously as she reached down with her slender, pale hand toward the withering, gasping flames. She then, with a subtle hesitation, wrapped her fingers around the top tip of a dark long flame protruding from the top of the fire. She looked at Corvaire and smiled.

"It's not hot!"

"I don't think it'd be too hot to any of us in this downpour," Corvaire said. "But the important part is you have contact with a part of the fire. At first when you're learning your magic set, you must realize that you have your Indiema, but so does the element or animal you're working with. That fire you're touching has risen from many, many lost fires. When you make contact, your Indiema resonates with it, doubling the bond with you and it. And the stronger your Indiema, and the stronger its Indiema, the stronger the spell. And fire has been around a very long time."

"What do I do now then?" she asked.

"Repeat after me," he said. "And when you say the words, don't only think about the fire in front of you. Think of all the fires that have kept you warm when you were cold and think about your grandparents and all of the fires that kept them warm at night. Think of the way that makes you feel. Are you thinking of that?"

She nodded, with her mossy green eyes staring wildly into the fire.

"Sparcus Naratul," he said. "Speak it softly but mean the words when you say them."

Her eyes narrowed, as Stone's heart pounded in his ears.

Ceres' mouth moved, and she gently said the words, *"Sparcus Naratul."*

Each of them glared eagerly at the fire, hoping it would swell up in dazzling, warm flames.

A minute passed while they each waited.

"Did I do it right?" she asked.

Corvaire nodded with a laugh. Adler laughed as well, but Stone felt his heart sink, and the chill returned in his body.

"I told you it wasn't likely," Corvaire said. "But don't fret. If it's there, you'll get it someday, and that spell will be as easy to you as spreading warm butter on fresh bread. Now, I'm going to get some shuteye. Let me know if Mud catches that beast." He laid on his side and was quickly snoring again.

"How does he do that?" Stone asked.

Adler shrugged. "All I know is I'm jealous. I'd give anything to get a lick of sleep in this horrid rain!"

Chapter Five

The rain didn't fade, the ground didn't feel any less muddy on their boots, and their hoods were completely soaked through. Mud came back an hour or so ago then, and laid next to Ceres, snuggling in cozily with her. Whether he was trying to warm her or get himself warmed was anyone's guess.

Adler had somehow managed to trudge off to sleep as the thick raindrops fell.

Stone shimmied his way next to Ceres, who laid her arm around him unexpectedly.

"This is one of the worst things one could be expected to go through," she said, as she shivered and shook.

"Yes, yes, it is." He rubbed his hand on her back to warm, her, but found himself pressing the rainwater from her cloak down her back instead. "Yes, yes If only we could fall asleep like them and wake up in the morning. Life would be so much more pleasant. To just be able to sleep through all of this… I could only dream…"

"If only I—" she said, but then stopped abruptly in a soft voice.

"It was your first time trying… ever! You didn't even know there was such a thing as real magic before you dug me up from my grave. Have a little patience, you'll get it."

"But how good would a hot fire be right now?" she asked with her eyes staring into his.

He looked down at the dying fire whimpering its last breaths before them as the wet logs grew wetter.

"It would be nice. It would be very nice to warm my hands. I won't deny that fact."

"Should I try again?" Ceres shivered under Stone's arm.

"I don't think Corvaire—or anyone—would approve of you trying it on your own," he said.

"But what would you give to be warm? You know we're not going to get any sleep. We're going to sit here all night until our bones shake from our bodies."

"Good point," Stone said, his head was being pounded by the downpour, and his eyelashes were hanging heavy drops from them. He wiped them away.

"Do you maybe think you should try?" She prodded the fire with a stick, trying to stir it back to life.

"Me…? You think I should try? Why would I do that?"

"Well, you are the one the Mystics said would save us all. Maybe with a little flicker of your fingers and a couple of words spoken, you could do it. Maybe it's just worth a try?"

"No," he said. "You heard what he said. If I've got any chance at figuring out what spells I would ever be able to cast —I need to figure out what magic set I would even use."

"Oh, come now," she said in a stark voice. "You could try. What real harm are you going do?"

She looked at him with wide, fluttering eyes.

"You heard what he said," he responded, moving away from her ever so slightly. "If I try to use magic from the wrong set, I could lose all of my magic—if I have any at all that is."

"But you don't know when you were born," she said.

"What chance do you have to finding it, if you don't even know where to start looking?" She rubbed her chin. "Maybe we could try using the set from the day you came up from the ground. That was Sonter! It could be that one!"

"No, no." He shook his head as the drops fell off his hood. "It doesn't feel right."

"Well," she asked, moving her head close to his. "What does feel right? With all of this going on around us, what does, huh?"

The first thing that came to his mind then; he did not say aloud.

You. You, Adler and Corvaire seem right. And Mud, too!

"I think we all need to stick together," he said. "That's something that seems right."

"How about a cold fire?" she asked. "That feel right to you?"

He paused, looking down at the blue flames that were barely able to bend around the wet logs.

"I can't," he said. "I can't. What if…? What if I'm one of the other sets? What if I was Wendren? It's the most powerful, I could be losing out on that. What if I'm Corvaire's Primaver Set? I could control lightning itself like he did. I can't miss out on that. I just can't!"

"Well, then, figure out a damned way to get that fire going," she said. "My toes are going to chip off!"

"What if… what if you tried again? Even if while they're asleep?"

"I'd rather you," she said.

"Why?" he asked. "So, I can burn the plains to barren dirt?"

"No," she said shyly, with her hands behind her back, swaying from side to side, letting her blond hair trickle past her shoulders.

"Well, why not?" he asked. "I already told you it was all

right if you tried one more time. Just don't kill any of us please."

"No. I can't."

"Why not? It was your idea," he asked.

Ceres sighed, letting her shoulders slump, and then picking them back up. "I don't want to fail again."

They both sat there silently in the rain for many moments.

The stars were far past the thick clouds above, the moon's white light was nowhere to be seen, and Ceres rustled her way into Stone's side. He pulled a cup of water up to his mouth and drank.

"You ever think about how life could be so different?" she asked, while still gazing into the dying fire. "How different would our lives have been right at this very moment if we were still with our families?"

That struck Stone like an arrow to the chest.

"I—I don't know," he said. "I don't know if I'm ever going to know that feeling."

"Oh!" she said. "Come off it. You know you had a family."

He waited for her to say more.

"Come now," she said. "You really believe you were born of dirt? How could you have survived that long down there without water and air? Something happened to make you be able to live under the soil. And that's something we are going to figure out—you and I…"

"Do you really think so?" he asked as the rain fell onto their heads and the wet grass.

"I know so," she said.

That caused one of the warmest feelings he'd ever felt deep down inside. It was a feeling he could only describe to himself as *hope.*

"We're all here for a reason," she said, looking foggily at the dwindling fire as it popped and crackled. "Especially you. Ya heard it from the mothers' own mouths."

"I couldn't have gotten this far without you—without all of you," he said. "Even Mud included. I'd be dead back there in Atlius or in the Everwood. Even that fairy, Ghost, helped you too."

Ceres glared out into the dark prairies. Stone noticed quickly, and his gaze followed hers.

"Stay low." She wiped the rain from her face and held her hood over her brow to peer out into the shadows.

Stone scanned the area but saw nothing.

"What is it? Is it the creature again?" he asked. "We should wake the others… have Corvaire let us get another peek at it…"

"No," she said quietly. "It's not the creature… it's something else. It looks… familiar."

It was then that Stone caught the faint glow that surely Ceres was alluding to.

It floated toward them like a firefly slowly buzzing down a shallow creek bed. It swayed back and forth as it made its way to them. It didn't take long at all for its blue wings to be completely visible in the deluge. Its wings fluttered angelically as if from an old tale, and her slender, pale body gleamed in moonlight that wasn't there. Her long, violet hair flowed behind her body like dry hair in a misty wind.

"Ghost!" Ceres said to the fairy. "What are you doing here?"

"Adler, wake up," Stone said, kicking his sleeping friend's boot.

"What?" Adler stirred. "What are you doing kickin' me this time of night?" But as soon as he rubbed the sleep from his eyes and saw the beautiful fairy bobbing in front of Ceres, he stirred to life.

"Ghost—" he gasped, getting to his feet quickly.

Stone saw that Mud was awake—sitting and wagging his

tail as he too was looking at the majestic fairy with the long purple hair and blue butterfly wings.

Ghost flew up to Ceres' collar and pulled on it, nudging her to follow.

Each of them knew not to hesitate when listening to the fairy who seemed almost divine in her intuition.

After all, she was the one who led Ceres to find Stone and dig him up, and she was the one who helped them to save Adler from those bastardly soldiers who shoved that horrible drug up his nose, taking him off while they were tied up.

"Corvaire," Stone said, but not hearing an answer as Ghost pulled Ceres away, he leaned down and nudged his shoulder. "Corvaire, wake up. Wake up."

He lifted himself off the ground with a grunt, looking dizzily at Stone. "What is it? Did that creature show its face again? I'll blast it to the Dark Realm so I can have but a little bit of shuteye."

"No," Stone said. "We've a visitor here with us—a friend. Come, she wants to take us somewhere…"

"A friend?" Corvaire wiped the sleep from his eyes. But once his keen vision returned to him—he saw her. "Oh." His eyes opened wide and the whites of his eyes glowed as the moonlight cracked through the thick clouds above if for only an instant."

"Come," Ceres said she followed Ghost's bobbing, something like a hummingbird and a bat's movements in the air.

"Always trust a fairy," Corvaire said. "Everyone knows that."

"This one is Ghost," Adler said. "She's our friend. She saved my life."

"She's taking us somewhere," Stone said as the blue lights of her wings bounded through the fields.

After a half an hour or more, Stone understood where she was leading them. Up ahead then, was a wide stream, and then beyond that was a thick forest with lots of brush and thick bushes.

They had to wade through the stream that rose to their waists, causing each of them to irk once the cool water raised up past their knees, and Adler carried Mud across, who surely would have been just fine to swim.

Once they left the stream and moved to the tree line, Ghost made quick gestures with her little hands to move into the woods as her tiny eyes gazed out behind them—back out into the fields.

Each of them ran in, ducking low as the rain continued to fall, causing a loud percussion-like melody throughout the woods.

"What is it?" Ceres asked Ghost. "What's out there? Is it that shadowy creature we saw before who jumps around like a rabbit?"

Ghost shook her head. She then put one of her slender arms out forward, and with the other one—pulled back with a small fist at its front. Her fingers then unlocked, and she shot her pulled backhand forward in a quick motion.

"An archer?" Adler asked. "Is that what she's telling us?"

"Damn," Corvaire said. "Get into the thick brush now! Can't believe I didn't sense their trail…"

"Who?" Stone asked. "Who are they?"

"Get into the brush…" Corvaire growled at him with intent eyes.

Each of them moved carefully to move deeper into the wood, lying behind thick foliage, large boulders or tall tree trunks.

"Do you see anything?" Stone asked the others. "Who is out there?"

"They're out there," Corvaire said. "Don't look for *them.* Look at the grass. Look closely at it."

Stone moved his head to the side to peer out through the

trees and rain, looking intently at the grass. At first all he saw was long fields of long, green grass swaying in the wind and behind battered by the falling rain, but then—he did notice something out of the ordinary. Thin streaks moved through them like snakes spreading out from its nest.

"What is it?" Ceres asked. "What are they?"

It was then that Stone saw what was behind the slinking grass. A bolt of lightning shot to the ground in the distance—behind the moving grass, and that's when he saw the unmistakable outlines of men standing out in the fields. Some had bows across their backs, and some had their swords drawn.

"Hounds," Corvaire said. "They're tracking our scent."

"Who are they?" Stone asked.

"Too difficult to tell at this distance," Corvaire said, glaring around the side of a tree. "One thing is for certain though." His dark hazel eyes peered into Stone's as the heavy rain fell. "They are looking for us."

Chapter Six

With his wet finger curled around the side of the thick tree he was hidden behind, Stone watched the men stroll through the tall grass, following behind the hounds. At any moment one of them could catch their scent, and the dogs would surely lead them right into the woods, he thought.

They hadn't dug in deeply into the trees, so it wouldn't take long for the hounds to rush in and find them. There were over a dozen soldiers, and as Stone was finally, fully able to see them through the rain—he saw the red 'V' on their sigils as they walked toward them.

"They're from Verren." Ceres stirred. "What're they doing out here looking for us."

"I'm not so sure they're only looking for us," Adler said. "You really need that many soldiers to hunt down three men—and a woman—our size?"

"I believe you're right," Corvaire said with a furrowed brow. "They may not be looking for you, they may be a scout party for something else..."

"They're after stragglers from the battle," Adler said with

certain surety on his breath. "Not only are they looking for the injured soldiers of Dranne who scattered, but I'd wager they're looking for deserters from their own troops too."

"They must've seen our fire," Stone said. "Even as frail as it was."

Ghost floated behind the tree with Stone, clinging to its wet bark, peeking around the side at the advancing troops.

A shrill nervousness ripped through Stone then as a loud *snap* echoed to his right, and he quickly saw that Adler had his boot atop a small branch at the base of the tree he was behind, and it had broken before he was able to leap off.

A horrid look shot onto Adler's face, and each of the hounds on the other side of the creek looked in their direction.

"Get your swords ready," Corvaire said. "Ceres, stay back and put that bow to good use."

As the hounds made their way toward them, leaving the plains and wading through the water to their side, they got up back onto the grass—all four of them—shaking the water from their fur.

Stone was nervous as his shoulders shook, not only from the deep chill in his chest—but he really didn't want to kill innocent dogs. They had no ill intention toward them, and they could just as easily be friends if they weren't hiding in the woods at night from them.

The hounds crept forward, sniffing wildly.

"They've found our scent again," Ceres said.

The soldiers on the other side of the grass had stopped at the water's edge, glowering into the dark wood as the hounds were at the trees' edge.

That's when Stone heard the quick shuffle of moving brush and fast feet through the forest floor. A shadow rushed right in front of him, heading straight for the hounds—who'd all halted their advance in curiosity. The furry creature ran directly at the hounds, whose back fur raised, and their teeth shown as they snarled. That's when the black-furred dog darted to the side with an astounding speed, leaving clumps of dirt flying behind it.

The hounds' paws left the dirt and they quickly trailed after Mud, who was leading them up the banks of the stream. The dogs were soon out of view as the hounds barked and panted. Stone was now looking at the soldiers, who were looking at the dogs run off, wondering what to do next. They seemed unsure to cross the flowing water or not. And as the hounds were still chasing after Mud, who Stone hoped was nimble enough to escape the four larger dogs, he watched the soldiers of Verren intently.

They were speaking between themselves, but at that distance, their words couldn't be heard. One was about to cross the water, while another barked something at him, and they quickly got into a verbal scuffle.

"You have any magic that can push them away?" Ceres asked Corvaire. "You got anything that will make them forget about tracking us?"

Corvaire shook his head.

"Be patient," he said. "We don't want to have to kill some of the soldiers of the kingdom we're heading off to in cold blood."

"We could go deeper in the forest," Adler said. "If the hounds don't come back, then…"

"Just be patient," Corvaire said. "And keep quiet."

The two soldiers continued their squabble, before one yelled erroneously at the one entering the water and trampled off as the remaining soldiers followed him off in the direction of the dogs—but on the other side of the stream.

Stone breathed a sigh of relief, as he watched the soldier entering the water turn back up the bank and follow his comrades with a bitter expression on his face—trampling off.

"Hope Mud's gonna make it back," Adler said. "We owe that mutt a cow's tongue for that one!"

"Why are these kings fighting in the first place?" Stone asked. "I thought they had an agreement to cease their fighting while the Neferian were here attacking the kingdoms?"

"They've been fighting between each other for so long," Corvaire said. "I don't think they know any other way to rule now. I don't even think they know why they are truly fighting one another anymore. Maybe for some more land? Some more citizens to rule over and tax? Tritus and Roderix II are two of the most blood-thirsty, bitter souls in all of these lands. The Worforgon would be a better place without either of them. Their queens would rule far better—and I don't know a thing about them—how much does that say?"

"How did it start, though?" Stone asked. "Surely someone knows why all these men and women are dying."

"There was once a queen who ruled most of the lands," he said. "And when she died, and the once-great capital of Aderogon was destroyed, there was an… opportunity. The kings then took up their arms to try and take the lands through force. King Tritus was one, and King Roderix the First was the other. Another king fell during that time, losing all his lands and heirs—that's how bloody this war has been."

"There's no end in sight, is there?" Stone asked.

None of them looked to have the answer.

"Come," Corvaire said. "There's only a few more hours of night, let's just be on our way. No sense in trying to sleep out in these damp woods. Better to rest in the sunlight and get warm."

They made their way back out of the forest, moving back out past the stream, hoping Mud would find his way back—and soon. It didn't sit well with Stone—leaving his dog behind like that—especially with the bravery that dog had shown time and time again.

They walked through the fields that night and day as the sun refused to let out its full brightness. The day remained gloomy and chill as they walked. At one point, Ceres even prayed to Crysinthian to return their three horses back to them: Angelix, Grave, and Hedron—who'd been left behind while they climbed the mountain to get to the Mystics at the top of the mountain.

Stone didn't think the god was listening to her that day, as no horses came. But luckily, they saw no other sign of the soldiers, and in a gleeful moment of thrill, Mud came bounding through the tall grass like a fawn and knocking into Stone, toppled him over as the black dog with the white-spotted eye licked his face.

An hour later they'd come to a wide road leading north, which they took to, and walked up the trail with the other travelers that coursed the veined roads of the western lands. Many were weary, downtrodden and in need of desperate luck. Others were pitched in wagons and pulled by horses or asses. Some appeared to be knights making their way back from the battle—each Stone and his friends were quick to put their hoods up at the first sight of any soldiers—as they'd had close to zero good encounters with any type of man in armor—save for Corvaire.

The longer they walked, day in and day out, the more signs appeared for the city up ahead, and after many days of weary walking, they saw the high tips of the kingdom appear upon the northern horizon. The crowds of travelers had grown to clog the road and they found themselves walking out wide, in the already trampled grass as more walked to the city than away.

"What do we say when we get there?" Stone asked.

"We say we have business with the armorer Holm Yederan," Corvaire said. "I've met him a few times. I know enough about him they should let us through, and if we've got a couple of coins to put some more weight on their purses, they shouldn't ask too many questions anyway."

On their way, Stone marveled at the size and construction of the vast city. Its outer wall wrapped immensely around its perimeter with high walls of thick, gray stone. Many towers lined its defensive walls, and the keep was distant at its epicenter. It was a sharp-looking, light-colored palace with sweeping buttresses, thousands of windows of an array of dazzling colors. It had hundreds of its own banners flapping in the wind and at its center was the white Tower of Empireodon.

The city of Verren had amassed its own sort of refuge city. Thousands had made shanty homes or canvas tent homes outside of its walls—while they hoped and prayed that they'd be let in someday for protection from the many dangers that then ran rampant in the lands.

They were funneled into a long line formed by the soldiers on the outside of the black metal gate that led into the city. Many were turned away, far more than were let through, and Stone noticed something quickly: the more ragged the clothing of those trying to enter; the dirtier their faces—the quicker they were turned away.

Stone and his friends wet their hands with the little water they had on them in their canteens and splashed it onto their faces and under their armpits. All of them pulled their hair back from their faces, and the soldiers took a quick look at them and asked then what their business was.

"Got business with the armorer, Holm," Corvaire said. "We've got gold to spend." He reached out to shake the soldier's hand with two tabers lodged in it.

The soldier shook his hand, looked down at the two coins and motioned with his head for them to proceed in.

"That was all it took?" Stone asked with a great sense of relief. But looking back he saw a woman sobbing with a small baby wrapped up in her arms talking to the soldiers who were motioning for her to turn around from the city and leave.

"Corruption has a loud voice," Corvaire said. "Even when it whispers. You'll learn that here. Don't think of anyone within these walls as a friend. Desperation has swelled, while hope has waned in this old castle."

PART II
ORPHAN ALLEY

Chapter Seven

The day remained overcast and dreary as they entered the city. Their excitement for a soft bed and warm bath was combated by the overwhelming smell of heaps of putrid garbage and mangy cats roaming the streets. Stone would trade a soft bed for the fresh breezes of the prairie, but in the tight quarters of the over-populated roads, he found he missed the openness of the rolling lands they'd left behind.

In the busy square, loud vendors shouted out with lively-moving hands to get the attention of the thousands of people that were walking the wide road that went straight through the heart of Verren, leading up to the palace of King Roderix II. It seemed to Stone people of every walk of life were living here. There were people with fine silk robes, people with servants carrying their newly purchased wares. And foul-smelling sailors and parents carrying their young ones as they shopped for food for their families.

"Follow me." Corvaire pulled his hood up over his face.

"I'd like to pick up one thing before we head off," Ceres said, eying the many tables full of all kinds of wares: clothing, swords, shields, beaded jewelry, ivory, sashes, spears, and candy.

"We can return later," he said. "Once the crowds have died down. But let's get settled in first, before I go and talk with the armorer."

"You sense that?" Adler asked Stone, as they were the last ones following Corvaire's lead. "You sense that we're being watched?"

Stone hadn't sensed it, but he looked around, not noticing anything—but he knew he wasn't the trained assassin that Adler was.

"Not us necessarily," Adler said. "But can you feel the eyes in the shadows, lurking… waiting for something?"

Stone looked around again, and that time, he had to admit he did feel that something was out there— watching.

It was then Mud rushed up between them, and then darted into an alley to the right.

I knew he'd make it past those soldiers without any issue.

"Come now," Corvaire said. "This way."

"Sure I can't stop just for a quick moment?" Ceres asked. "I won't be long, I promise."

Corvaire was insistent on keeping going and making their way to his safe place within the castle's walls, but he seemed to notice the glowing need in her eyes for her quick stop at one of the vendor's tables.

"Fine, but only for a moment," he said. "It's not a good idea to linger long on these roads for us."

Ceres pushed through the crowd toward the table she'd already had her eyes on. While she did that, Stone watched her hands as she made her way through. He'd never seen anything like it. It was as natural to her as walking itself. Her slender hands glided into pockets and purses like she was swimming in a gentle pool. He couldn't even tell if they were pulling anything from the pockets or not. But he did notice she didn't do it to everyone—there was a mother carrying a young child that was left free of Ceres' *inspections*.

Once at the table, her eyes were wide, and her lips were wet as she perused the many candies. The others followed her, and Corvaire and Adler scanned the area, keeping an eye out for anything that may prove aggressive toward them. She picked out a handful of truffles, some chocolate covered nuts with salt sprinkled on them, and a couple of clear candies twisted to look like rope. She handed the gruff-looking vendor the coins he asked for and they were back off.

Corvaire led them off the main road and onto a side road with white-brick homes and shops with the banner of Verren pitched on every corner. The road they were on was less crowded, but the dark alleyways were now visible, and it seemed almost every one of them were inhabited by many—and to his surprise—many were children.

"Why are there so many in there?" Stone asked.

"War creates orphans," Adler said. "Many fathers and brothers died in that battle back there that we saw. Kings don't care who fights or dies for them. It's all a numbers game to them."

"Its… it's so sad," Stone said. "There are so many…" The dirty children sat sitting against walls and were digging through piles of tossed-away things. Their eyes were so innocent, and they struck him like he didn't expect. It reminded him he had no family himself, and he could just as easily have been one of them if he were that age.

"It's just the way of the world," Adler said. "There's no helping everyone who needs it."

But Stone didn't want to hear those words. He thought differently.

There has to be a way to help everyone. If it means I have to find my magic through The Elessior, and find the strength of my Indiema, then that's what I'll do.

Corvaire led them down four of five roads, snaking their way up through the city until they arrived at a run-down, old tavern that looked like it hadn't been occupied in at least a couple of years.

"You've got to be kidding me." Ceres brushed her hair back as to look up at the disrepair in the window trim, the creaking door that swayed at its entrance and the torn curtains behind the broken glass windows.

"There are going to be *so* many dead cats in that place," Adler scoffed, while rubbing his temples.

Corvaire smirked. "Come on, now. I'm sure it won't be *that* bad."

"I think I'm just gonna go and head back that way," Adler said. "I saw a tavern that didn't look like a fart could blow it over."

Stone laughed.

"It will be an adventure," Corvaire said with a glint in his eyes.

Adler sighed, but walked toward the broken-down structure. Stone followed.

"I'll wait here," Ceres said. "You two make sure it won't topple over from your weight first."

"Come now," Corvaire said. "It may be more pleasant on the inside than you imagine now."

"Hard for it to be much worse," she said, walking toward it with a deep sigh.

"After you," Adler said to Stone as they were standing before the split door that hung off the hinges.

Stone shrugged and pushed through the door as it cracked free from the rusty hinges and fell to the floor, causing a plume of dust to bounce up.

"It's up the stairs," Corvaire said from behind. "Go on."

Stone went first, having to stride up the wooden staircase to the left, while stepping over the stairs that were non-existent every few or so. The stairs creaked heavily under his boots.

"No dead cats, yet," Stone said. "That's promising."

"If we find a dead body up there instead..." Adler said. "I'm out of here and back at that tavern faster than you can say—"

But as they got to the top of the staircase, they were both awestruck by the sight of low-burning candles along the wall. There were six doors—one at each end and four along the back wall.

"Pick a room," Corvaire said. "There's enough for us to each have our own."

The floor was pristine and intact—a smoothly sanded oak. The candelabras were a shiny brass, and the doors were all snug and closed.

"What is this place?" Ceres said softly as she joined the others at the top of the stairs.

"This is one of our safe houses," Corvaire said. "You'll find almost everything you need here: clean linens, some clothing, soap, quills and ink."

"How is this place not inhabited by those who could use a place like this?" Stone asked. "How is it that it sits empty like this?"

"Magic," Corvaire said. "It's hidden to those who aren't looking for it. To anyone else this would appear just like the downstairs."

Guilt gnawed at Stone's stomach.

There are so many children living on the streets that could be happy in a place like this. They could feel safe.

"Remember," Corvaire said to Stone then, sensing his mind was troubled. "We've got a larger-picture quest on our hands. Once we've accomplished that goal, we'll have saved hundreds, maybe thousands or more. Then—then, we can focus on helping everyone one by one."

Those words reassured him a bit, but he couldn't stop thinking about the children who needed help right then.

"I want the one on the end!" Ceres ran toward the room. "Any chance there is water up here?"

Corvaire shrugged. "I don't remember." He winked at Stone. "You'll have to go and see."

Ceres rushed into the room and let out a scream of glee. "There's silk sheets in here!" she said from the other side of the door. "I'm never leaving this room again!"

"We'll meet back up this evening," Corvaire said. "We'll have a sit-down supper and discuss what's to come."

Stone turned to Corvaire and asked, "Do you mind if Mud stays up in my room with me?"

Corvaire smirked. "Just as long as you clean him up first. You might have to change that dog's name once you get all of that road filth off him."

Before Stone entered his room, he went back down the broken staircase, out into the open city again—looking for the dog with the white-spotted eye. He walked back down the road they'd taken to get there. He kept his hood up over his eyes just to be safe as he called out for Mud.

He didn't see the dog but continued to walk, peering into the alleyways as the innocent gazes of the lonely children looked longingly at him.

Stone turned and walked toward one of the alleyways as the children scuffled to run away. "It's all right," he said. "It's all right." His palms were held out openly as he knelt. "I'm not going to hurt you."

The seven children slowed their retreat and paused to look at him.

"Here." Stone dug into his purse and pulled out the few coins he had. "Take this, get yourself something to eat. You must be hungry."

"What do you want?" a young boy asked.

"Nothing," Stone said with a smile. "Just get yourself fed."

"No one gives out for nothin'," the boy said. "We ain't going down to the cellars to work, if that's what you're after."

"The cellars?" Stone asked. "No, no. I want nothing from you. Who would want anything from you?"

"You really just giving us your coin?" the boy asked.

Stone nodded.

The boy inched his way warily to him, as Stone held out his hand with the six coins on it: one twint, two tabers, one quort, and two dinins in it. It wasn't much, but that twint would be enough to feed them all for a few days at least.

The young boy snatched it out of his hand and took it eagerly back for the other children to inspect. One even put the twint up to his mouth and bit on it to make sure it was real.

"Now remember," Stone said. "Get some food." He looked at what they were wearing then. "I'll come back tomorrow with more, hopefully. You need to get some warmer clothes and some shoes."

He then heard the rustle of a dog's paws running up to him.

"There you are," he said as Mud rubbed his muzzle on his shin. "Let's get you cleaned up. I've got a surprise for you!"

Chapter Eight

The following morning, after a short night full of new, soft linens, hard-soled boots, and deep slumbers after warm food and cool libations, they all left the shanty house. A new sun's rays felt warm on their skin as the blades of grass at their feet dripped with fresh dew. The smell of fresh coffee and bread flowed down the road from a bakery only a couple of doors down.

Corvaire had freshly shaved his beard off, as had Adler and Stone. Ceres had the time to shave her legs the night before, and Mud had been given a bath with frothy, soapy water. He didn't fight it, and that made Stone feel the dog either enjoyed being pampered like he was, or he had come from a home somewhere in his past—with someone who cared for him.

They were being led toward the keep and the high-reaching castle with its sweeping buttresses and many windows that reflected a golden sheen down upon the city. Inside the tallest Tower of Empireodon, Stone assumed King Roderix II glowered down upon his castle—and all who dwelled within its walls. Corvaire wasn't leading them to the keep though, for just outside its outer wall was the armorer the Majestic Wilds spoke of just before their deaths. And once they approached the keep's outer walls, they could quickly smell the smoldering heat and iron from the forge.

Ash Forge, so-named by the swinging sign just above its front door was a small shop with a handful of steps up to the wooden shop, accompanied to the open-air forge next to it with two people working in its inside while one of them dipped a red-hot blade into a barrel of cool liquid with a short and sharp *hiss*.

"Drâon," the stout man at the back of the forge said as they approached. "Hardly recognized ya."

It took Stone a second to remember that was Corvaire's first name.

"Holm," Corvaire said, walking into the shop with his hand out.

Holm, who was two heads shorter than their friend, reached out with both hands and embraced him. "It's been a hound's age since you've been here. You're early." Holm pulled back and gave him a sour eye. "You knew I wouldn't be down with these for a few weeks now. I'm backed up as it is. War's good for nothin'… save coin."

"I didn't choose to come this soon," he said. "Something's happened up in the city in the mountains."

Holm sighed. The stout man had a bushy brown beard, was balding but had long braids pulled back where there was hair. His arms were bulging with thick muscles and nasty scars, and they were bare with not a hair to be seen.

"Leave us a moment," Holm said to the other man working at the front of the forge—who put down the sword he'd just bathed on the anvil and walked off into the streets after a nod.

"What happened?" Holm asked quietly, tapping on the leather of his long apron.

"The mothers…" Corvaire said. "They fell. Arken came in

the night. He was after them… And finally, after all these years, he got the revenge he'd sought."

Holm shook his head as he dropped his chin to his chest. "Seretha, I'm so sorry," he said. "Vere, Gardin—you'll not have died for nothing. That bastard will get his someday."

"That's why we're here," Corvaire said, turning to the side and motioning with an open hand to the three of them. "The weapons you're forging are for them. Holm Yederan, I'd like you to meet Stone. And this is Ceres Rand, and Adler Caulderon."

Hold nodded. "Stone. Stone what?"

"Just Stone," Stone answered.

"I like it," Holm said. "Sounds like a powerful lad in your ranks. Tell me, what've ya got up yer sleeves. You all three wield The Elessior? Ya got training in fighting? Fencing? Grappling?"

"Stone here is a near master swordsman," Corvaire said. "Adler is a member of the guild, and Ceres is training in the Sonter Set."

"Who's yer mentor?" Holm asked, looking at Stone. "Which school did ya yield from?"

"I—" Stone began.

"He doesn't know much about his past," Corvaire said with his fists on his hips. "We're still working to figure out where he came from, and how he learned to use a sword the way he does."

"He's not…" Holm began with raised, bushy eyebrows.

"Yes, he is," Corvaire said. "At least Seretha and the others believed he is."

"I've only met them less than a dozen times," Holm said, "but I never knew them to be wrong."

Corvaire nodded, as a horse-drawn carriage strolled past the forge, and Holm gave it a nasty glare.

"Shouldn't be talking so loudly about such things 'round

these parts," he said. "Always there are eyes and ears in the shadows. But I suppose it don't matter much now the mothers are gone."

"Listen, Holm," Corvaire said. "We can't wait here weeks for their blades. We've got to be off to find the new mothers. They're our best chance of finding a way to stop the Dark King. He made his will known that he's going to kill Stone. And we can't let that happen. There's little we can do in a fight against him. We need those weapons."

"Problem is," Holm said. "Seretha wanted them made of Masummand Steel. Gotta get that carted in from Broadstone in the southern Worgons. It's on its way, but it'll be at least another week until it arrives."

Corvaire glowered. "Don't know if we can wait that long. It's not safe here for them here. They've killed some that deserved it but wore banners. If that knowledge reached Roderix, they'd *never* leave this city."

"Aye." Holm folded his broad arms over his thick chest and round belly. "Rare it is to find a soldier without their eagerness for the spoils of war, and far too many tickle their demons with powders and resins. They probably had it comin' one way or another."

"What other choice do we have?" Stone asked. "We could hide out if we must in the house."

Corvaire groaned. "I don't like it."

"Plenty o' other metals here," Holm said. "Hardened steel, galvanized, even Ironium."

"No." Corvaire sighed. "If the Mystics said Masummand, then we will wait for it."

"I'll be able to forge them in two days' time," Holm said. "I'll push everything else back. I'll get 'em done as fast as we can."

"Very well," Corvaire said. "And as for payment…"

"Already taken care of," Holm said.

Corvaire nodded. "I'm certain it was."

"How much does such a sword cost?" Adler asked. "I've heard of Masummand. It's the finest steel in all the Worforgon. As rare as red diamond."

"Often these blades are bought and sold in coin," Holm said. "If you catch my drift."

"They're bartered for," Corvaire said.

"Royal weddings," Holm said. "Traded for the betrothed, or even for assassinations. Things like that."

"What did the mothers trade for?" Adler asked, "If you don't mind my asking, of course."

"Why, what else would it be for?" Holm asked.

"What do you mean?" Adler furrowed his brow. "I don't understand."

Corvaire turned to look into each of their eyes. "What do you think this is all about?"

Ceres then spoke, "They've traded with someone, and in return the mothers offered the assassination of King Arken, didn't they?"

Corvaire and Holm nodded.

"You were the bartering chips," Corvaire said.

"In return," Stone said. "We have to kill the Dark King… but what if we fail…"

There was a long, still silence, filled only by the bustling of the crowded roads brimming with people shuffling from one place to another.

"Fail… was not part of the agreement," Corvaire said, hanging onto the word fail with a bitter note. "We're going to see this through to the end, and in exchange, you'll be blessed with some of the sharpest and most durable blades to be forged in these lands in decades. There is no 'fail' here. We're going to kill a king."

"Anything that's worth doing…" Holm said.

THEY SAID their farewells to the famed armorer and fell back into the crowds of Verren. Thousands of people made their way through Verren's roads like veins pumping life from the heart.

Ceres glowered at the many soldiers that stood in large packs like rats at the main intersections, looking more for laughs within their group than looking out into the roads to protect those innocent travelers on their way in. Stone knew she hated anyone who wore the symbol of a kingdom or king, and his own resentment toward them wasn't far off. Corvaire had instructed them to keep their hoods low as they were in the public view—and that they did.

There was a ruckus behind them, and just as Stone turned to see who was yelling, a furry animal ran right next to his left leg, carrying a turkey leg in its mouth. The man hollered at them to stop Mud from getting away with someone else's supper. Stone shrugged and walked away as the man cursed them. The six soldiers up ahead took a quick glance at them and the man, and two walked up to the man reluctantly. One of the soldiers looked into Stone's eyes as he passed, and Stone looked away… but not too quickly to look as if he was evading him.

Once they were a few roads down, into an area with fine-looking homes with angled stone stairwells leading up to them and their second story with wide patios rimmed with iron gates.

Then Adler broke the silence, with the question that was certainly on Stone's mind, and Ceres' too based on her quick interest in hearing the answer. "Who did the mothers make the deal with to get the Masummand Steel for us? Who had the coin to get it mined and brought here just for us? Or was it another favor for someone else?"

Corvaire glanced at him quickly, and then looked away with a dark demeanor on his face.

"Corvaire?" Stone asked.

He'd never seen that expression on Corvaire's face. His hair slightly covered his shadowed eyes and his jaw clenched. *What's wrong with him?*

"I don't know," he said gruffly.

"You don't know?" Ceres asked, leaning in with her arms outstretched.

"You'd think if anyone knew it would be—" Adler said but was quickly cut off.

"I didn't ask." Corvaire turned his head slowly with his eyebrows lowered.

They continued walking, as Mud ran up to them and walked next to Stone as they went.

"You didn't ask?" Adler asked softly.

Corvaire groaned, but then laughed. "You really have no qualms about stirring the pot, do you?"

"Not really, no," Adler said. "I'd say it's served me fairly well up to this point."

"Up to this point," Corvaire said. "And no. They didn't tell me, so I didn't ask. Some things don't need to be shared. Why does it even really matter to our quest? Or is it because you have to ask questions all of the time?"

Ceres said, "I think it's physically impossible for him to not shut his mouth, especially when there's some irking to be done."

"Does it not matter to our quest?" Stone asked. "Do you really think that?"

"I don't know, Stone," Corvaire said, with his voice then at its normal temperament. "Seretha told me she had gotten the Masummand for your weapons. And I nodded. That's it."

"But you knew how rare it is," Adler said. "You're of the

line of Darakon. You must know almost nearly everything about these lands."

"Not everything," Corvaire said. "But you don't learn by picking at those wiser than you. You just... listen."

That seemed to shut Adler up well enough for the moment as he crossed his arms over his chest.

"Yes, the mothers bartered for you to kill the Dark King, so that someone wealthy enough could front the gold to get you the weapons you'll need for the fight ahead. If there's anything with the possibility of hurting him, swords of this make might do it."

"But..." Stone said. "Dragonfire itself couldn't hurt him or his Neferian."

"I said, there's a chance."

"And we're going to learn our magic," Ceres said. "Can we study more this evening?"

Corvaire nodded.

Ceres was brimming with enthusiasm as she skipped down the road, and Mud rubbed his muzzle into Stone's calves as they made their way back.

Just before they arrived back at the shanty house, Stone pulled Ceres aside and bade the others to go on without them. "I've got a quick favor to ask of you," he said.

She raised her eyebrow, and brushed her blonde hair back, showing her freckles in the light of dusk.

"Do you have any coin you can spare?"

"What?" she asked.

"I... I have seen what you've been doing in the squares and on the market roads, I was just wondering if you could give away a bit for a good cause?"

"What cause?" she asked.

He took a step back and put his arms behind his back. "I don't know if you'll agree with it or not. But if you'd just give it, I promise it will go to a good place."

"Are you in need of something? Surely you're not talking about just giving it away. I've worked hard my entire life to learn my craft. I don't do it just to toss it off like some ol' knickers."

"Please, just a little… a few quorts?"

"I'll give you more than that if you'll just reveal this prolonged mystery to me. I'm not giving ya' shite otherwise."

He sighed. "Fine, follow me."

He didn't have to lead her far, though.

"Where are you taking me?" she asked, looking down the long roads as they started to glow in warm torchlight as soldiers walked down lighting the many along them.

"It's just right here."

"Right where, where are we…?"

He turned into the alley he'd given his own coins down into.

Her mouth fell open at the sight. "This is why I was asking," he said.

Looking down the alley, where the night prior, there were less than a dozen children with dirty faces and gleaming, hungry eyes—there were now dozens—and they were all looking at Stone.

"I said I'd be back," he said with a wide grin. "And look who I brought with me this time. This is my friend, her name's Ceres. She's an orphan too. She's like us."

"She don't look like us," one of the children said. "She… she looks like one of *them*."

"One of them?" Stone asked.

"Yeah, the lucky ones…"

Stone glanced back at Ceres; whose eyes were wet with tears. He grabbed her by the hand and pulled her closer to the alleyway with the children just inside its mouth.

"I'm one of you," she cried. "I just… I learned how to look like one of the lucky ones."

"Did you all get something to eat last night?" Stone asked. They nodded, and he even caught a couple of smiles. "I see you brought some friends." He laughed.

"Nobody's nice to us," another young girl said. "They treat us like rats."

"You're not rats!" Ceres said with her fists balled. "Don't you let no one treat you like that. You're stronger than they know. You're survivors. You don't need anyone to get what you deserve."

"They're still very young," Stone whispered into her ear. "They maybe *do* need someone's help."

"I'm sorry, I was so distracted staring at purses and candies as we walked, I didn't see what was really needed in this city. Here." Ceres unstrapped her purse from her side, and brought out a hidden one from between her breasts. "Here. Get washed up, and get some new clothes. Oh, and don't forget to get some more food. To look like one of *them*, you've got to *look* like one of them."

Ceres and Stone walked into the alley as they handed coins to each of the children with open hands. All in all, Stone counted thirty-one of them.

Thirty-one children we helped feed tonight, and all it took were a few stolen coins from those who wouldn't even look one of these starving, innocent children in the eyes…

"I'll get more tomorrow," Ceres said as they walked back to the shanty house afterward. "We'll come back again, tomorrow."

Chapter Nine

In the early morning rays of the rising sun, the pack went out again into the streets. On a balcony above, a young woman strummed upon a lute as she sang a song about a long-lost son. A group of elderly men sat under a shaky, small pergola smoking musty-smelling tobacco from pipes while they drank tea, and two children drew pictures on the stone-road with bits of black chalk as they giggled.

Adler didn't know where they were going, but he knew the rough area of the Assassin's Guild in Verren. He figured it would come back to him the closer they got. They were heading north through the city, but away from the keep, as they wove their way northeast to the outskirts of the city, and to one of the more, under-served, parts of the castle city. And Stone noticed the farther they got into that corner of the city, the less-polished the roads were, the more women of the night tempted on the intersections and the more foul-breathed men trudged down the streets, staggering and stammering.

Corvaire wasn't keen on Adler's wish to check in to the local chapter of the guild, but he also knew how the guilds operated—so he didn't resist too heavily—but he insisted on going along.

"You know where it is yet?" Ceres asked. "I'm getting drunk just off the fumes of that man's breath."

"It was on… Primy Road? Or was it Rhythm Road?"

Ceres sighed. "Those don't even sound alike."

"We're on Bloomington Road now, and there's a Grimer Street right over there," Stone said.

"Grimer Street, yes!" Adler said. "That's the one, it was on the tip of my tongue."

Ceres hung her head as her long blonde hair covered her annoyance. Corvaire clapped his hand on her back as they walked in that direction.

"Yes, yes," Adler said. "It should just be down this way a quarter-mile or so."

"Well, we'll just follow you," Stone said.

"Where the red inn falls in the shadow of the rising sun," Adler said to himself, "a small, brown pub lays in front of a stone, round distillery."

"You mean that red inn?" Stone pointed to their left, at the tavern, whose front awning was shaded from the sunlight.

"Aye," Adler said with a keen eye.

They made their way down to it, and quickly found the brown pub and distillery behind it. A sign marked it as The Seasons Distillery and Pub. The swinging door to the pub was open, so they walked in. It looked like a regular pub. Drunkards were howling laughter in one corner, and a group of women huddled by the hearth while they sipped on wine. At the long bar were a couple of old men, not talking to one another.

"This is the place." Adler winked.

"What can I get ya?" the barkeep asked as they approached.

"Was hoping to look at the distillery," Adler said. "Heard they make a mighty fine gin."

"Sorry, the place is flooded," the barkeep said, while cleaning his yellow teeth with a pick. "Bad weather we've had."

"The rain smells quite dry, and the wind look wet, wouldn't you say?" Adler said.

"Come on back in a half hours' time," the barkeep said. "We'll see if we can get 'er cleaned up enough fer ya. Or enjoy a drink while ya' wait."

"It's a little early for a drink," Ceres said. "I may go for a walk."

"Suit yourself," Adler said as he sat at the bar. "Stone? Corvaire? Who's willing to play me in a few games of cards?"

Corvaire seemed indecisive of who to stay with.

"I'll keep you company," Stone said. "You want to go watch after her?" Corvaire nodded.

A half an hour passed after a couple rounds of cards and more than a handful of drinks for the both of them as Ceres and Corvaire came back into the room, letting in a swath of bright sunlight that Adler tried to shoo away.

"I'll show you in, now," the barkeep said.

Adler and Stone both got up, wiping the wrinkles out of their clothes.

"What a lush," Ceres said. "You'd better hold it together in there."

"These are my people!" he said with a wide smile and glassy eyes. "They're gonna be happy to see us."

They followed the wide-shouldered, wide-hipped barkeep into a door at the end of the tavern, down a short hallway, and through another door with two guards on its backside. The guards didn't look like soldiers though, they were two women in light armor, dark armor with long, thin swords ready to draw if the need arose.

Inside the guild, again, there were long tables with many

empty seats and a few patrons having drinks or playing games of cards. There were two doors at the back of the room. And there wasn't a single window in the room. The torches made it seem like it could be anytime of night or day within there.

"Let's make this quick," Corvaire whispered.

"Someone will be out to see you soon, have a seat anywhere," the barkeep said as he turned and went back through the door which they'd come—leaving the squeal of rusty hinges behind him.

It didn't take long for them to be seated before they were greeted by a woman who'd gotten up from the far table. She had gray hair pulled back and had a large, rough burn mark on the side of her face. She wore brown leather armor wrapped in black straps. Her exposed arms were weathered and lean.

"How can I help you?" she asked in a raspy voice as she sat next to Corvaire, eying him up and down. "You look familiar. Have we met?"

"Don't believe so. I'm Adler Caulderon. We're stopping through to gather some equipment before we move on. We'll be here a week further."

"Caulderon…" she said. "Armonde's protege. I'm Lucik Haverfold, this is my guild here."

"Honored to meet you," Adler said. "These here are my traveling companions: Ceres Rand and Stone. The dark chap is Corvaire."

She eyed Corvaire again. Ceres and Stone nodded to her.

"Here to re-supply?" Lucik asked. "What sorts of materials are you gathering?"

Stone was unsure how honestly Adler was going to respond.

"Weapons," he said. "We're in need of newer swords for going back out into the wilds."

"Can't blame ya' for that," she said. "Blasted kings are

wanting to continue their idiotic fights again. Soldiers being deployed while the Dark King is flying around, burning whatever he chooses."

Adler didn't respond or know what to say.

Lucik leaned in, whispering to them then. "Listen, I know why you're really here. Soft voices travel quickly here." She looked around. "You need to be careful here—or anywhere as far as I'm concerned."

"What do you mean?" Corvaire interlocked his fingers and put them on the table as he leaned in as well.

"The fire on the mountain," Lucik said with cat-like eyes.

"You know about that?" Adler asked.

She nodded. "The guild knows. And there were four that came down from that mountain—only four as that sea dragon dove back into the waves. Arken burned the ancient city, leaving none alive. Except you four, I take it."

"Who saw us?" Adler asked. "They saw Grimdore too? Was it our assassins that saw us?"

She shook her head. "No. There were spies from both armies who saw the flames high up. King Roderix and Tritus are both looking for you. As it seems, the Dark King is too."

"Miss Lucik, do you know of a creature that lurks in the dark plains? That can bound like a frog but is the size of a man, with leering eyes?" Stone asked.

She sat back and rubbed her chin. "Don't believe so, never heard of such a creature. No troll can move that fast. Nor an ogre or a druid."

"What?" Stone couldn't tell if she was lying about such other creatures. But her expression was serious.

"Could be something Arken sent out after you," she said. "He's sure to be searching for you. He's known for his grudges—hence why he's here at all. Atop his Neferian, he's going to burn every last structure to the ground to get his revenge against people long dead."

"Do you think he knows we're here?" Adler scratched his arm.

"Don't know," she said. "But better swords aren't going to do much good against his riders. You don't happen to have any more dragons with you, do ya?"

"Just that one," Adler said, "and she's hibernating. We do have a fairy that helps us from time to time, and a dog."

"A dog?" She laughed. "I hope it brings you luck out there."

"Can the guild help us?" Stone asked. "If there are three kings scouring for us, we'll need every advantage we can muster."

"I don't know why Tritus and Roderix would wish any harm upon you," Lucik said. "They're cruel, but more than anything they value information. But they will seek you out, especially with you being in one of their kingdoms. I'll see if there's anything else I can find that may be useful to you. Normally, young Adler, we'd pair you up with a new master, but it looks like you've found someone else special."

"I'm no assassin," Corvaire said in a low voice.

"No, you're one of the Darakon, aren't ya?" she asked.

Stone was surprised, but Corvaire just glared at her.

"How do you know that?" Adler asked, as Ceres tried to shush him as soon as his mouth opened.

"A Darakon was found," she said. "Unexpectedly. And she was deceased."

Marilyn…

"In Atlius of all places," Lucik said with wide eyes. "She burned up an entire room of soldiers, just because they were after three young people your age: two boys and a girl. One boy with pale skin and a widow's peak, a man with shaggy brown hair and blue eyes, and a girl with blonde hair, green eyes and freckles. That ring a bell? I guessed you were another of the Darakon, but there's something in your eyes, something that tells an old, mysterious wisdom about you. I believe if these three are important to the fate of what's happening in the Worforgon, then I think they're in good hands with you, Corvaire."

He nodded.

"Have you all enough food and drink? You need coin to get you through your stay?"

"We should be fine," Adler said. "Wouldn't mind a little warning if you hear of anything after us in the city. We try to keep to the shadows, but with Roderix after us, it wouldn't hurt to have some insight beforehand."

"We'll have our ears to thin walls of the city," she said. "You're welcome to some drinks here to kill time if you please. But I'd keep these sorts of conversations to soft voices."

"Thank you very much, Lucik," Corvaire said. "But I think we'll be back on our way."

"I understand," she said, standing and bowing. "Good luck. I hear there's a shipment of Masummand on its way here. With any luck you may receive some mighty fine weapons from your visit here." She winked. "Farewell." And she made her way back to the far side of the room, sitting at the end of a pew with a few others.

They exited back the way they came.

"More drinks?" Adler asked as they walked past the bar again.

"The sun is still barely up," Ceres scoffed.

"What else do we have to do today? Sit in our beds, twiddling our fingers?"

"Sounds better than being in a cell," she said.

"Why would we be in a cell?" he asked. "We've done nothing wrong, yet…"

"Did you not hear anything Lucik said in there?" Ceres shoved her finger between his eyes. "Anything going on in there?"

"Hey." He swatted her hand aside.

"Come on," Stone said. "Let's be on our way. Let's use our time to train. There's much to learn, besides how many bottoms of bottles we can find while here."

"Fine," Adler moped.

They made their way back through the street to the shanty house, and while in Corvaire's room, discussed what it was they were going to prepare for while inside Verren. From downstairs, where the front door was barely hanging from its hinges—a sturdy knock was heard from the door.

"Was that a knock?" Stone asked.

"Go check," Adler said.

Corvaire glared out the window but couldn't see who it was.

"I'll go see," Ceres said.

"I'll go with you," Stone said.

"You can't go without me," Adler said.

"Corvaire," Stone said. "Maybe you should keep to the shadows in case something goes awry. But stay close."

He nodded.

They made their way down the staircase, with their footsteps creaking all the way down.

Before they even got to the door, they could see who had knocked—and Stone was glad they'd decided to bring their weapons along.

On the other side of the wooden door that hardly covered the entrance was a band of soldiers.

"They didn't burst through," Ceres said. "That may be a good sign."

"How could anything about this be a good sign?" Adler asked.

They walked up and Stone opened the door.

"Afternoon," the soldier at the front said. He was tall and had a broad stature. "I'm here to deliver a royal decree from the chancellor of the king. You are summoned to meet before him on the morrow, failure to appear will mean incarceration." He handed Stone a scroll with a red, wax seal upon it. As soon as Stone wrapped his fingers around it, the soldiers turned and walked away back to the street.

"We're summoned," Stone asked with wide eyes, "to meet King Roderix tomorrow?"

THAT EVENING, just as the cool wind cascaded through the city, rustling around the many nooks and crannies of Verren, Stone and Ceres prepared for another trek to the alleyway to check on their friends in need.

Their heads had been full of worry since the arrival of soldiers at the door to their shanty house in the corner of the city. They'd been discussing how the king knew they were here in the first place, or how he knew where they were staying. He wondered how Lucik knew so much, and they worried for what the king was going to say or do to them.

But there was one thing that kept coming back to their conversations: the king didn't send soldiers to arrest them. He'd given them a whole day, and the opportunity to willingly go to the Tower of Empireodon to meet with him and his chancellor. There was no violence in his intent—no aggression—at least not yet. So, they decided they would meet with them—at least that's what Stone's decision was, although Corvaire made the argument to flee in the night. Stone thought it would be best to see if the king had any information for them as well—because maybe his will to defeat Arken was more than his wish to capture Stone for some reason. One thing was for certain though between them—they would not mention their hunt for the new Majestic Wilds.

Once he and Ceres were down in the lower part of the house, they saw Adler slouched over in a beaten-up rocking chair by the window.

"Is he drunk?" Ceres asked. "Did he go off by himself?"

"Huh?" Adler stirred awake. "Drunk? Me? No, I just drifted off… after a few pints." He rubbed his eyes and yawned. "Where're you two off too? Didn't you go somewhere last night at this time?"

"Should we invite him?" Stone asked.

"Only if he promises to keep his mouth shut, which there's a fair certainty he couldn't do anyway."

Adler stood up spryly from the chair. "Where? I want to go. I promise I'll keep quiet. I'm dying of boredom in this place."

"C'mon, then." Ceres waved for him to follow as they all left the house. Corvaire was left upstairs as he'd been in deep contemplation about their meeting the next day.

Adler followed them to the mouth of the alley, and just as they turned to look down it, Alder was about to say something, but Stone turned and waved a finger at him.

"This isn't about you, or some joke," he said. "Just be company for once."

Adler's mouth dropped open as Stone and Ceres walked up to the alley that was brimming with children—not an adult to be seen.

"I brought more for you tonight." Ceres smiled. "I see some of you got some new boots. Excellent. Hope that eases your feet, and I see you've washed up! You're looking more and more like one of them." She pulled out her heaping purse and reached in to give Stone some of the coins, and then turned. "Hold out your hands." Adler cupped his hands as she poured coins into them. "Try to be fair and even."

He didn't say a word as the three of them walked into the alley filled with over a hundred children, handing out coins into their little fingers as the smiles of the children shined, and another lively conversation between them and Stone and Ceres continued into the twilight.

Tomorrow, we've got to come with more!

Chapter Ten

Stone awoke with a disturbing pit in this stomach. He lurched forward in bed, gripping his belly, unsure if he'd made the correct decision to go and adhere to King Roderix the II's request—or not so subtle request.

Corvaire had insisted that they should flee the city, but Stone didn't want to risk another enemy, now that King Arken himself had stated that he'd find and kill Stone anywhere he went. Perhaps, the king was understanding and temperamental enough to know that Stone only wanted to do good. Maybe he'd even help.

Getting up out of his bed and wiping the sweat from his brow, he walked past Mud, who looked up at him as if he was ready to be fed. Stone instead opened the smooth door, exiting out into the hallway and knocked delicately on Ceres' door. He could hear her stirring from the inside with a moan.

“What?” she asked, her voice was muffled into her pillow. "The sun’s hardly up. What do you want, Stone?"

"How'd you know it was me?"

"I can hear your dog next to you."

Mud wagged his tail while looking up at Stone, and it

thumped against the wall. His paws were also pattering against the wood floor.

"Come in," she said with a groan.

His sweaty palm turned the latch and he opened the door slowly to see a warm glow creeping in past the thin drapes at the back of the room. Ceres lay on her side with a thick, cotton blanket strewn over her. Her bare arm fell over the soft cotton, and her elegant hair draped over the side of the pillow. Her head was tucked into the soft, white pillow.

"Ugh," she said. "What is it? Can't this wait? I didn't sleep hardly a wink."

"I didn't sleep too well either," he said. "That's why I'm here, I wanted to ask your opinion about today . . ."

"No." Ceres sat up. "I don't want to go to the keep. I don't want to meet that warmongering king. And no, I don't want to get in the middle of this idiotic civil war of his!"

Stone took a lumbering step backward. Almost in fear that she was going to leap out of the bed and smack whatever expression he had on his face clean off. "I, uh . . ." he mumbled.

"But you're the one who the mothers said was the one to defeat Arken, and you're my friend, so I trust you." Her maddening gaze turned softer. "We're here with you. Until the very end. And if there's something, like this, that I think is completely dumb, expect me to tell you, but it's going to be your decision in the end. Trust your gut."

"I wouldn't expect any less of you," he said. "I want you to tell me the truth. But right now, my gut's saying this isn't the right thing to do."

"Is it too late for us to flee?" She leaned back on the bed with her arms propping her up behind her.

"We've got to wait for our new weapons," he said. "That's one of the main reasons for us obeying his will. Where would we hide out for a whole week, or more?"

"Well," she said with a cock of her head to her shoulder. "I guess we're going to meet our first king . . ." Her freckles and soft skin held the warm glow from the early morning sunlight.

"I actually don't think that's the first king we've met . . ." he said.

"Well, I know you're not talking about Adler," she said. "That boy doesn't have one lick of charisma in his bones. And no, Arken doesn't count. He's more like your friend's creepy uncle than a king."

"What do you think we should tell Roderix?" he asked. "How far should we go? Obviously, we're not going to talk about the Mystics."

"No, no, no. We'll tell him just enough, but not too much. And remember, Stone, we're going to be right there with you. You can feel safe with us. And don't be pressured to say too much. Oh, and don't sweat like you are now—it looks bad." She laid her head back down, but then rose again. "Oh, and don't tell him about the prophecy . . . or about you waking up from the ground. And don't tell him about the magic I've been working on . . . You know what? Maybe we should talk to Corvaire a bit before we head off to the keep."

WITH WILD WIND pouring down into the city that morning and roaring around every corner within the city's walls, they walked out of their shanty house back out into Verren. Each of them had to hold their hoods up to keep them from flying back down. The glow that was in Ceres' room hours earlier had faded with the full clouds that had washed their way over the sky. The wind was chill, and Ceres had even run back up to her room to collect a thicker shirt.

They made their way toward the keep, and its high peaks of the Tower of Empireodon. The many windows of the tower reflected a murky gloss that made the tower's stones look bright and polished.

Walking past the alleyway with the many orphans, Stone was pleased to not see a single child within the cluttered space. Adler wore a puzzled expression, like all they'd done the night before was just a dream. Ceres smiled, and Corvaire hadn't noticed, as he glared up at the tip of the tower ahead.

Stone hoped those orphans were out getting warm milk, washing up behind four walls with soapy water, and eating buttery pastries.

Once they walked up to the front gate of the keep—a massive iron gate was opened with dozens of soldiers meandering between its opening. The gate itself was a dark iron that interwove around itself like vines flowing around thin tree branches. The long cobblestone path before them led past the gate and through a long courtyard with dozens of types of flowers of mostly the colors of Verren: with many yellows, golds, and oranges flowing like a painting down the long garden beds. Along the insides of the road that led to the keep were bushes brimming with red roses. There must have been tens of thousands of them, Stone thought. Yet under the overcast sky, they held a more ominous glow than a bright Sonter day would yield.

"Go on through," one of the soldiers said in a dismal voice. Obviously, the soldiers were expecting them. Many of the reddened eyes of the soldiers stared at them as Corvaire led them past. "You'll be greeted at the front gate of the tower. You'll be stripped of yer' blades and be told about what you can and can't do in his presence."

Stone nodded as they walked by. They made their way quickly up to the second gate as Corvaire walked briskly—surely, he just wanted it to be all over and past them.

"Remember," Corvaire said. "Nothing about the Wild Majestics." His gaze was on Stone, who nodded back. During their walk to the keep, Stone had asked him what to say and what not to say. Hidden between Corvaire's words though was something like, 'just don't say anything stupid.'

At the front gate of the keep were two huge men with heavy armor and gold helmets covering their faces. Each of them hefted double-sided axes of spectacular design and craft. Above were rows of archers, chatting away, but staring menacingly down at them.

The two soldiers shifted their feet wide, as the rattle of the metal of their armor clanked and tinged. One of them motioned with his head toward a wooden box next to him, and on the other side of the iron gate before them of the same design as the other one, and Corvaire went and put his sword in there, as well as a dagger from his back. Each of them went over and placed their swords in there too.

Corvaire put his hands up showing he wasn't armed. "Good enough for you? Can we go up now? Or you just going to stare at us all day?"

One of them grunted, letting his ax sway at his side. But then pulled a ring of keys down from his hip and pushed one of them into the lock behind him. Twisting it, the lock popped open and the gate opened outward.

"So, we heard you were going to explain some rules to us?" Adler asked them.

"Rules?" one of the giant men said.

Adler swallowed hard as he found himself in the shadow of the large man.

"You address him as your highness," the soldier said in a low voice. "Only that, and nothing else. And if you disrespect him in anyway, you'll find yourselves bound and heading fer' a long stint in a cold, damp cellar."

"Okay, okay, I got it," Adler said.

They went through the gate, into the cold feeling, yet elaborately decorated interior of the keep. There were red and yellow silk banners hanging from the highest parts of the room, with old carpets climbing all the way up both staircases on either side. The banisters were a dark-stained, smoothly sanded wood, and there were hundreds of paintings on the walls. Some were of splendid landscapes, but most were portraits of kings and queens past, and snotty looking children painted to look royal.

There were handmaidens and butlers walking around in the back of the room, seemingly getting ready for something—perhaps a grand dinner or something similar? Stone thought.

"I suppose we head up," Stone said. There were many floors on the way up, but they were on one side of the tower, as the crisscrossing staircases wove their way up the other side. From the bottom, you could see nearly all the way up from its inside.

Once they arrived at the front door to what appeared to be the highest part of the keep, with an insignia chiseled onto the thick door itself, Stone got the annoying pit in his stomach again. He gripped it and winced in pain.

"Stone?" Ceres went over and put her arm around him. "What's wrong?"

"Nothing," he said, standing up straight again. "I'm fine. Let's get this over with."

Two guards with the royal colors of the city draped over their shoulders and down their backs opened the door that glided open with a squeak. The illustrious room on its other side was immediately visible to them. Smooth, white marble floors with thin streams of grays and black flooded down them. Thin red curtains draped the many tall windows on both sides of the long room. And on either side of the carpet that led to the throne were exquisitely carved statues of women only covered by loose-fitting garbs and muscular men that had no clothing.

As the four of them walked down the long carpet with

angular patterns of reds and yellows of many shades, Stone saw that there was no one at the throne, and the pit in his stomach vanished. There was another waiting up there though: a tall man in violet robes with fine-fitting, tan pants and tall leather boots of the finest design. On either side of the man stood heavy-built soldiers.

They walked up to the man finally, looking into his beady, blue eyes with many wrinkles cracking out of both of them. His thin mouth feigned a smile. "Welcome to Empireodon," he said, bowing. "I am Kellen Voerth, Chancellor of the kingdom and to the king."

"Where is the king?" Stone asked. He was standing in the center of them, with Ceres on his right and Adler and then Corvaire to his left—who had his arms folded. Adler had his hands in his pockets, and Ceres' were behind her back.

"King Roderix II had something to attend to," Kellen said. "Many things for kings to handle these days. But you can take my word as that of the king himself in his absence."

"So why are we here?" Stone asked. "You summoned us to meet with him, and here we are."

"Want to get right to the point?" Kellen turned and paced in front of the throne of black obsidian and a single, white broadsword protruded from its back, like it had been shoved into the stone by a giant. "I can appreciate that. What with the wars going on and the arrival of the Neferian. Many things to kill one out there at the moment."

Stone clenched his fists in his pockets. *Is he trying to threaten us?*

"You've been summoned here because we know where you've come from," the chancellor said. He paused as if to wait and see if they'd respond.

"Where we came from?" Stone asked, trying to see what he knew.

"The mountain," he said. "We saw the fires burning up

there from King Arken himself, and we saw you four come down upon the back of that other sea dragon." Another long pause.

"What we don't know," he said with a raised eyebrow, "is what you were doing up there."

Stone was feeling uneasy and was unsure of what to say.

"You," Kellen said, pointing to Corvaire. "You're of the Darakon? No?"

Corvaire nodded.

"Marvelous," he said. "We've only had a handful of yours in our castle in the last century. Privileged. And know that if you ever wanted to make heaping mounds of coin, the king would reward you handsomely for your services here."

"Don't kill for coin," Corvaire said gruffly.

"What were you doing up on the mountain when the Neferian attacked?" he snapped. "It's far too much of a coincidence that you go up there, and then the ancient city of Endo is burnt to the ground."

He does know about Endo…?

"We went up there, you know?" Kellen said. "We saw the ash. We saw the blackened stone. We saw the burned bodies."

"Yes," Ceres said. "It was a horrible tragedy what happened up there. But it didn't have anything to do with us. Arken attacked because of an old grudge, about something we don't even know."

"A grudge…" he said. "Against the Old Mothers?"

There was a heavy silence that drug on for an excruciating moment.

"You know of them?" Corvaire asked.

"Of course, we know of them," Kellen said. "They're one of the best kept secrets in all of the Worforgon. We always have. My question to you—heir of Darakon—is how do *you* know about them?"

"They brought my sister and I to them," he said. "We were

like those soldiers that stand behind you now. We were their guards. Nothing more."

"They taught you nothing?" Kellen scoffed. "Hard to swallow that."

"Do your guards not hear things from this conversation?" Corvaire asked. "Or do they walk around spreading those whispers? No. Why are you so interested in the mothers anyway?"

Stone was relieved that Corvaire was taking a stern approach with the chancellor and was curious if he'd have the same tone with the king himself.

"We had a pact with them," Kellen said, as a slight tick happened as the right side of his mouth twitched. "They were free to do their witchy things up there, as long as they did their part to keep us safe from magics. The last thing we need is a bunch of peasants walking around crippling others for no other reason."

"That's the last thing we need?" Adler finally spoke. "I'd say the last thing we need now is a war when King Arken and his riders are burning our homes."

Kellen shot him a wicked glare. "How about this?" he said. "One more peep from your mouth with that tone, and we'll send you to the dungeons and slice your tongue clean off?"

Stone nudged him not to speak again, but deep down he was proud of his friend's courage.

"Let me get to the point," Kellen said. "The mothers… are they dead?"

"We don't know," Corvaire said. "We fled just as the Dark King attacked."

"Don't lie to me," he snapped.

"They may have gone deep into the mountain," Corvaire said.

Kellen stroked his pointed chin. "I'm not sure if you're

telling the truth or not… but know, that it is treason to lie to the king."

Stone could tell Adler was brimming, and about ready to burst. He nudged him again to keep his mouth shut.

"You'll return tomorrow at the same time," Kellen said. "The king will wish to meet with you then. Do not leave the kingdom. That's a royal order. It's to keep you… safe."

Chapter Eleven

That evening after they left the castle of Empireodon and the chancellor Kellen with his stark warning about leaving the city, they sat in an inn just south of their shanty house. They'd each just returned from the mouth of the alley where they gave away a newly collected fresh batch of shiny coins to the many mouths that yearned for them.

Stone was happy to witness the many, then-clean, faces that popped out of the shadows with wide smiles. Many of them had their hair trimmed and wore shirts and vests that weren't tattered at every edge. But he couldn't help himself, he wanted to do more. He wanted to help them more.

He felt almost guilty sitting at a table with warm meat and fire-roasted vegetables to eat. Stone wasn't sleeping there in that alley in the cold, although he remembered the feeling of sleeping out in the rain without a tent. He didn't want those children to sleep on the streets with no one to tuck them away and tell them that everything was going to be all right.

"Why're you looking at me like that?" Ceres paused with her mouth open and teeth ready to chomp into a bite of pork shank.

"What?" He leaned back in his chair with his eyebrows raised.

"Don't worry," she said. "I know we're going to get more coin tomorrow. I know you're thinking it without you even having to say it. So, don't."

The inn was dimly lit with candelabras on each of the round-top tables, except for the roaring fire from the hip-high hearth at the longest side of the room. A long banner of the castle was draped across the top of the bar top, and swarthy men guzzled ales and laughed, or they moped bitterly. There was a woman with a low-cut top laughing in a high-pitched voice as she lay her arms over one of the men's shoulders as he howled in laughter.

"I like this place," Adler said with a thinly veiled slur in his voice. "Barkeep, another! One fer' me and one for me friends here."

"I'm all right," Ceres said. "I've got some more practice to do before I'm off to sleep. Corvaire told me a couple more things so I could practice by myself without hurting myself."

"Like what?" Stone rested his elbows on the table.

"There are a couple of spells he taught me that aren't that harmful, so even if I get them wrong, I can just get up and walk away once they've worn off."

Corvaire nodded, stroking his chin and taking long puffs off his pipe.

"Any luck with any of them?" Stone asked. "I know it's only been a few days . . ."

"I thought I felt something while we were walking today," she said. "But there was nothing there."

"You'll get there," he said. "I wish I knew my magic set so I could practice with you. But better safe than sorry."

An hour later they were back in their rooms and Stone lay awake staring at the top of his room, letting his eyes trail along the finely carved lines between the dark wooden beams. His hand lay over the bed and stroked Mud's clean fur. Even with the Dark King Arken after him, and his meeting with King Roderix the next day, all he thought about by himself in that room was how to help feed those children and give them good lives. But he also knew there were so many others like them out there in the world. There were so many that needed help.

THE NEXT MORNING, after a long walk to the keep under a gloomy sky with chill wind that whooshed into their faces, they entered back in through the gates opened by the soldiers. Stone and the others walked up to the room where they'd met Kellen the day before and made their way to stand side by side in front of the king's empty throne. This time there was no chancellor either. They stood there, glancing at the cold glares of the soldiers with their weapons ready at their hips.

There was a stir at the back of the room, next to a tall, exotic-looking plant with sharp draping leaves. The door behind it cracked open, and out strode the king. Stone recognized him as the king from the crown of gold he wore. His face was stern, as the lines on his forehead where thick and his eyebrows angled down.

"All hail King Roderix the II," one of the soldiers said loudly. Kellen had to duck through the door behind him to fit through. The king went and sat on the throne strongly, staring at the four of them before him, his hands held onto the arms of the chair like a soldier clasping his sword.

"Your highness," Stone said, with a bow, as they all did.

"My king," Kellen said as he rushed up to his side, as he named them one by one to him.

"Yes, yes," the king said. He was of dark skin with a bald-shaved head and a thick, black beard. His gown was of reflective purple with a golden belt and cuffs. At this hip was a sturdy, fine sword that Stone guessed was made by their own smithy. "You were there when Endo Valair burned to ash. Kellen has brought me up on what you said to him yesterday. And what more do you have to say to me?"

"I—I don't know," Stone said. "I think we said all we knew about that night."

"Why are you here in my city?" the king asked in a low voice.

"To acquire weapons," Corvaire said. "Before we head back out there. I believe we may have business in the north."

The king squinted at him.

"Honest," Stone said. "That's the reason we're here."

"You're here for only weapons then?" the king asked with a raised eyebrow. "You've met with the smithy Holm in my city. But that's not the only reason you're here. Is it?"

"I'm not sure what you mean, Sire," Stone said.

"Let's just cut out the shite," the king said with the whites of his teeth showing as he snarled. "You spoke with the Wild Majestics before they were murdered by Arken. They sent you here, didn't they? I want to know what happened up there. I want to know what they told you before their demise."

Each of them looked at each other, wondering what to say next to calm him. The door creaked open behind them as three pairs of footsteps rattled in.

"I was with the Wild Majestics," Corvaire said after clearing his throat. "These three were not there when they fell."

Adler looked back at the three men who'd entered.

"You know them?" Stone whispered to him.

"No." Adler turned his attention back to the king.

"You are to stay in my kingdom until you have given me all knowledge you have of the lost Old Mothers, man of Darakon."

"Your Majesty," Corvaire said, with a slight bow. "All

respect given; I cannot stay with the castle much longer. There are things I must attend to out there: matters of urgency."

"What is more urgent than serving your king?" the king spat.

There was an unnerving silence as they all stood there waiting for the next one to speak. Adler turned his head and looked back to the three men, waiting their turn to speak with the king.

"You are not my king." Corvaire let his hands fall strongly at his sides. Even without his weapons on him.

"I am your king, and you'd do well to remember that. I have no notion that even from whichever family line you are a descendant of, that you'd not do well to rot in my cellars with such a treacherous tongue. You will tell me what I wish to know. And you will tell me now."

Stone's head turned back and forth between Adler's focus and that of the argument going on between the king and Corvaire.

"You are not my king, and this is not my kingdom," Corvaire said. "I mean no disrespect to your rightful throne. But my family doesn't hail to any banner or crown. We've sworn our allegiance to the lands and all the people who live here. It has always been the way of my family. I'm no enemy of yours. I'm here to help, but I'm not here to bow."

"How dare you," Kellen finally intervened. He'd been standing over to the side with his face growing flush from anger. “You can’t speak to our king like that. You should be hanged for such an insult upon his royal head!”

"It’s true," Ceres said with her arms out. "We're here to help. We've come far to fight with you against the Dark King. He's the true enemy!"

"What is it?" Stone whispered to Adler, who was still focused on the men behind them.

"I don't know, but there's something about them."

"Where are the soldiers at the doors?" Stone asked.

"We're not here to argue or insult," Corvaire said. "We're here to help, just like Ceres said. But you have to trust us we are doing what is best for you and your people."

"You give us no sign or a reason to trust you," Kellen said. "What say you, King Roderix II?"

Adler took a step back toward the men.

"Adler?"

"If you hail not to me," the king said. "Then you hail to no one. I am the one true king. And if you refuse the will of your king, then these lands have no use for you. I alone know what's best for these lands, and even with your—"

Adler rushed at the men, who had been slowly spreading apart. All attention in the room fell upon him as the man at the center with a long, blue cloak lifted a slender crossbow from underneath it. Stone ran after his friend.

"What is this all about?" the king yelled.

It was then that the trigger of the crossbow clicked, just as Adler fell onto the man and the bolt went flying past him. As Kellen threw his body over the king, the bolt flung right over the king's shoulder, and the two kingsguard unsheathed their swords, running at the other two men in long cloaks. Stone fell upon the one in the center, and with their combined weight, they caused him to fall backward, with both of them falling onto his chest.

Corvaire flew into action as well, running at the man on the right side of the room as he drew another crossbow. Ceres ran to her friends.

With all of the attention upon the man underneath Stone and Adler, and the other one drawing his weapon as the king yelled upon his throne as he got to his feet and drew his sword—no one seemed to notice the third man slinking along the walls at the left side of the great throne room.

As Corvaire and one of the king's guards ran at the man,

his bolt was launched and the kingsguard thrust his body in its path, stopping it with the side of his chest as Corvaire grabbed the crossbow and battled to break it free from the man's hands. While he was scuffling with the man, and Stone and Adler laid blows with their fists upon the one at the center, they could hear the king and Kellen yelling from the throne.

Stone looked back to see a black, wet substance sliding its way up the throne and over their legs, moving like water flooding out from a spilled glass—only upward. It was then he looked over to the third man whose bare arms were raised as his fingers twirled through the air above him. His hood was flung back and hung at his back. His eyes were glowing in a hazy black and he was chanting words that were unfamiliar to him. He then saw the same black liquid was sliding up the other king's guard's legs, and even Corvaire's.

"What kind of sorcery is this?" the king yelled. "Kill him! Kill him!"

The kingsguard took a dagger from the back of his belt and flung it end over end at the man with a quick whistling sound, but the man tapped it away with a flick of his wrist. The other kingsguard lay clutching at his bloody chest with the end of a bolt still protruding through.

Stone tried to get to his feet, but to his dismay he saw that his own feet were being consumed by the thick, tarry liquid, as was Adler's and Ceres'. He fought to break free from it, the harder he fought, the more it seemed to creep up his legs and stuck to his fingers and knuckles.

The third man's sight was squarely upon the king, who now had the black substance creeping up his waist and inching its way toward his chest.

"Someone's got to do something," Ceres said. "We can't let the king die in front of us like this. We've got a' do somethin'!"

Corvaire was still fighting to grab the crossbow from the burly man he was tussling with.

"Can you . . .?" Stone asked her. "Can you try to use your magic?"

"I can try." She closed her eyes, took a deep breath and chanted a couple of words that Corvaire had taught her over and over.

"Hurry," he said as the sticky liquid crawled up over his hips, and the man underneath them got back to his feet, rushing over to grab his crossbow that had been thrown toward the open door in the scuffle.

Ceres' brow beaded with sweat, as she held her arms out at the third man. Her hands were tense and thin veins popped up on them.

Just as the man in the middle of the room was about to grab the crossbow, and reset it with another bolt, Corvaire reached up with his right arm, balled his hand into a fist and struck the other man squarely on the jaw, as his knees went limp, and he fell back to the floor.

The black liquid was now swelling around the king's neck as he panicked, clawing at it as his finger and arms only grew more entrenched in the slime. But then Stone saw something interesting happening in the middle of the room—from within the cracks between the stones was a dim blue light growing, and he could feel the hairs on the back of his neck begin to prickle.

"Ceres, I think you're doing it!" he said, as he could feel a wide grin widening on his face.

The man with the blue cloak had the next bolt in his hand, ready to clip into the crossbow, as the red rug that led to the throne started to sizzle and smoke. Thin streaks of blue illuminated from underneath it and crept up from the cracks around it. Tiny streaks of blue light started snapping up in quick bursts as the sticky, black liquid had covered the king's beard and was inching its way toward his mouth as the fear and rage was brimming in his dilated, reddened eyes.

"Let him go!" Kellen yelled.

"What are you waiting for?" Adler asked Ceres. "Do whatever you're doing, but just do it now!"

"I don't know what I'm doing!"

He heard the click of the bolt into the crossbow, and his heart sank, and his stomach turned as he was still unable to break free from the liquid, then covering his own chest.

"Do it!" Adler said.

And as if by command, the liquid was pouring into the king's mouth with the crossbow aimed at him. The blue light in the floor erupted into a furious display of crackling light that shot out at the man with the crossbow's arms. The blue light that looked like blinding bolts of lightning burned away all of the red rug at the center of the room and caused the crossbow to explode in the man's hands as he shook violently from the surging power pouring into him.

The man who'd been casting the spell that had bound them all stopped his spell and scanned the room for what was causing such a destructive force.

"Ceres . . .?" Stone asked.

"I—I don't think it's me . . ." She looked at her palms and backs of her hands with wide, blank eyes.

Stone looked up at the third man, whose full attention and his mouth agape as he looked past Stone. Stone looked behind him to see Corvaire illuminated in thin, snapping streaks of lightning that ran over his body. His eyes were glowing a brilliant blue hue, and his stance was wide.

The man lurched forward, twirling his hands again as he hissed out. Just as he began starting another incantation, Corvaire said, "This is as far as you go."

With that, another explosion erupted from the floor in the room and burst out at the man, sending the coursing energy into him. The man shook violently and screamed as the energy tore through him, causing his own eyes and mouth to let out the intense blue light. Black smoke smoldered out of his ear and nostrils before he fell to the ground lifelessly—his body smoldering with wisps of smoke as the blue light receded back into the stone floor and the black slime rolled down their bodies like thin oil falling back to the ground.

The king coughed and choked up the liquid as he fell to his knees and Kellen went to his aid. The king's guard hurried over and stabbed his sword through both of the men's chests as the lights that had consumed Corvaire faded, and he was left standing like a statue of a hero from ages past.

The king's guard went over to the third unconscious man behind Corvaire and went to thrust his sword into him, but Corvaire stopped him with a wave of his hand. "You'll want that one alive. I'm sure the king would want some words out of that one's mouth if I had to wager upon it."

The king then collected himself, and while pushing off Kellen, stood back up of his own accord. The oil rolled down his once-fine garbs and fell to a pool of oil beneath him. He glared at Corvaire for a long moment, unsure of what to do with him as he wiped the oil from his hands.

"Man of Darakon," he said finally. "I give you my thanks for saving me. For this, you are in my debt."

"Sire?" Kellen shook his head. "Don't forget his insolence. And he used magic!"

"You'd be dead too if it wasn't for him. Knight Drâon Corvaire. I thank you."

PART III

NEW TIDINGS

Chapter Twelve

The king was alive—and so were they—*thank the heavens!*

Stone figured the absolute last thing they needed was a warring king to die right in front of them—who knew... they may even have taken part of the blame, even if they were weaponless.

Yet, after the king and the chancellor had given them their praise—albeit, Kellen's was far from sincere and of a reluctant nature—Corvaire held a heavy look of concern in his eyes and he was more quiet than usual as they left the keep in the late afternoon.

"What's the matter?" Stone finally asked him as they strode down a narrow, wet alleyway lined with empty clotheslines.

He just growled.

"Let's go get something in his stomach." Adler brushed his chestnut hair back with his fingers. "I know my legs are already sore from that scuffle..."

"Scuffle?" Ceres moaned. "You are an idiot. We almost died. The king of Verren almost died right in front of us."

"I'm just glad we're all okay," Stone said. "That was a close one. And not to mention, hadn't this occurred to you yet… but how many people out there know magic?"

"That is concerning," Adler said. "I've been thinking about it this whole time we've been out of the castle."

"Just means we need to learn ours," Ceres said, cracking her knuckles. "Better to bring a sword to a sword fight than a dagger."

"Or a stick," Adler said with his arms out. "We know absolutely no magic. We'd be dead if it wasn't for him. We need those weapons! I wonder how close Holm is to gettin' and forgin' them…"

Stone heard his own stomach groan then, which Adler seemed to notice too with an upturned eyebrow.

"I hear that sound," he said. "I feel the same. Nothing like spoiling yourself after a battle won!"

"Who—who were they?" Ceres asked coldly. "Were they assassins from your guild?"

"Don't know," Adler said. "Not high enough up the ranks to know them all."

"I assume they were from Dranne?" Stone said. "Who else would be after the king?"

"They were not from Dranne," Corvaire finally said with a bitter tone.

"How do you know that?" Stone asked.

"That magic," he said. "That type of magic has a certain… insignia on it. Did you notice how the black tar turned to a thin liquid after that mage was killed?"

Each of them looked at each other and nodded.

"That is not The Elessior."

"What do you mean?" Ceres asked. "There's another type of magic?"

"Yes, it's called the Arcanica." His voice was grim.

"So, aside from The Elessior, there's another that the man used?" Ceres asked. "What's different about it?"

"So, your magic is Sonter Set, Ceres. You will use the powers of plants and trees and wield the magic of fire. This is used by harnessing your Indiema. The Arcanica though, uses not your ancestry as your power, but rather, uses death itself as your power."

"Death?" Stone gasped.

"What do you mean?" Adler asked.

"The more you kill…" Corvaire said with a cold gaze. "And that mage back there… as you saw… was powerful."

Stone noticed Corvaire was limping then and his skin looked flush.

"Corvaire, you need to rest," he said.

"Aye. Need a good meditation is all. That spell took it out of me. My Indiema's all spent."

"You need food, and rest," Adler said.

"No, I just need to get back to the house and meditate. I'll be fine. You go and rest yourselves."

"Corvaire, the Arcanica," Ceres said, as they left the alley back out onto one of the main roads of the city which was wide and well-lit. She lowered her voice. "What's so dangerous about it?"

"Those who practice it are from the deep south. Hardly ever come this far north. I fear that it wasn't an assassination attempt from King Tritus, I fear it was from their leader down in their village. I wouldn't doubt that there was an attempt upon Tritus' life at the very same moment."

"What would be the point of killing the two kings?" Adler asked.

"Your guess is as good as mine," Corvaire said, as he walked in the middle of them down the road and Mud came running up, walking next to Stone's legs. "They could want the war to end, or they could have been working under the direction of one of the other royal families, or who knows what else?"

A dark thought rolled into Stone's head then, something he wished was not the case. "Corvaire… is there a chance that they could be working with… *him?*"

There was a long pause, and Corvaire exhaled deeply.

"I don't know, Stone. I don't see a reason that Salus Greyhorn would work with Arken… but the Arcanic Mages are strange fellows."

"I know that name," Adler said. "Armonde told me about him. He's the Vile King, right?"

Corvaire nodded.

"The Vile King is real?" Ceres asked, pausing in her tracks.

"As real as you and me," Corvaire said.

Stone was unsure what to think about this. *How many kings are out there?*

"You see," Corvaire said. "The thing about Arcanica magic, is that its set is based upon the element of water, and the natural poisons that exist in the world. Water is one of the most powerful forces in all the world, and poison can be derived from many sorts of plants and beasts. Awful stuff…"

"So, the Vile King may be siding with the Neferian?" Ceres asked.

"If he cut off the heads of the snakes that led the kingdoms," Corvaire said, "they'd be thrown into chaos, which is what he really wants. He wants people to suffer like he has."

"If we have the opportunity," Ceres said. "Perhaps we could talk ta' the queens of the other kingdoms, maybe they'd agree ta' work with us… and forget about these warring kings."

"Like who?" Stone asked.

"Queen Bristole of Valeren," she said. "Maybe?"

"That's thousands of miles to the south," Adler said.

"I said if we get the chance," Ceres said. "At least she's known for her rationale."

"Tritus' wife Angelica won't be no good to us," Adler said.

"She couldn't get a whisper to his ear if she had her lips sown to it."

"There are other royal families, too," Ceres said. "Maybe one of them."

"Let's just focus on finding the new Majestic Wilds, when and if they arise."

They walked around another couple of corners, cutting between the crowds, and Ceres lined her empty purse with fresh metal.

As they got back to their shanty house, and Corvaire prepared to head back up the stairs to his room and recover, Stone nudged him on the arm.

"What's this all mean for us? I mean… saving the king here, but being wanted by Atlius and being hunted by Arken?"

Corvaire groaned. "We are in the favor of the king now."

"That's good, right?" Adler said. "We don't have to hide in the city now."

"But now we're out in the open," Ceres said. "Don't you think it's better to keep to the shadows? Aren't you an assassin?"

"I don't like being associated with any kings," Corvaire said with his black hair flapping over his face. "We don't need more eyes on us than we already do. And my mind still wanders back to that creature in the shadows out in the fields. I think we haven't seen the last of it."

"At least we have Ghost to lead us to safety when we need it most," Ceres said.

"Where are all of these creatures coming from?" Adler asked.

"Life is complex since Ceres rescued me from my coffin."

"I don't think it's gonna get any easier, either," Ceres said. "You go, Corvaire, rest up. We'll bring you somethin' to eat later."

The knight walked into the shanty house and made his way

up to his room. They turned to walk back toward one of the roads with a couple of places to put their butts on seats and fill their bellies. Stone peered down the orphan alley but saw not a single child there. He passed with a grin as Mud trotted behind.

They walked into a tavern after a pair of soldiers nodded to them as they entered.

"That's gonna take some gettin' used to," Ceres said.

"Come, come, sit!" the innkeeper beckoned with wide eyes as she took off her pearly-gray apron and tossed it on the counter. "This is our best table over here by the window!"

She shooed away a pair that was sitting at the table who seemed perturbed until they saw who was being invited to sit. They got up quickly and bowed their heads to the three of them.

"What're ya thirsty for?" she asked, while cleaning off the table and motioning for the waiter to come over quickly. "We've got a new port wine from the north coast you might enjoy. How about a puff of some nutty leaf from the fields west of the Worgons? We brew a strong ale that might rest your weary selves after saving the king hisself!"

"Ale, please!" Adler said while sitting eagerly and folding his arms over his puffed-out chest.

"I'll have a dry wine if you've got one," Stone said, "and some water. Loads of water."

"Tea would be nice, thanks," Ceres said.

"Tea?" Adler scoffed. "We just won a victorious battle. We should be chugging mead like champions!"

Stone glanced around and saw every set of eyes in the room was watching them. Some looked appreciative with soft eyes, others looked frightened, but couldn't look away. "Word spreads fast. Why do they look so scared?"

"Because they know *how* we defeated the mage," Ceres

said. "I doubt a single person in this room knew magic was real before today."

The barkeep rushed back to them with their drinks and three full jars of clear water. "I'll have the cook whip you up the freshest things we have to offer. And there will be absolutely no charge. I demand it. You have our deepest thanks for what you did today."

Adler raised his glass. "You see? Things are gonna be just fine while we're here. We're heroes."

But Ceres and Stone gave uneasy glances around the room.

"I don't know if it's better to be in the shadows or upon a pedestal," Stone said. "But I know I don't like the way this feels right this moment."

"We'll just stay close together," Adler said. "Shouldn't have any issues with soldiers while we're here now." He chugged down his ale and hollered out. "Whew, that is strong! Another please!"

"What a pig," Ceres said.

"I'm going to enjoy this while it lasts, excuse me," he said. "I've got a feeling we're not going to have this royal treatment much longer, especially when we get back out into those wet fields."

That stark reminder seemed to stir something in both her and Stone.

Stone gulped down his drink with a finger in the air, and Ceres pushed her tea away. "The ale is strong you say?"

Chapter Thirteen

After a long night of howling wind that battered their windows accompanied by light, tapping rain, Stone, Corvaire, and Ceres stood out back of their shanty house. Their boots stood in the sticky mud scattered with thin strips of green grass in the shade. The color had returned to Corvaire's face and he was freshly shaven with his black hair pulled back like Stone's—an unnatural sight to the two.

"Adler coming down for this?" Stone asked with his knuckles on his hips looking up at the fake facade of the structure.

"Nope," Ceres said with a grin on her pale face, letting her blond hair shake from side to side. "Said he had some sharp pains in his head. But I think he's just tuckin' his tail between his legs at the thought o' learning magic."

"Like I said before," Corvaire said with a cold stare, "it normally takes years to learn this, and you aren't children anymore. Magic is normally taught at a young age."

"I know," Ceres said. "But I'm going to get it. I know I am."

"I want to," Stone said. "I just don't want to ruin my chances by practicing the wrong type."

Corvaire just nodded, while Mud laid in a patch of sun behind him, itching his ear.

"Okay, Ceres," he said. "Let's try something simple again."

"Yes," she said.

"You know she just wants to learn the spells that Marilyn cast before." Stone laughed. "She wants to learn how to cast that red haze and those vines that sprouted from the ground to keep those bastard soldiers in place."

"We'll get there hopefully," Corvaire said. "You pay attention too; this will apply to you when and if we ever figure out when you were born."

"I won't deny I want to learn them all," Ceres said with her arms up at her sides and with a bashful look on her face.

"So, you are of the Sonter Set," he said. "Yes, Juniper's Red Haze and Vines that Bind are spells you would be able to cast, but to get there you need to get very in touch with the way plant life feels and acts, and you need to get comfortable with heat and how it works."

Stone asked, "Is her magic stronger if she uses it in the Sonter season?"

"No."

"Oh," Stone said.

"Let's try this," Corvaire said. "The first thing you need to get adept at is getting your Indiema strong. And when I say strong—I mean chain links strong. You've got to reach deep into your feelings for your ancestors and build that emotional connection to the point where you could almost hold an entire conversation with a person centuries dead."

"Do you talk to the dead?" Stone asked.

"No. Well, it's more like singing a song with a friend than having a conversation. You hold the same tunes and join in it together as almost one voice ringing out."

Ceres closed her eyes.

"First, think about your mother and father. Do you remember them?"

She nodded.

"I know they've both passed. How about any siblings?"

She shook her head.

"All right, well let's start with your parents then. We need to find some powerful connections to them."

Ceres' lips quivered.

"It's okay to cry if you need. That's a good thing here."

Stone had to look away.

"Think about your favorite memories of them. Think about the way your mother smelled at night as she tucked you away to sleep. Think about the way the skin on your father's hands felt. Were his hands rough? Dry? Do you remember the feeling of putting your small feet into his large boots?"

Ceres' eyes were still shut, but tears streamed down her cheeks.

"Good," he said softly.

"Now, what about the bad things about your parents that still haunt you?"

"Corvaire…" Stone said worriedly, rubbing his thighs with his sweaty palms back and forth. But the older man waved him away with his hand.

Stone thought Ceres was about to fall over from grief.

"It's good to think about this, not all of our strongest emotions are soft. You need to think about those painful memories that sting even to this day. Do you remember the last time you saw their faces? Were they smiling or not? Did your father hit you? Did your mother sleep with another?"

Ceres shook her head. "No, none of those things. They were kind and sweet to me. I just…"

"You just what?" he asked.

"I just… it's my fault they're gone."

"Was it something you did? Or do you only blame yourself because you couldn't stop something?"

Ceres fell to her knees and continued to sob with her hands then covering her face.

"You don't have to tell us; I just need you to think about it. Focus on that pain until you can see their faces as clearly as if they were right mere inches from your face. Think about your grandparents if you ever knew them, or if you didn't, what did you parents tell you about them? How old were they when they passed? Where were they born? Were they kind too, or harsh?"

"They were kind farmers," Ceres said softly.

"What color was their hair?"

"My grandmother's hair was just like mine. My mother always said I got my freckles from her too."

Corvaire knelt in the mud and pulled her hands down. He opened her hands on her lap and placed a single dandelion in them.

She opened her eyes and looked down at it. Her eyes were completely glassed over, and her lips quivered as she looked at the many, tiny golden petals.

"Touch it," he said. "Feel how soft it is? How delicate it is?"

She caressed it with one hand.

"Keep thinking about your family. All the things you've been through, and all the things you couldn't do because they passed on to the Golden Realm. Do you feel anything in you when you touch it? Do you have any sort of connection to it?"

Ceres' brow furrowed in concentration, but Stone caught a look of frustration in her face.

"A dandelion is considered a weed. It's a pest among flowers. While a single rose is touted as beautiful, an entire field of dandelions are thought of as a weed that's ground should be occupied by flowers of grass. Have you ever felt like that? Like you should be replaced by something else? Something other people consider better?"

Ceres' lips quivered again, and she closed her eyes and nodded.

"But a dandelion gives life to so many. Bees and birds feed them with pollen, and they give that pollen right back. We might not have the roses we have if it wasn't for those fields of weeds."

"I—" Ceres said. "I feel something…"

Stone saw Corvaire eagerly awaited what she was feeling.

"It's like… it feels my pain. It feels warm in my hands and I don't feel as sad."

"Good. Now repeat after me… and when you say it. *Mean* what you say. Feel the words as the breath leaves your mouth… *Floris Neptulum…*

"Floris Neptulum," she said, pronouncing each vowel and syllable.

Each of them gazed eagerly at the dandelion.

But nothing seemed to happen.

"Again," he said. Which she repeated the words, and they all watched as the small, yellow flower lay motionless in her hands. She repeated the words again, and again.

For the next ten minutes, Ceres continued to repeat the word. She used different tones, different speed, and even tried singing it once. Corvaire said nothing though, he only watched the dandelion with a weary gaze.

"What's it supposed to be doing?" Stone finally asked.

"You'd know if you saw it," he responded.

"I'm not going to get it, am I?" Ceres asked.

"This spell you can try on your own without risk of injury to yourself and anyone around you. It's one of the beginner spells, but just keep in mind that it could be a long time before you start to see anything happen. If you even have the ability to use The Elessior. Now, I'm going to go off and take care of some things. We'll talk again later." Corvaire rose, with his muddy knees showing, and walked off.

"I can't do it," Ceres said with a whimper. "I want it more than anything… anything…"

"What color were your mother's eyes?" Stone asked.

"Blue."

"What was your favorite thing that she made you for supper, or breakfast?"

"Cauliflower stew with bits of bacon in it."

"What were the last words she said to you in person?"

"That she loved me…"

That brought tears to Stone's eyes even.

"What would you say to her right now if she were here in front of you?"

Ceres sobbed, caressing the dandelion's soft petals.

"I—I'd tell her how much I miss her. I'd tell her that I'm okay. I'd tell her that I'm going to be fine and that she can rest in peace." Heavy tears fell from her cheeks onto the flower. "I'd tell her I'm sorry. I'm sorry for ever being a dumb brat, and not being grateful for everything she did for me. And I'd do anything to hold her hand again, to have her run her fingers through my hair, for her to kiss me and tell me that everything is going to be just fine…"

"Now, Ceres," he said, wiping the tears from his cheeks. "Say the words, like you're speaking them to your mum."

With her eyes still closed, she whispered, "*Floris Neptulum.*" She hadn't opened her eyes but repeated it again—this time louder. And then again, she said the words as if she'd said them a hundred times before. On the next time, Stone reached over and grabbed her shoulder. She stopped and opened her eyes to look at him. Stone swayed his head for her to look down at her hands.

As she turned her head back down to look at the flower, she leaned in closely to inspect it. Stone did the same.

In her pale, cupped hands, and in between the many tiny petals, a trickle of golden light appeared.

"Say it again," Stone said.

Ceres said the words again, and just as the last syllable trailed out of her mouth, the dim lights grew brighter. She said it again, and the petals popped to light with a vibrant, bright glow that blossomed to the tip of each of its thin petals. The whole top of the dandelion shimmered in beautiful warm light that lit each of their faces. Ceres smiled widely with her mouth open. Stone had never seen her so happy.

"I did it," she screamed, jumping to her feet. "I did it! I did it! I used magic!"

She wrapped her arms around Stone, who returned the warm embrace.

"I'm proud of you," he said, as a slow clap started back by the shanty house.

They both quickly turned to see Corvaire leaning up against the dark stone clapping his hands with a grin on his face.

"Bravo," he said. "Bravo."

She fully turned to him, holding out the glowing dandelion for him to see. "I did it! I did it!"

"Yes, you did. Well done, girl. Well done, indeed."

Chapter Fourteen

With Ceres still gushing with excitement from her first display of her Sonter Set of magic, she was both emotionally drained and spiritually. Corvaire insisted she'd spend much of the day meditating in her room to recover her Indiema. She'd asked him why such a tiny amount of magic drained her so, when she'd seen him and Marilyn use spells that were many times more powerful before they needed to recuperate. He told it is was because she was new at it, and not to try to practice for the rest of the day. Even the smallest of spells would require time for her to recover. He warned her against trying to use any spells in battle—should one arise—because there was a strong chance that it would render her vulnerable from her weakness after.

Stone was elated by her prowess, and happy for his friend. But after witnessing that—the thought in his head grew more frequent—*will I ever be able to use magic myself?*

Adler stirred awake, and after a quick soak, Corvaire said he was off to check on the progress of their new weapons. Stone and Adler decided to accompany him. Walking past the mouth of what they'd been calling 'Orphan Alley' he was pleased—yet surprised—to see not a single set of weary eyes down it.

Every one of them is still off doing things… and haven't returned?

Once they were back at Ash Forge, with its musty smells of smoldering iron and hot-burning wood, they entered back in to see Holm Yederan sending his hammer down onto a red-hot piece of long steel as sparks flew onto his shoulders and chest that were covered by a slick piece of charred leather. It took him a moment to make out who was standing in his doorway.

"Master Corvaire." He raised his dark spectacles over his thick, brown eyebrows and onto the bald spot on the top of his head, with long brown braids below it. "Only in town a few days and already the most famous person here now. Bravo!"

"Not my intention," Corvaire said in a low tone. "Don't want the attention. It was more self-preservation what I did."

"Well, either way, saving a king's life is nothing to scoff at. You're gonna be treated different wherever you go now. I'd expect ya to pay for perhaps half yer' drinks the rest o' yer' days?"

"I'll admit," Adler said. "Even for me… I don't care for the attention…"

"Don't worry," Holm said with a wink while sending the steel blade into a water bath with a stark hiss and bellowing steam. "The mothers already paid upfront fer' your weapons, so there'll be no awkwardness about that…"

"Speaking of…" Corvaire said.

"Aye." Holm took a rag from a table next to his anvil, and wiped his brow clean from the beads of sweat and walked over to them. Stone was a full head taller than the stout man with the wide shoulders. "There was an issue with the transport… I was gonna come and find ya later this afternoon…"

"Issue?" Corvaire said with a raised eyebrow.

"Damned caravan got stopped by some soldiers down

south, asked for a bit o' tax for all the metals they were importing."

"Importing?" Stone scratched the stubble on his cheek.

"'Twas a scam was all it was." Holm tossed the rag onto a different, round-wooden table next to where they were. "But either way… when a pack of armed men in armor ask you to be payin' them… you pay or fight… and my men ain't all fighters."

"So…?" Corvaire growled.

"They insisted on wanting a fair percentage of the goods, but didn't know what they had, and refused my man's offer, so the soldiers 'accompanied' them to the nearest town to get the metals appraised. Everything is fine, they've left after two days, but it was an unexpected setback is all."

"And our Masummand Steel?" Corvaire asked with a leery eye on the armorer.

"They couldn't figure out what it was, none o' them. They charged an extra tax but didn't take it. Perhaps deep down they knew not to mess with it. Lives get lost for taking that kind of steel."

"So, when will it be here?" Corvaire asked.

"Two or three days, depending on the weather. It'll be worth the wait though. And a couple days to forge your weapons. Already got the hilt, guard and pommel made, just need to craft the metal. Normal steel I could do quicker, but we're talking about Masummand Steel here. Not many can even manipulate the hard steel without it cracking or splintering."

"I still can't believe we're getting Masummand Steel weapons," Adler said to Stone. "We're going to become some great warriors with those."

"I don't want to be any more known than we already are," Stone said. "I just want to find the new mothers and find a way to kill Arken and get rid of these Neferian. Then our quest can be done, and I won't have to worry about looking over my shoulder everywhere we go."

"Agreed," Adler said. "The sooner Arken is dead, the better."

"Easier said than done," Holm snarled. "That bastard's as cruel as they come. Got a heart of ice—if there's one at all. Hard to imagine a pack of kids to be the one to do him in… even the dragons can't get that done."

"Grimdore can," Stone said with a stern voice. "She survived a fight with Arken's own Neferian. I know she can kill one of them—when she's recovered that is."

"I certainly hope you're right about that," Holm growled. "I hear there's been six of them counted in the Worforgon. And more dragons are flying in from the Arr every week now."

"Six Neferian?" Adler gasped, his eyes were wide and his face flush.

"Yep," Holm said. "That includes the giant one that Arken rides.

"We'll kill all six, somehow…" Stone said. "Or get them to fly off back to where they came from…"

Just then, a soldier entered into Holm's forge with a scroll sealed with the insignia of the king. He bowed his head, handing it to Stone, who once he found it in his hand, the soldier bowed and left.

"What is it?" Corvaire asked, and even Holm was on his toes to peer at the letter.

"He wants to see us again tomorrow."

"We're getting to be regular guests with him these days," Adler said. "We may have to get you some nicer clothes, Stone, for all these royal visits."

"What's wrong with my clothes?" Stone sneered.

THAT EVENING—YET again—even after Ceres had recovered and found time to lessen some pockets in the market streets, they arrived at Orphan Alley to find not a single eager set of palms.

Adler asked where they'd all gone off to, but neither of them had an answer. That night Stone tossed and turned in his bed—unable to sleep at the thought of something unfortunate happening to the already misfortunate.

After several hours of late, light sleep, and after a dream of being back in his cold, dark coffin, he awoke to the sound of heavy raindrops on the roof of their shanty house. He stood, as Mud yawned, and went to look out the window. The air was damp and the daylight dreary through the thick, dark clouds hanging low in the sky.

They met downstairs and went off to eat before they started the day. They weren't expected to meet with the king until noon, so Ceres went off with Corvaire to practice her magic, Adler went off to get his hair cut and go purchase some new clothes for him and Stone—which Stone laughed at because he thought he'd been joking the day before.

While left alone, and after they'd all eaten, Stone tossed a tightly woven ball of twine for Mud to fetch out front of the shanty house. He just wanted to take his mind off things for a while, and Mud had seemed extra eager to get some energy out—and the dog sure did seem to enjoy playing in the rain. But while he wanted to rest his mind, he kept getting distracted by the many people who either nodded to him as they walked by, or came up to him and thanked him for what he'd done to save the king's life. He would smile and nod as they walked off, sometimes looking back over their shoulders at him as if he were a famous traveling bard or something.

Mud wanted to keep playing, but Stone just went back to his room, drying him and the dog off. He sat at the table in front of the open window as Mud dozed back off to sleep on the thick carpet on the floor. His sleep hadn't been the best the night before, so he found himself staring off into the city through the window. The rain continued their way down onto the city, as the clouds seemed not much higher than the tallest peak of Empireodon Castle.

He rested his chin on his hands with his elbows placed on the table, letting his mind finally wander without prying eyes. He watched merchants wheel their carts away from the market as the rain surely kept away eager buyers. Small children played in puddles. Horses neighed and drank from troths outside of inns, and an elderly woman covered her head with a leather shield curiously as she walked slowly down the side of the road.

Up on the castle's tower the thousands of windows glowed in soft candlelight that sparkled in the gloom like fireflies resting upon a mighty tree in the deep forest, shadowed underneath its thick canopy. It was then—in the space between dreams and reality—a warm feeling rose in him, causing him to fall deeper into the dreamworld. He was back in his coffin, not knowing if he was alive or dead, but he felt something in his hand—something soft and warm. A shiver ran through his body.

He didn't know if he was dreaming or if his whole adventure with his friends was not real, and he was really still back in his coffin, but he did know that the hand that was holding his in the darkness made him feel completely safe and loved. There was someone in the coffin with him, but in the shadow, and underneath the many hundreds of pounds of dirt, he couldn't see.

"Who are you?" he whispered. "Why are you here with me?"

There was no response, but he could hear the soft breathing of the person next to him.

"If I'm going to die here, you shouldn't die with me. This is meant for me."

"You were never meant to die in here," a soft, delicate voice said. Her hand squeezed his.

His stomach pitted and his chest tightened. "Who are you?"

Her other hand went up and caressed his arm. Nothing else mattered to Stone then. Everything else out there in the world could wait. All that mattered to him was her—whoever she was.

"I have to leave you," she whispered.

"No," he gasped. "Don't leave me alone in this place again. I don't want to be alone anymore."

"You're not alone," she said, and he could sense she was smiling. Her hair smelled like lilacs. "You have them, now. They are your family, and they love you like I did."

"M—mother?"

"I'll always be with you," she said as she squeezed his hand tighter and caressed his arm.

Mud's barking stirred him awake, and there was a soft knocking on the door.

"No…" he sighed, looking around the room anxiously.

"You ready?" he heard Adler ask from the other side of the door.

Stone leaped to his feet and opened the door wide. Adler was taken aback by his friends' energy.

"Stone? What's the matter?"

"I saw her! I saw my mother!"

Chapter Fifteen

"What do you mean, you saw your mother? Where? Here?" Adler asked, with his eyebrow raised under his freshly cut hair.

"I dozed off. I saw her. She spoke to me. I had a mother, Adler. I had a mother!"

"That's fantastic news," Adler said, walking into the room. "What'd she look like?"

"I don't know. It was all dark, but I felt like I knew it was her from when she was holding my hand in the coffin. I knew it was her. I felt… I felt like I was home."

"I'm really happy for you," Adler said. "Want to talk about it while we walk to meet Roderix?"

"No," Stone said. "I just want to keep this feeling as long as I can."

They joined with the others out front of the house and made their way back up to Empireodon in the rain.

Once they made their way back up to the highest reaches of the white tower, they were met once again by the chancellor, Kellen Voerth. The throne room was still stained with blood that had been mopped mostly away, but the memories of the battle remained. The rug that had run down the center of the room to the king's throne had been replaced by another of the same material—as the other had been singed and burnt away.

"Chancellor," Stone said to the tall man.

"Stone," he replied.

The gloom of the dark clouds outside filled the windows of the tower with an eerie, shadowy backdrop.

"Will the king be joining us?" Stone asked.

"No, but he sends his regards once again," he said with a slight nod. "He was called off for an urgent matter. King Roderix has many concerns to deal with this day and age."

"I understand," Stone said. "Do you mind getting straight to it?"

Kellen looked disturbed by that, as did his friends with their quick glances at one another. But his mother's appearance was fresh on his mind and he wanted to go somewhere by himself and think about what he'd seen. *The less time here, the better.*

"This was a royal summons," Kellen shouted. "Not an invitation."

"I understand how this works," Stone said. "And I know the sooner you tell us what you want to tell us the sooner we can get back to our lives. Now, what is it you want?"

Adler chuckled, turning his normally pale skin to a flush of red. Ceres looked as if her bottom jaw was about to drop to the floor.

"I'd wish you'd understand you'd not be allowed to talk to the king like that. You'd be thrown into the deepest of our cellars."

"I wouldn't. But you're not a king. And we didn't only save yours, we saved his. I don't think he'd be as quick to throw us behind iron bars with the breath he continues to draw into his lungs because of us. Now. Do you have something for us, or should we show ourselves out?"

Kellen's fists were balled up so tightly they were shaking.

"Maybe we should just go," Corvaire said, clearing the tension in the air.

"Hold," Kellen yelled, as they'd turned to leave. "The king wished me to give you something, invite you to another, and give you a warning as the third."

Each of them turned to face the tall man who'd seemed to sort of recollect himself with his duty.

"He wanted to give us something?" Stone asked. "What?"

"Well. He's already given it to you. Those orphans you were giving those coins to."

"What about them?" Stone asked with a stark dread welling up inside of him.

"They've been taken off to an orphanage next to one of the cathedrals on the other side of the city. There they will receive food, water, clothing, and education."

"Did they have a choice?" Stone asked. "Or did you just take them?"

"We invited them, which almost all of them took."

"What of the others?" Stone asked.

"Argh, this was a gift of the King of Verren. I'd expect you to be a little bit more gracious."

"What about the other orphans?"

"I don't know, they're probably back on the streets begging for scraps."

"It's okay." Ceres placed her hand on his shoulder. "It's a good thing."

"Moving on then," Kellen said. "The king is rallying his troops for an attack, and he would be grateful if you were to join his army for the battle. He'd reward you handsomely for your skills."

"Do we have a choice in this?" Corvaire asked firmly.

"He just wants us for your magic," Adler added.

"You do have a choice," Kellen said. "But I personally urge

you to accept. Having the king's favor at your back will be of a lifelong advantage. And the king has many friends that you do not."

"We graciously decline," Stone said.

Kellen frowned, causing the many wrinkles on his face to crease. "The king will not be pleased to hear you do not wish to help him in his heroic capture of these lands to free the oppressed."

"We have our own battles to fight at the moment," Stone said. "Although you can tell him we appreciate the offer. He is a good king. Now what of the third thing he asked to relay to us? A warning you said?"

"Yes, he knows you were planning to leave the castle as soon as you acquire the weapons you are waiting for. But it has come to his attention that something new has come to these lands from where Arken came from. There's more to worry about than the dark dragons. They've been spotted on the plains and in the mountains on horseback now."

"More Runtue on horseback?" Stone gasped. *First the invasion came by air, and now they're coming by land? How could this get any worse?*

"How do you know that name, Runtue?" the chancellor asked.

"That's what they used to be called," Stone said. "The kings named them and their dragons the Neferian. We don't know all their past, but we know more than most."

"Where were these riders spotted, exactly?" Corvaire asked with narrow, glaring eyes.

"One pack was four-hundred miles to the east," Kellen said. "They ride swiftly from what our scouts have told us."

"How many are in that pack?" Corvaire asked.

"Ten."

Stone's gut ached as if a rock had been thrown into his inner core.

"And the other pack?" Corvaire asked. "You said there were two."

"Another was in the Androx Mountain range, just east of Mÿndmorden."

"Is that where the king's army is going?" Stone asked. "To fight the Runtue?"

"No."

"What?" Stone barked. "Then where is he sending them off to, if not to fight the real enemy?"

"That is none of your concern, for you do not wish to aid the king in his ultimate quest—you need know naught of the destination of his forces."

"What is wrong with you?" Stone snapped. "Why don't you fight together to save us all? Why are they squabbling while there are people dying! There're six dark dragons out there. How long until just one of them ends up here?"

"I'll warn you to watch your tongue," Kellen said. "You've gotten leniency so far. But that will only keep you safe for so long. Don't pretend to know the ways of kings. None of us can. This was only a warning to you for when you go back out there. Since Arken has promised to remove you from this world, it's possible the riders are out there to search for you. King Roderix wished for you to have knowledge of this."

"We thank him for that," Corvaire said in a calm voice. "Is that all?"

Kellen bowed while glowering at them, and they were quickly off back into the heart of the castle. And once they were out of earshot of the king's guard, Stone whispered. "Fools. They're all fools."

"Revenge is a bitter stain on the heart," Corvaire said. "They've been fighting each other so long they don't know any other way. And after this long there's no way they're going to agree to a truce. They're going to fight until one of them is dead or an entire kingdom gets washed away from history."

"We need to find someone with some sense to help us defeat Arken," Ceres said. "There's got to be someone with a brain who's got some power."

They walked back down the stairwell, and Stone still held a resentment for the conversation with the chancellor. Once they were back down to the ground floor of Empireodon and walked back out into the rain, Adler asked, "Where to next?"

"The orphanage he spoke of," Stone replied. "I want to see them with my own eyes."

Getting to the other side of the city took them over an hour by foot, but it gave them the chance to see a nicer side of Verren. The cobblestone roads were smoother—with less cracks—and there were less beggars and peering gazes from the dark corners and alleyways. Faces seemed cheerier, bellies were rounder, and smiles were whiter. But there was a much stronger presence by the king's soldiers that far west.

While they walked there were many eyes upon them though, just not from the shadows. Almost every single person wished to sing their praises as all they wanted to do was get to the orphanage and see how the children were being treated. Some gave them gifts even, after each of them tried to decline, but most refused, and they were forced to take them. Necklaces of silver or ivory, a couple of rings with gems of reds and greens, even a pair of wool socks from one elderly fellow.

"Should we just walk through the alleys?" Adler asked. "I'm not going to be able to carry all of these things."

They were even given a set of handkerchiefs, died in a lavish purple color. Stone tied one around Mud's neck, and they continued on. It was then they saw the high spire of the cathedral directly west of them, and straight ahead. It was then that Stone knew it wasn't going to be a small place of worship.

Stone didn't know much about Crysinthian, but he knew Adler and Ceres believed him to be the one true god that watched over the lands. Honestly, to Stone though, he thought, if he's watching and protecting all of the Worforgon—where was he now? When did the world need him more than right at that moment?

Once they got to the front gate of the cathedral, he heard it was known as Halen Veticus Cathedral, and was famous in that part of the world as being one of the oldest ones that still stood after all the wars that had ravaged the kingdoms in the last century.

He could already see from the outside of the gates the many children playing on the grounds outside of the cathedral. The younger children were laughing and running around on a circular path. There was sandpit for them, a wooden structure to hang on and climb up, and women of faith watching them while speaking amongst themselves. The older children stood on the outside playing games with small balls that bounced and sets of cards.

"Doesn't look too bad from here," Adler said.

The guards at the front gate let them pass without a word, and they walked into the courtyard. Halen Veticus was a huge church, Stone thought. It was a long, rectangular building with a second-story arcade with hundreds of pillars lining it. It had colorful, stained-glass windows running down it and its spire at its center must have reached one-hundred feet high. The courtyard was a vast park with lush, green grass and dozens of varieties of flowers brimming with color in the damp afternoon. The sun had peaked its way through the clouds and a warmth flowed throughout the courtyard.

The orphanage was supposedly next to the cathedral, so they walked toward the playing children.

"Good day," one of the nuns said. "Can we help you?"

"We came to check on some children that just arrived here by the king's orders," Stone said.

The nuns looked to each other. "You know them?"

"Some of them, yes."

"Well, follow me," she said. They walked behind her toward a side building that was newly constructed—as it didn't fit the elegant design of the old cathedral. The orphanage was a building of gray stone and mortar, but it looked large enough to fit many inside.

She led them through the front doors to the dim interior lit with many candles.

"This is a place of god," she said strictly. "There will be no use of his name in vain, or you will be asked to leave. And I know who you are, and what you did for Verren. But here, we are all treated equally, and we treat each other as such. But the Great God Crysinthian's name will not be tarnished here."

"Understood," Stone said, as they all walked past her, and he found one of the children from Orphan Alley.

The child ran up to him, as did many others from their bunks.

"Hi," Stone said, "how are you all?"

"You're famous now," the child said. "Everyone knows you. And because of you we are here, and not sleeping in the streets anymore. They say we may even have chances of finding new parents here."

"You—you like it here?" he asked.

The child smiled. "Yes, I think we all do. They feed us, and we each get our own bed. All we have to do is pretend to pray to their god. Not too bad a deal."

"Well, I'm pleased to hear that," Stone said. "What about the others? We asked about the children that didn't want to come here. What happened to them?"

"All I know is they were told they couldn't stay in that alley anymore, and they had patrols that kicked them out if they tried."

"They probably just wanted it to look good for us," Adler said. "Like all of them were taken care of. Not the worst thing to do to a child without a home. Hopefully they found some other place to keep safe."

"Do me a favor," Stone said as he knelt to meet the eye level of the kid. "If you hear from any of them—tell them where we are. They can come anytime to see us if they need help. Will you do that for me?"

The child nodded.

They stayed there another twenty minutes chatting with them, and as they left, they pleaded for the nuns to take good care of them, which they waved away coldly. And Stone and the others walked through alleyways back toward their shanty house. They decided they didn't need any more jewelry or adornments than they'd already received.

Chapter Sixteen

The following morning each of them awoke to the loud horns that blew down from Empireodon, echoing throughout the city. The king's forces were mobilizing, and they all went down to the main road from the keep watching the soldiers in full plate armor walking toward the front gate of the city.

There were thousands of citizens lined on either side of the road, tossing flowers onto the road and next to the soldiers' feet. Many whimpered as they walked by with the sound of their shuffling boots hitting the cobblestone—others cheered.

"Idiot," Corvaire sneered. "Why send them out to fight in a war that no one is going to win—"

"We could be standing next to them," Adler said. "I'm at least glad we were given a choice."

"Don't be so glad, yet," Corvaire said in a low tone. "There's still a chance they'll drag us into this. I've lived too long to know to not think kings want to control those with magic—as much as they say they don't want it to be around."

"How many of them do you think there are?" Ceres asked, watching the soldiers walk by.

"I'd say two and a half thousand," Corvaire said. "If he's not careful, he'll have no army left. After all, they did just get massacred by that dark dragon in the valley. He's just spiteful after almost being killed in his own castle. He's blinded by rage, and so many are going to die because of it."

"They'd be better to go out after those Runtue riders that are out in the wilds," Stone said. "At least then, I wouldn't have an issue joining in on their fight. That would be against the real enemy."

"We're going to have to be really careful when we leave the city," Adler said. "They may only be on horseback, but we'll most likely be on foot—unless one of these people gives us four horses, and I don't think that's going to happen."

"We could ask the king," Stone said, looking up at the white tower, where Roderix was most likely looking down upon them from.

"Yes, that's a possibility," Corvaire said. "I'm guessing Kellen wouldn't like that too much though. And with that bastard hissing into the king's ear, I'm almost eager to just get our weapons and be on our way."

"Hopefully it won't be that much longer," Adler said. "Anyone in the mood to kill some hours away?"

Ceres sighed. "Is that all you ever think about?"

"What else is there to do?" Adler shot back with a wide grin.

"Practice with your blade, try some magic, go read about whatever you want in the libraries here. There's literally so many things to do besides hang out at a tavern."

"But none of those things sound good," he said with a shrug. "And there's always tomorrow for those things! What do you say?"

Stone still wanted some time away to think about his dream with his mother in it. But he didn't mind the thought of wasting away a few hours with Adler, and as he looked up to Corvaire, he didn't seem to mind too much either.

"Don't tell me he's gotten to you again?" Ceres asked him.

"We may not want this fame," Adler said. "But I sure wouldn't mind some drinks that don't lighten my pockets too much."

"He makes a good point," Corvaire said.

Ceres was left flabbergasted with her mouth agape, but then regained her composure and brushed her blond hair back behind her ear. "Well I'm not going to leave you to have fun without me. I'm going to practice my magic after, mark my words!"

"Okay, Ceres," Adler said. "You can do whatever you want afterward. Who knows—if we get into the harder fluids, I might even try some magic myself?"

"I wouldn't recommend that," Corvaire said.

"Maybe I'll check with you again after you've had a couple," Adler said to him. Corvaire groaned.

Minutes later they'd walked into a nearby tavern where it went from stark silence from the patrons once they saw their entrance, to a near-deafening exuberance—and the drinks flowed. It was no run of the mill afternoon waste of time that Adler had been known for by his friends. Stone thought it perhaps had to do with the many fathers and sons going off to battle that people wanted to forget about also.

Mugs were laid on the table before them—as they didn't even have a moment to sit. Dozens of people flocked into the dim tavern from the streets as many surely heard the clapping and dancing from inside. Stone shook so many hands it was difficult to keep track of who he'd met and who he hadn't. Time passed like this, and none of them even got much time to talk to one another. Stone found himself drinking a clear liquor that tasted like rum but was thick like syrup.

At one point, Ceres grabbed him by the wrist and pulled

him out into the road, where it was surprisingly almost dark out. His head was foggy, and his focus was solely on her as she stared into his eyes.

"You doin' all right?" he asked.

Her green eyes were glistening with the light of the candles burning from inside the tavern. Her normally pale face was lightly flushed with a rosy hue, and her delicate blond hair trickled in front of her face.

"You seem liked you're having a good time," he said. "Can't believe it's almost dark out. How long have we . . .?"

"Shut up, Stone." She leaned forward with her lips leading the way.

He pursed his lips, ready for the kiss, but then her fingers nudged his head to the side, and her lips found her way onto his cheek. It made Stone's heart beat wildly and all his worries wash away like a warm bath after too long in the woods.

She pulled back and looked at him with loving, caring eyes.

His lips felt as if they were locked together with lock and key, if his mind even had been able to find the words to say. So, he didn't say anything.

She grabbed him by the wrist again, pulling him back into the tavern, where time again slowed—or hastened—he was handed another drink by someone and he looked up in amazement as Adler was up on the bar top, dancing in a line with a woman twice his age. A lutist and a fiddler were playing a tune, while many of the patrons sang. Elation lit up in Stone as he watched his friend dip the woman backward and saw Ceres over to the side clapping her hands and swaying from side to side, watching them as well.

Corvaire was leaning up against the corner wall, in the more dimly lit area of the tavern.

Stone went over and nudged him on the arm. "Everything all right over here? You're not dancing?"

The joke didn't have the intended result.

"No. You have your fun. I'll stand here and have a clear head tonight. Now go, be with your friends."

Stone again, didn't know what to say, so he stumbled off back to where he'd been, just in time to see the end of the song. Adler gave a low bow with one arm out, and then kissed the woman on the hand. To Adler's surprise she laid a big kiss on his mouth while holding the sides of his face, while the entire tavern erupted in cheers and laughs. Adler was left with a big smudge of red lip gloss on his face. Stone laughed so hard his eyes watered, and he looked over at Ceres where she held one hand over her mouth and was laughing so hysterically she had to hold onto the table to not topple over. Adler feigned a shrug with a wry smile and leaped down from the bar top.

"Looks like you made a new friend," Stone said to him.

"Yer just jealous." Adler put his mug up to his mouth but found it was empty. "Another!" His voice was like a king commanding his court.

"Easy there," Stone said. "Have you had anything to eat since this morning?"

"One of those ales was a bit. Chewy." He laughed.

Ceres came through the crowd and fell onto Adler with her arms around his neck from the back.

"Adler," she said, with a slight slur in her words, "you're a real pecker if I'd ever met one. But that was one o' the funniest things I've ever seen in me' life!"

"All right," Stone said. "Let's head out of here and get you two something to eat."

"But." Adler tried to fight, but no new drink found his way to him as he glanced around. "Argh. They're all drunk! Let's head out of here."

They made their way to the door, where Corvaire was waiting stoically for them, and Mud sat patiently on the road, waiting for them.

"Oh, I love him so much," Adler said as he went over and

petted Mud's head, and then kissed him on the nose, but then pulled back quickly. "What did you get into, dog? Tastes like you had rotten rat guts for supper."

"Stop." Ceres laughed. "I'm going to lose my appetite."

Stone and Corvaire led them to an inn a couple of buildings down the road and ordered them an assortment of meats, cheeses, breads and fresh fruits. Of course, Ceres ordered a plate of sweet cake with honey. The smell was intoxicating as it arrived at the table, and Stone realized he himself hadn't eaten since far earlier in the day.

After he'd shoved the food into his mouth and sat back after drinking a full mug of water, he looked up and saw a strange look in Ceres' eyes. It was as if she was focusing on something intently behind Stone, who turned around in his seat but saw nothing.

"Ceres," Stone asked. "Something wrong?"

"I—I don't know," she said slowly.

Adler stopped eating, and paid attention as well. "What's the matter with you?" he asked.

"Something. Strange," Ceres said in a hollow tone.

Stone slowly stood, but her gaze was unwavering.

"There's something there," Ceres said in that same, off-sounding voice. "There's something out there."

"What is it? What do you feel?" Corvaire asked.

"What? What is it?" Stone asked. "Is it Arken? Is he coming?"

"No," Ceres said. "Doesn't feel like him. It doesn't feel dark. It's a light. It's a faded light, but it's getting brighter."

Stone flinched back as Ceres' gaze snapped to the right, getting up from the table, slowly walking toward it.

"You see it?" she asked with a blank expression on her face. "I—I think it's—" Then, she cried out in crippling pain, wincing back and falling to the floor with her hands clutching the sides of her head.

"Ceres!" Stone said as he ran to her.

"What is it?" Adler asked Stone. "What is this? Are we under attack? Is this magic?"

Ceres then opened her eyes slowly, as if awakening from a deep slumber.

"Ceres, are you all right? What just happened?" Stone cradled her in his arms.

Corvaire, who was hovering over her, leaned in to inspect Ceres.

"Ceres?" Stone asked slowly.

"She's awoken," she said.

"Who? What?" Adler asked with a puzzled look on his face.

"She's awoken," Ceres said with a wide grin. "One of the mothers."

Stone and Adler both watched in awe as Ceres rose to her feet, staring at the wall at the northern end of the room. She raised her right arm and pointed at the wall.

Ceres then looked down at both of them, as a wide grin grew across Corvaire's face.

"One of the new Majestic Wilds… She's awoken."

PART IV
INTO THE WILD

Chapter Seventeen

"We've got to go gather our things," Corvaire said, rushing out the door of the tavern and out into the torch-lit roads of Verren. Adler splashed water on his face.

"What, tonight?" Stone said, walking at a brisk pace to keep up with Corvaire. "Our things are on the other side of the city. And we need rest before we go out." Ceres and Adler caught up with them, as Mud trotted behind. "Can't we leave in the morning? Do we know where they are?"

"North," Corvaire said, looking ahead down the road back toward the eastern part of the city. They could feel many eyes on them as they walked. "And yes, we're leaving tonight."

"Corvaire," Ceres said. "We may need just a few hours of sleep before we go. I feel woozy from what I saw. I feel as if I need to."

Stone turned then, just in time to see Ceres fall to her knees, barely catching herself with her hands. Her gaze was distant and foggy. He and Adler ran to her, as Corvaire stopped with a concerned look on his face. "She all right?"

"I'm okay, I just need some rest." She almost toppled over to her side.

"We need to get her to a bed," Stone said, holding her up off the ground.

"In all that's been happening lately, I'd completely forgotten that she's one of the Litreon," Adler said, scratching his head. "Will she be able to help us find the new mother?"

"Yes," Corvaire said, "but it will use her Indiema. And since she's so new to it, it will be quite exhausting on her, I'm afraid. We'll have to use it sparsely."

Stone helped Ceres up to her feet and Adler put her other arm over his neck, aiding her to walk back to their shanty house.

"Corvaire," Stone asked. "If she felt the new mother being born, how many others felt the same thing? How many Litreon are there out there?"

"Don't know," he said. "Don't think anyone knows the answer to that question. Even Seretha and the other Majestic Wilds didn't know."

"What will others do to her if they get to her first?" Adler asked.

"We're not going to find out the answer to that question, Adler," Corvaire said. "Because we're going to get to her first, and we're going to get her safely back to Endo Valair."

"Endo?" Stone asked. "Why Endo? It's burned asunder. And Arken knows where it is. He'll be able to find her."

"Endo didn't burn," Corvaire said. Sending them all into a confusing whirl of uncertainty.

"It what?" Adler said. "We saw it burn."

"Endo Valair didn't burn. The city atop it did."

"Endo is underground?" Stone asked. "In the mountain?"

"Keep your voices down," Corvaire said as they all walked. "But yes, the knowledge of the Majestic Wilds didn't die with Seretha, Vere, and Gardin. There's more to their wisdom and legacy than you know. We've just got to get another mother there. Others will seek her out and attempt to exploit her magic, but we've got to get her back home—where she belongs. She will be able to tell us more about how to defend ourselves against the Neferian possibly and help us to unravel their secrets."

"We're going back to Endo?" Adler said with both eyebrows raised.

Ceres let out a low moan.

"After we get the girl," Corvaire said.

"But Corvaire," Stone said. "We can't leave now. We'll be leaving our new weapons behind."

"We can retrieve them later. This takes far more precedence. We must leave at once."

"What about horses?" Adler asked. "We were thinking about asking Roderix for horses."

"We can steal some along the way."

Stone and Adler looked at each other with cocked heads. They didn't ever mind Ceres pickpocketing from the rich, and never too much, but stealing horses out in the open. That was a good way to end up on the wrong side of a prison gate.

"Can we talk about this?" Stone said. "If we wait until morning, and get horses given to us, we'd still be faster than going out and walking now."

"And what do you say when the king asks why we need horses? And why we're leaving so quickly—before our weapons are ready? Doesn't that seem a little suspicious? And what if he has a Litreon here in the city? That person may not have even known they were one. There hasn't been a new mother in a long, long time."

Adler and Stone were silent for a good ten minutes after that, with all that was reeling through their heads, and about the logical statement that Corvaire had made. They both knew all that was on the line then—it was a race. A race to see who would get to the new mother first. And another thing was troubling Stone greater than the idea of having to take an exhausted Ceres back out into the plains: *what if Arken knows about the new mother?*

They wove through the roads of Verren, as the white Tower of Empireodon loomed over them with its many windows lit in dazzling torchlight, and Stone couldn't be sure, but he felt heavy eyes on him from up above. *Is the king going to be troubled that we're leaving in the night without saying anything to him? We don't have a choice. We have to go, tonight.*

They finally made it back to their rooms, and Stone and Adler laid Ceres onto her mattress as she let out a soft moan again.

"Gather her things, and yours," Corvaire said as he ran into his room and packed.

"Give her an hour," Stone said. "One hour won't hurt that much. We could all rest our legs for a bit before we walk all night in the dark."

He didn't hear an immediate answer, but eventually he heard Corvaire say, "One hour."

Stone pulled up Ceres' sheets over her, and went back to his room, where a wave of exhaustion swept over him, and he laid in his bed and drifted off to a deep sleep. What only felt like minutes later though, he awoke to Adler shaking his shoulder.

"Time to go," he said. "We've got to start getting ready."

Stone looked around, blinking. "He said one hour."

"That hour passed," Adler said. "Come now, I've made some hot tea. That should help." On the floor, Mud remained asleep, snoring softly.

Before Stone went to packing though, he went out of his room and around the corner, poking his head into Ceres' room.

"I just woke her too," Adler said from behind him.

Ceres sat on her bed, looking down at the floor in a daze.

"How are you feeling?" Stone asked.

"Been better, but I'm fine. I think that tea will help."

"We can take it slow at first," he said.

"No, I'll be all right. Just need to wake up." Ceres she rose and walked over to the dresser at the far side of the room. Stone looked down the hallway to see Corvaire coming out of his room with his pack on his back, and his sword fixed at his hip. His thick cloak was on and his dark hood pulled up over his head. This was the Corvaire that Stone remembered most—the hardened adventurer and soldier. He wasn't meant to be cooped up in cities and castles with kings and chancellors. He was a fight—a warrior, destined for greatness.

"We leave in ten," he said in a strong voice. "Make sure you feed the dog."

He strode past them and went down the stairs with heavy footsteps.

Stone and Adler went to their rooms and packed, shoving things back into their bags. Stone picked up his sword from the table and unsheathed it four inches, scanning the blade. He wished he'd had his new blade but pushed it back into its leather sheath and belted it to his hip.

By the time he'd left his room and gotten Mud to wake up, the others were downstairs waiting for him. They were all sipping on the tea, and Adler poured a cup for him.

"Ready?" Corvaire said. "We're going to have a different way out of the city without as many eyes as the front gate. We should be on our way. We'll want to get some good distance in between us and the city before the light of day."

"Corvaire," Adler said, pulling his cup down from his lips. "There is one thing I've been thinking of. More of a concern, really. What about those Runtue riders out there? What if we run into them? Without our new weapons, what do we have to fight them off with? You have magic, but who knows what they can do?"

"You've got a sword on you, don't you?" Corvaire said. "Start with stabbing them with the sharp end."

Adler sighed.

"Look, lad," Corvaire said, walking over to him and clapping a hand on his shoulder. "If we run into them; we fight. I don't know how powerful they are, or how fast their steeds run, but I do know this—if Arken gets to the new mother first, we've lost a huge asset in our fight against him. And to be honest—our lives mean nothing compared to hers."

"What do you mean?" Ceres asked. "Stone is the prophesied one."

"Yes, and perhaps not," Corvaire said. "The prophecy was vague—intentionally? I do not know. But, '*the dead will aid in his end.*' That doesn't mean that Stone was or is going to be—the only one that could fulfill it. The Wild Majestics are superior, extremely powerful beings. Their knowledge alone of things is enough to turn or win a war."

"That's unfortunate that their magic didn't work against Arken and his attack on them," Adler said.

"Yes, that was why I stayed to fight him, and sent the mothers off to hide," Corvaire said. "Now, follow me."

They followed him out of the house and crept around the corner, dipping into an alley behind a row of homes, alongside a tall wall darkened in the shadows. Each of them crept low and followed after him quickly with soft footsteps. He cut left down another alley, each of them scuttling through the dark with their hoods up. Mud scampered behind. Corvaire was leading them north, past the tower of the king, weaving from alleyway to alleyway, scanning busy roads before crossing them. He was mostly looking for the leering eyes of soldiers, as he didn't want word to get to the king of their hasty exodus before they were long gone.

For what felt like an hour to Stone, they continued on their way, until they finally got to the northern exit of the castle. And for some reason, which Stone couldn't figure out—while they were trying to figure a way to get past the two soldiers and safely out of the city—Mud ran up and grabbed a thick sausage off the table next the soldier and ran back into the road on the inside of the gate. The soldier hollered and ran off after him with his spear out. The other soldiers walked slowly after him, laughing.

"Dimwit soldiers," Corvaire groaned. "Smart dog, though, owe him a bone for that one."

They ran out of the castle gate and ran down into the brush on the side of the road that left the city. And just like that, Stone found himself back out on the plains, and back at the mercy of whatever was to come.

Chapter Eighteen

The sky was blanketed with pinpricked shimmering stars once they'd gotten a few miles out of the city. They'd moved back up onto the road as they walked while the grasses rolled on in the gentle breeze. Bats flew overhead chaotically, and the moon lay just over the horizon line, looming largely above the road in front of them.

Stone was still dazed, yet Ceres seemed surprisingly awake as they walked. While he should have been concerned about the dangers that lay out on the road, his thoughts were more driven to the memory of his mother in his coffin, and the kiss that Ceres laid upon his cheek earlier that same night. He wanted to ask her about it, but didn't have the nerve—and not in front of the others.

Step by step they strode through the night. They hardly talked, but each of them surely worried about who else out there would have the knowledge of the first new Wild Majestic in a very long time. Back in Verren—they'd been heroes—but out in the wilds of the Worforgon, they were at the mercy of whatever lurked out there in the vast plains. And now, with the new sighting of the Runtue on horseback,

Corvaire seemed even more rigid than normal. His feet walked the road quietly, and his gaze was vigilant upon the plains, causing them to run down into the grasses multiple times as he'd thought he'd seen something. Mud would just sit and wait for them to get back up to the road, each time walking next to Stone.

After a long night and little sleep back in the city, the sun rose, and they heard a rooster crowing off in the distance. Adler sat heavily on a boulder on the side of the road and dropped his pack. He wiped the sweat from his brow and let out a heavy yawn. That caused Stone and Ceres to yawn too.

"Wish we still had our horses," Ceres said. "Maybe we should've tied them up when we were at the base of the mountain when we went to Endo. I miss Angelix."

"I miss Hedron," Adler said. "I'm sure you wouldn't mind having Grave back either."

Stone nodded.

"We can rest a bit," Corvaire said. "But we must be back on our way soon. Ceres we're going to need you to use your Elessior to find the new mother soon."

"I—I feel I'm too weak still," she said, wiping her brow and sitting with her legs crossed. "We need real rest. But I get the urgency we're under. I just don't know how long we can keep walking like this without rest. Are you not tired?"

"I am," Corvaire said. "But this is more important than me."

"Why don't you go on without us," Adler said. "You find the woman, and we'll catch up with you later. I don't want to keep you from doing what you need to do."

"What I need to do is protect you," Corvaire said, letting down his pack. "*And*, I need to get to her before anyone else."

"We will go with you," Stone said. "When will we be able to rest? Do we have any idea how far off she is?"

"Only Ceres can tell us that."

"What do you think?" Stone asked her. "Do you think you can try to find her?"

"I can always try."

"Do you feel her now?" Corvaire asked.

Ceres closed her eyes and took a deep breath. "I—I don't think so."

"You're willing to try?" Stone asked. "Even if you need to meditate afterward?"

"Like I said. I'll try."

Corvaire went over and knelt before her. "There's no spell to cast," he said. "There's no words to recite. It's a feeling deep down inside you. It's like a thread that pulls you two together. It's thin and weak at first, but it should grow tight, and form a strong bond between you—until you finally find one another. Can you feel it? I've heard it described like a needle poking you into the inside of your chest."

Ceres took another deep breath and reached up to touch her chest with her left hand. "There's something there, but it doesn't feel like a needle. It feels more like a tiny marble."

Stone and Adler leaned in.

"This marble," Corvaire said in a clear voice. "Does it feel like it's moving you? Does it want to pull you toward something else? Like there's another marble out there?"

"I—I don't know. I can barely feel it. It feels like it's just resting there."

"Ceres," said Stone. "Think about your mother again while you're feeling this. Remember something about her that made you feel happy."

A warm smile went across her face. "It is sort of wanting to move, I suppose. Forward. It's pulling me forward."

"So, she's still north," Adler said. "How far? Can you feel how far away it is?"

Ceres was silent, with her eyes still focused and her eye

moving around quickly behind closed eyelids. "I—I don't know. It's so faint—I have no idea."

"It's all right," Corvaire said. "We'll try again later. We can rest here for an hour, but then we must be back off. We're going to need to find a way to travel faster than this. At this rate, she could be hundreds of miles away, and if any of the kings or queens know of her existence yet, they'll send their fastest riders out after her."

"So, we're going to steal horses?" Stone asked. "Is that what you're saying?"

"I don't know yet. Whatever it takes though. Whatever it takes."

Over the next hour the three of them rested as Corvaire had given them all bread and dried meat that he brought from Verren. He then lay back and slept soundly on the side of the road as the sun rose slowly higher into the sky. Chirping birds fluttered overhead and in a large tree off to the east.

Stone laid there with a cloth over his eyes, shielding the light of the sun. As much as he tried to drift off to sleep though, every time he shut his eyes, he only thought of his mother holding his hand, telling him that she was with him. The memory wouldn't go away, and he didn't want it to. He just wanted to see her face. He wanted nothing more than that.

That's when they heard it though—that familiar, yet far-off roar that made the hairs on the back of his neck tingle. His mind raced as the roar that sounded like erupting fire and broken glass echoed throughout the hills and valleys, causing the birds to quickly hush and fly off west.

"Down into the grass!" Corvaire jumped to his feet. "Quickly!"

They rushed down in the tall grass, each gathering all of their items, as to not leave a trace back up on the road.

"Is it Arken?" Stone held a hand up over his brow to shield the sunlight. At that far of a distance it was difficult to spot the beast, especially with the thick, white clouds in the sky to the east.

"Can't tell," Corvaire said.

"Does it matter?" Adler said. "Even if it's not, we've still got no chance if that thing spots us."

Then a sudden, new worry came to Stone then.

"North," he said. "Is it flying north?"

"Can't even see the blasted thing," Adler said.

"If it's after the new mother," Corvaire said. "We've already lost."

"Would it," said Ceres softly. "Would it kill her?"

"Don't know what Arken's plans would be for a new mother," Corvaire said. "He had a hatred for the Old Mothers because of what he felt like they did to him. I don't know if he's got a reason to kill this new one—or if he'd try to turn her to his side. After all, she will have potent magic that would be useful to him, if that's what he's after."

"Look!" Adler said, pointing up to the distant sky.

Stone trailed his finger to see the mighty Neferian emerging from the thick clouds, letting out another roar that caused every living thing within the vast miles to shiver in silence.

"It's turning back south," said Adler. "It must not know what we know!"

"I pray to Crysinthian he doesn't," Ceres said.

"It's not Arken himself," Corvaire said. "And this may be a good sign, for if this Neferian rider doesn't know about the mother, that's almost sure that Arken doesn't know yet either."

The dark dragon glided through the sky mightily. Its giant wings flapped easily as it flew back down southbound. Its long dark body was covered with hundreds of horns and spikes, and its long claws peaked out of its fingers at the tips of its wings. The rider atop its back sat proudly upon its back as it rushed through the air.

Stone petted Mud's head and neck, trying to calm him and keep him from barking up at the beast.

"We must get moving again," said Corvaire, standing back up out of the brush with his hand on the grip of his sword. "We don't have time to be standing around like this. We've got to find a way to get to her quicker than this."

They followed him up out of the grass and made their way back to the road once the dark dragon was out of sight. They walked with a quicker pace then behind him.

"Corvaire," Stone said after a few minutes of walking. "Would you tell us why Arken hated Seretha and the others so much? What did they do to him that made him hate them so?"

Corvaire groaned.

"Please," Ceres said.

"It was so long ago," he said. "Seems immaterial at this point. Arken's consumed by his hatred. Hate is all he knows now. But very well."

Stone took a deep breath, intent on listening to his friend.

"As you know," said Corvaire, "Arken said Majestics betrayed their friendship, and a promise they had made to him. But I've mentioned that he betrayed them. And remember—this was a very long time ago."

He scratched his cheek and looked up to the sky where the Neferian had vanished off into the distant skies.

"Back then the Runtue and the other people who lived here mostly cohabited. They'd barter and trade with one another, and they looked the same. They were mostly living in the southern provinces back then. Their lifestyle was similar, and they farmed the same crops and ate the same foods. But there was one stark difference between them and the other people here."

"What was that?" Ceres asked.

"God."

"Crysinthian?" she asked. "What about him?"

"The Runtue didn't believe in him."

"Who'd they believe in?" she asked with her brow furrowed; puzzled.

"They believed in a set of crystals that gave power to those who found them," he said. "To them—the crystals were the divine artifacts, not the people who wielded them."

"Fascinating," Stone said with wide eyes. "Was there any truth to that?"

"Oh," Corvaire said, running his fingers through his dark hair. "Depends on who you ask."

"I'm asking you," Stone said with an intense gaze.

"There is evidence that there is some truth to it, yes. But there's also truth to the God Crysinthian."

"So, they ended up fightin' religious wars?" Ceres asked.

"Yes and no," Corvaire said. "The Runtue were legendary warriors, and their generals and combat expertise were vastly renowned. They had battles over the ages, but the old kings decided it would be best to strike a truce with the old leaders of the Runtue people."

"So, that's where the betrayal comes in?" Stone asked.

Corvaire sighed. "King Arken Shadowborn was the last king of the Runtue before what at the time was called, The Shadow Purge. It's been wiped from history's ear. But it was a secret attack by the kings to destroy Arken—who they'd decided was getting too powerful for them to allow. For they believed he'd been driven mad to find one of those crystals, and reign over his people with powerful magic for a very long time. And above all—the kings of the Worforgon fear magic."

"I gathered that from our time in Verren," Adler said. "Can't say I blame them much. That shite is more trouble than it's worth."

"It's saved your shitter more than you care to admit," Ceres barked.

"Anyways, continue," Stone said.

The Wild Majestics at the time: Seretha, Gardin, and Vere—were the greatest sorceresses in the lands, but they were benevolent. They never used their magic for evil—or to pick a side in the battle between Arken and the Kings. Arken, even, would travel to Endo and share dinners with the Old Mothers. They had a bond. He had the Wendren Set of magic after all—just as they did. They'd share their findings and abilities with one another. They were friends and became even more than that."

"More than that?" Adler asked. "They were lovers? Which one?"

Corvaire tilted his head and lowered an eyebrow at him in response.

"All of them?" Adler said, leaning back with his face flush.

"They shared a connection," he said. "But they refused to pick sides in the dispute, and over the years, after pleading with them, Arken grew impatient and angry that they wouldn't help him defend his people. And so he asked for one thing from them at least: if there came a time that they *had* to pick—that they would pick him and help save his people. In exchange, the mothers conceded that they would, if and only if—he didn't start the conflict in which this decision would have to be made. For they promised an allegiance to the kings that they would stay out of the battle, and the kings would let them live in seclusion like they preferred and teach the magic to others that the kings wanted to exterminate completely."

"So, they were allowed to use and teach magic," Ceres said. "As long as they didn't use it in the conflict between the kings and the Runtue?"

Corvaire nodded.

"But that's when things went awry?" Stone asked.

"Arken broke his promise first, didn't he?" Adler asked.

"Arken thought he found a crystal's location," Corvaire said. "But it was in a Lord's small castle outside the city of

Valeren. So, one night, Arken and his people laid siege upon the castle, and it wasn't without causalities. Many died, even though the Lord's life was spared. Yet the kings saw this as an attack on all of the kingdoms, and Seretha and the others cursed Arken for attacking the way he did and refused to take his side."

"So, that was their betrayal?" Stone asked. "Doesn't sound like one to me, sounded like they did what they said they'd do."

"Did he find what he was after?" Ceres asked. "The crystal?"

"I don't know. But, yes, Stone. Seretha said they wouldn't pick a side, and that they didn't. But by that time Arken had grown bitter and angry—just as the kings had over those fragile years. His temperament clouded his judgment, and when the kings' armies attacked them in the night during The Shadow Purge. It was meant to kill King Arken, destroy their villages, and scatter his people."

"So, what happened?" Stone asked. "Arken is obviously still alive."

"The Shadow Purge turned into a massacre," Corvaire said, itching his thigh as a crisp wind blew through. "The Runtue expected the attack, as they'd seen the large enemy approaching from far away. But the kings didn't bring a battalion to lash out an attack—they brought their armies in—all of them. It was a bloodbath. So much hatred had brewed for so long, those armies trampled, burned, and attempted to wipe the Runtue from the lands—and nearly did so. As I said, the Runtue were skilled warriors, and they killed thousands, but most of them fell that night."

"Soldiers, right?" Ceres said with a rash gulp.

Corvaire sighed again. "They armies tried to wipe them out. All of them."

Ceres covered her mouth in horror.

"I despise soldiers." Adler shook his head.

"What happened next?" Stone asked.

"Many died, but many escaped through underground passageways. One of them was Arken. And as it broke the Old Mother's hearts to stay out of the fray and watch Arken's people murdered—they'd made a promise, and that promise they kept. So Arken escaped and his warriors regrouped, attacking his enemy from the shadows for weeks."

"The mothers told us how the story ended," Stone said. "They caught Arken, and instead of killing him and giving him a soldier's death, they took both his eyes, his hands, and his legs and sent him off into the Obsidian Sea to suffer out on the waters, never to return."

"Yes," Corvaire said. "They planted a trap to catch him and catch him they did. Arken grew one eye back somehow, and has hands and legs again. There's something else at play here. Arken's become twisted in his anger."

"What a terrible story," Ceres said. "And now Seretha and the other mothers are dead because of this war so long ago. When will the killing end?"

"It ends either when Arken kills everyone and everything," Stone said with an intent glare, and flicker of light in his eyes. "Or we kill him first. We just need to figure out how."

Chapter Nineteen

Two days went by.

Two days of walking, desperately searching for a way to expedite their journey.

They searched for horses they could purchase or swipe if need be. But, Corvaire assumed, word had spread of the Runtue on horseback, and they only saw one solitary merchant upon a mule traveling south to reach Verren. He had little insight to offer other than there was no need to be out in the open then with all the madness happening around them with the Neferian, civil war, assassination attempts, and now invading foreign forces by land. There was even rumor that the dark dragons had burned small villages on the east coast of the continent.

Before they could even offer to trade for the mule—if only to have something to help them carry their supplies—the merchant gave them a gruff glower and told them, 'don't waste yer' breath.'

So, they trudged on.

"You rested?" Stone asked Ceres as they walked upon the

high-banked road with only wagon-wheel tracks lining a long trail of grass northbound.

Ceres' hair whipped in the breeze with the long plains to their right, and a scattered, thin thicket to their left. She nodded. Mud was lapping in a narrow creak down at the bottom of the bank near the trees.

"Care to try again?" he asked her. "See if we need to change course?" Adler and Corvaire were both interested in her upcoming reply.

"I wasn't able to yesterday, but yes, I do feel more rested. I can try."

They stopped then, standing behind her as she faced north with her hands both gently touching her temples. Stone watched as there was a stark silence between them. They heard the birds chirping softly in the trees, and saw an albatross flying high overhead as Ceres stood there for minutes like a statue, while they waited anxiously.

Finally, she grunted and dropped her hands back to her sides.

"I still feel that pit in my chest, like I can feel something, but it's not pulling me in any direction. I'm sorry. I'm tryin', but I just can't do it yet. I'm not strong enough."

"You will get there," Corvaire said. "You'll just need more practice is all."

She sighed and went over to grab her pack.

"Ceres, have you been able to conjure that spell you did back in Verren?" Stone asked. "I haven't seen you do it since. Maybe if we practiced with that."

Instead of grabbing her pack, she bent over and grabbed a round rock that might be useful for skipping across a pond. Ceres brought it up between her and him, letting it rest in the palm of her right hand. She closed her eyes, and all attention was on the gray, round rock then.

Her lips moved, but no words came out, but with a faint flicker of light, the rock trickled with sparkles of light, dancing over it like a magical fire with tiny gemstones reflecting in it. She opened her eyes with a smile, and the rock beamed to light.

They all stood watching, as their faces were lit in its white light.

"There you go," Corvaire whispered. "There you go. Very well done."

She wrapped her fingers around the rock and its light extinguished without a sound.

"Amazing," Stone said.

"You're growing quickly," Corvaire said with a grin.

Adler put his hands in his pockets, looking down the long road ahead.

"We'll have to teach you some stronger spells next," Corvaire said. "Much more difficult—much more rewarding."

"I want to be able to do the spell I need though," she said. "We need to be able to find the girl. Why can't I do that yet?"

"That's not so much a spell," Corvaire said. "It's more of an inherent gift. That's something nobody can teach you, because so few have it and can use it. You'll just have to keep trying, and hopefully it comes to you."

"We'll try again later," Stone said. "Should we be off again?"

They started their pace back up the road, as Mud sensed this, and ran off ahead playfully, only looking back when he was many yards up and about to go around a bend that was hidden by trees.

"I was thinking of something this morning," Ceres said to the others, "about Stone's magic—if he has any."

"What's that?" Corvaire asked, and Stone's attention was certainly roused as a tingle ran down his shoulders.

"We don't know when he was born, so we don't know his magic set, but... You said that magic from a certain set can't hurt a person usin' the same set. So—I've got the Sonter Set, and Corvaire, you've got the Primaver Set. Adler—who's too lazy and scared to try his out."

"Hey!" he protested.

"If you're willing, Stone," she said. "We could try to use our magics on you, and see if they have any effect. If they do, then that's not your set, so hopefully we can narrow it down."

"But we'd only narrow it down to two," he said. "That won't help because if I try the one that's not mine. I'll get further away from my own."

"But…" she said with a slightly raised pitch in her voice.

Stone looked at Corvaire who seemed to be nodding in understanding.

"Who do we know who will have magic from one of the other sets?" she asked.

The only person around who came to mind was Adler, and he was of the Utumn Set, but wouldn't dare try any spells. *Who else is there? Who else do we know who would use magic, and how would we know what set… Oh?*

"You gettin' it?" she asked.

Stone stroked his stubbly chin. "The new mother… All Wild Majestics are in the Wendren Set. When we find her, we could have her try to use magic on me. Then we'd know for sure which set I am. Then I'd be able to practice magic too."

An exhilaration shot through him then as he felt a wide smile brim on his face. He clapped his hands together, and found a newfound urgency to get to the new mother before anyone else could. *I could finally start practicing my magic. Maybe that's the key, maybe that's the way I'm going to be able to fight Arken and the Runtue. Maybe that will be the way I can save more people from dying!*

"You wanna go first?" Ceres asked Corvaire. "Might be a bit safer."

He nodded and motioned for Stone to stand before him.

"Hold your hands out flat like this," he said, holding his palms up at chest level. "You may feel a slight pinch."

Stone held his hands up. "Is this going to hurt? And you're just getting me prepared?"

"Just hold still."

Corvaire waved his hands around slowly, focusing intently on Stone's hands with his eyebrows arched down.

"*Maximillia Centrura,*" he said, and his eyes sparkled.

Stone felt that pinch quickly on the underside of his hand, which quickly turned to a searing pain like something had just bitten him. "Ouch." He winced, about to pull his hands back.

"Don't move," Ceres said.

Corvaire repeated the enchantment, waving his hands around between them as a faint light enveloped them.

"It hurts," Stone said.

"Stop moving around," Ceres said.

But as Stone felt something crawling on the back side of his hands, his eyes went wide as he saw its head stick out between his fingers on his right hand.

"Oh my," Adler gasped.

Another head then poked its head out of his left hand just below the thumb.

Stone was stuck in a state of shock as the thick, wet, slick bodies of the many-legged creatures crawled up onto his palms and walked between his fingers.

"Are those centipedes?" Adler said, taking a long stride backward.

"They're enormous," Ceres said with a smile. Just as she said that another set of black centipedes crawled onto his hands.

Stone stood there like a terrified statue, unable to look away from the foot-long insects.

"Are they venomous?" he asked, with his voice quivering.

"Oh yes," Corvaire said, still waving his hands around. "Not much point in conjuring up harmless ones."

"They aren't going to bite, right?"

"No, no, no," he said. "I didn't say that word."

"What word?" Ceres asked playfully.

"No!" Stone said. "We don't need to know it. Everything is fine just the way it is."

Ceres laughed, and Corvaire did playfully too. Adler remained a safe distance away as beads of sweat ran down Stone's brow.

"Can you take them off of me please? I think we got what we needed to know."

Corvaire lifted his hands above his head then and said the word, "Poof." And the centipedes faded away to a soft mist that floated off in the breeze.

"What did ya think, Stone?" Ceres asked.

"I'd rather have had him create a butterfly, or a roly-poly, but I suppose it did the trick."

"Argh, no fun in casting butterfly spells unless you're doing it for children," Corvaire said.

"I'll admit," Adler said. "For an assassin, that sure would be a useful spell."

"Look at you," Ceres mocked with her hands on her hips. "You found something you don't hate about magic. You may come around after all!"

"I wouldn't go that far," he said.

"All right, my turn," Ceres said, rubbing her hands together eagerly. "What should I cast? The Firefly Lights spell again?"

"No," Corvaire said, looking up at the clouds as they floated past. "We don't need his hands glowing. Let's think of something different. Something you could practice. Oh! Here we go."

"Not Searing Flesh," Stone said flatly.

"No," Corvaire said, waving that away with his hand. "It's called Orb of Life."

"Well, that sounds better," Stone said, wiping the cold sweat away with his sleeve.

"You're not going to like the first part," Corvaire said. "And if she can't cast it, you're going to have a slight scar."

Adler chuckled in the background, muted behind his hand over his mouth.

"Fine," Stone said. "Let's get this over with."

"Hold out your hand," Corvaire said. "Just one this time."

"Orb of Life," Ceres whispered to herself, with her eyes focused upon Stone's open hand.

Corvaire unsheathed his dagger from his hip as it whistled with a shimmering sound of steel sliding against steel.

"Whoa, whoa, whoa," Stone said. "What's this?"

"We need to draw a little blood to know if it'll work. I'll keep the cut small."

Adler's chuckle turned to out loud laughter. Ceres glared at him, but then focused back on the hand and the dagger.

Corvaire gripped his hand tightly, and before Stone could resist much, he slid the blade of the dagger across Stone's hand, leaving a thin cut. He pulled the dagger back, as well as his hand, and then the trail of blood pooled up on Stone's hand.

"Summon your Indiema," Corvaire said to Ceres. "Gather what you need from it, let it flush inside of you like filling an empty glass. Look deeply into the injury on his hand, feel the blood trickle down as if it were your own. Let me know when you get there."

Ceres glared at the blood, motionlessly and powerfully. She nodded briefly after a matter of seconds.

"Now, repeat after me. *Allias Metomorphus Allilé*."

She mouthed the words first, but not speaking them. She moved from side to side, bouncing her shoulders up and down.

"Whenever you're ready," Corvaire said. Adler had stopped laughing and was then watching—engaged and unblinking.

"*Allias Metomorphus Allilé*," she said with a strong voice. All of them watched, but after several moments, nothing seemed to happen.

"Try again," Corvaire said.

She said the words once more, but again, nothing seemed to change as the blood continued to pool and trickled down his hands onto the road with a *put put, put put.*

Ceres shook her head, trying to shake free from the pressure, or to clear her nerves, but she kept trying, and kept failing.

"What's supposed to be happening, here?" Adler asked.

"Quiet," Corvaire said. "Let her concentrate. Again, Ceres. Like you mean it. Feel the words as the air leaves your lungs. Look at that blood like it ran through your mother and father's veins. Stop it from bleeding like you want your own pain about them to heal."

"*Allias Metomorphus Allilé,*" she said again, but louder. Nothing happened.

"Again," Corvaire said stronger.

She said the words again. Nothing.

"Again! How much pain is in you? Let it out."

She said it again, much louder. But nothing changed.

Stone could feel his mouth was agape as he watched the intensity in Ceres as her face flushed and her green, mossy eyes turned a dark hue.

"Say it again," he said. "Stop the bleeding. Stop your friends' pain."

She tried again, but nothing.

"I—I can't do it," she said. "It's too hard."

"You will do it," he said. "Stone's dying. His life is leaving him. You're the only one who can save him. Use all of your strength. This is important, Ceres. Do it."

She shifted her feet underneath her, and closed her eyes, taking in a deep breath, and letting it back out to calm herself.

"I won't let anymore of the ones I care for die while I still draw breath," she said, opening her eyes and refocusing in on the cut. She said the words again, that time much calmer and Stone quickly felt the tingle from the cut in his hand fading.

"What was that?" Adler asked Stone. "That look in your eye. Did you feel something?"

Stone's hand shook.

"What's happening?" he asked.

"Say the words again," Corvaire said, and she followed his direction.

Stone's hand grew in a vibrant light. The source of the light wasn't clear at first, until Stone's eyes opened wide as a shimmering ball of bright light hovered above his hand. At first it was no bigger than a needle's tip, but as Ceres repeated the chant, it grew to the size of a grape, and then after another several seconds, it was fully the size of an apple.

Each of them watched as the glow of the orb lit his hand, and it reflected off the pool of blood like the sun shining down on a sea of glass.

"Is it working?" she asked as her own hands shook from the spell.

"I don't know," Corvaire said. "Let's look. You can put your hands down now."

She dropped her hands to her side and panted.

"There's still a lot of blood," Stone said. "And I don't feel anything different."

Corvaire walked over and pulled a rag from his bag that was already stained in blood from wiping his sword's edge with it many times. He pulled Stone's hand toward him and wiped the blood away with strong swipes.

"Look at it, now," he said to Ceres. "You tell me if it worked."

She walked over eagerly and inspected his hand, and a smile quickly formed on her face.

"It's gone," Stone said. "The cut's gone. You did it, Ceres. I'm either Wendren or Utumn. I'm…."

"Look!" Adler said, and each of them looked over to him. He had his hand out and pointed out to the plains, and all color had left his face as his eyes were unwavering from where they looked.

Stone followed his finger out to the plains, and a sharp pain shot through his chest.

"What are those?" Ceres asked, but then gasped and covered her mouth with her hands. "No, it can't be them."

"Get to the trees," Corvaire said in a low voice. "Now, get off the road now!"

They ran as quickly as they could down the slope off the road and into the thin forest.

"Do you think they saw us?" Adler asked.

Corvaire didn't answer, but looked deeply troubled by his nervous staring out of the trees.

"How'd they get here so fast?" Adler asked. "They were supposed to be farther east. I sure wish we had those weapons right about now."

Stone then asked Corvaire, "What're we going to do if they attack? What chance do we have against the Runtue riders?"

"I don't know, Stone. I don't know yet."

Chapter Twenty

He could hear and feel his heartbeat in his throat. *Thump, thump, thump, thump.*

They'd only just seen the Neferian rider as it flew off into the southern sky without seeing them, and now the Runtue riders were galloping upon the plains.

Arken's going to war with all these lands. He's not only sending in dark dragons; he's sending in his armies. Soon, there won't be anywhere left to run to.

"Stay still, and keep calm," Corvaire said, crouching down low.

Mud let out a low growl as he glared at the riders off in the distance.

"Those horses," Ceres said. "Never seen one move like that before."

Running down a long hill of tall grass, the riders were still coming straight at them. They glided down the slope like a raindrop on a wet window. The men atop the horses hardly even bounced up and down like a normal rider would. It was almost as if they were sliding down it.

Each of the riders were in full armor, but not a shiny, heavy armor. Their armor was a dark gray that looked more like stone than metal, and didn't cover their entire bodies. They wore a large chest plate that covered everything from their collarbone down, but after covering their shoulders—their arms were left bare—save for golden gauntlets that went nearly up to their elbows.

It was difficult to tell at that distance, but it appeared to Stone that the men had warpaint on their faces—with gold and black streaks vertically running down. The horses as well were black steeds with golden paint smeared on their legs. And just as Kellen had said before, there were ten riders riding down the hill, and were then coming up another bank.

"We'd have no chance against them," Stone said. "Unless we use some of your magic to deter, or kill, them."

"This is war," Adler said to him. "Arken's pledged to kill you wherever you go. It's kill or be killed, Stone. If we have the ability, we're going to kill every last one of them."

"I hope it doesn't come to that," Stone said. "They can't all be bad. They may just be following orders. Perhaps they don't know that their king has gone mad?"

"They're not veering off," Ceres said. "They're riding right toward us."

"Do they see us?" Adler asked.

"We've got to get out of here," Corvaire said.

"I second that," Adler said.

They crept back into the thick wood.

"Stay low," Corvaire said. "And don't touch the trees, we don't want to signal where we are."

"I'm scared," Ceres said in a trembling voice.

"Me too," Corvaire said. "Keep moving."

Step by step they walked deeper into the woods. Each crack under his boots made Stone wince, and every crumpled leaf made him try to step lighter. The riders had gotten to the point that he could faintly hear the sounds of the horse hooves upon the grass. It caused a sickening sensation in Stone's stomach.

"We all realize that we won't be able to hide from them if they're actually coming for us, right?" Adler said. "What do we do if they attack?" Mud continued to growl and snarl.

"I'll try to use the Searing Flesh spell," Ceres said. "That might do it."

"Don't you dare try that spell," Corvaire snapped, all while they continued to creep farther into the woods.

"Why not?"

"If you are successful in casting such a devastating spell," he said. "You're not strong enough to direct that kind of heat. It would most likely be emitted from your own being. You'd surely burn before any others would be affected by the spell. That took Marilyn since she was a teenager to learn and use properly."

"Better to die fighting than to just give up," she said.

"I said nothing about giving up," he said in a low voice.

The riders galloped up the hill and were running down another, still riding directly at them. They could definitely hear the sounds of the horse hooves then.

"I've got a few spells I could cast to keep them busy," Corvaire said. "The only thing is—I don't know anything about these riders. There's a chance that if they are sorcerers themselves, that my magic may not work against one or some of them. And if that one gets through; I'll be too busy casting to fight him off."

"I'll fight any that get through," Stone said. "You worry about the rest. I'll take care of any that your magic doesn't work against."

"Tell me other spells I can cast," Ceres said, her voice was quicker, as they all watched with wide eyes as the riders approached.

"No time," he said. "I could give you the words, but you'll

be too scared. Trust me. Hold onto your sword and stay behind Stone. He may need your help. And to be honest, the spell we may need most from you is the Orb of Life spell. You'll need to save your Elessior for that.

"They're still coming this way," Adler said. "I think they've found us."

"Perhaps," Corvaire said, turning his head and looking back behind them. "They'll have to dismount to get this far into the woods though. I'll cast a spell to keep them at back and stuck in the trees. We'll have a chance for you three to run if they don't have their horses. I'll stay, but if I can't defeat them with my magic, then you'll have to run for it. We can't beat them in a sword fight—and who knows what weapons they have on them."

"Do—do you think they'd come to kill us?" Adler asked. "Or do you think they'd hold us prisoner for Arken?"

"Don't want to find out either way," Ceres said. "Either one is gonna mean death in the end."

"Wait," Stone said. "They're slowing."

The riders had slowed down to a trot once they'd reached the road. Once upon the road, they stopped, and as each of them watched nervously from the woods, one of the riders dropped down off his mighty black steed painted with streaks of painted gold. The rider was tall; wearing a helmet of matte gray with his face uncovered and two long white horns that pointed backward from its sides. His face was wide and muscular, yet his skin tone was similar to Stone's. Not ashen and ragged like Arken's. He had thick swaths of the gold and black paint down his neck and arms.

He dropped to a knee and examined the road where Stone and his friends had just been, and Stone could feel his heart racing in his chest.

Please don't let them find us. Please don't let them find us.

"They don't know where we are," Adler said, in a slightly uplifting voice.

"Yes," Stone added.

The Runtue man ran his fingers along the ground, looking up at the others, speaking to them. Stone couldn't hear what he was saying, he only saw his mouth moving. He didn't know if he'd even be able to understand him if he could hear. A shrill panic shot up from Stone's stomach as he watched the Runtue raise his hand from the road and point directly in their direction. The man rose and spoke with the others, all while looking out in the woods.

"They know we're here," Adler said. "We should make a break for it."

"Wait," Corvaire said. "They may know someone is out here. But what we don't know is if they care. Are they looking for us specifically? Or do they think we're just an ordinary set of travelers? Would we really be worth their time to come all the way in here just to kill a small pack of merchants?"

"Good point," Adler said.

The riders continued their conversation between themselves as another one dropped from his horse to inspect the ground.

"Maybe we should send Mud out there to bark at them," Adler said. "He's good at scaring things off like that."

"He probably would if we wanted him to," Stone said. "But we're not going to do that. He's braver than all of us, but he's staying here next to me."

"C'mon," Ceres said softly. "Forget about us, just ride on. Just ride on."

A third rider leaped down from his horse and continued the conversation, and Stone's heart continued to race, and he felt its strong beating in his ears. Stone felt something strange then, and he turned to look behind them.

"Stone?" Ceres asked. "What is it?"

"I—I don't know," he said. "It felt like we were. Like we were being watched from back there."

Each of them turned to look, but Stone couldn't find what he'd felt, and started to doubt himself.

"Probably nothing," he said. "Just a strange feeling."

"I'd hope it's nothing," Adler said. "We don't want to be fighting on both sides of us."

"Yes," Corvaire said. "I feel something too. There's something out there."

While Stone and Corvaire were looking back into the deeper, darker part of the woods, Ceres gasped.

"They're all dismounting," she said, causing them all to look back at the road.

"Shit," Adler said. "This isn't good."

"Stay calm," Corvaire said, looking in both directions. "But get ready to draw your swords. But not yet, we don't want them to see the glare."

"What's back there?" Ceres asked.

Stone caught something from behind a tree then. It was so subtle, it almost looked like the shadow of the tree, but it was too round.

"There," Stone said, pointing to a large tree thirty meters off and to the right. "See that one? Ceres, shoot an arrow there."

"No," Corvaire said. "It'll make too much sound if it hits the tree."

"Shoot it into the grass next to it," Stone said.

"You might miss," Corvaire said.

"I won't miss," she said.

"Um, guys," Adler said. "They're at the woods."

Stone turned back around and saw the Runtue looking into the trees.

"Forget about what's behind us," Adler said. "We've got to worry about what's in front."

"Keep your bow up," Corvaire said to her. "But don't fire yet."

Mud burst out from the group, quietly running through the brush toward the tree behind them. Stone tried to call him back softly, but the dog was off and running, and all of their attention went to the tree.

Mud was nearly there then, and just as he was about to wind around it, a familiar shape burst out from behind the tree, quickly bouncing off deeper into the forest.

"Couldn't be," Adler said.

"It's that damned shadowy creature from the nights back in the fields," Stone said. "What's it doing here? How long has it been watching us?"

Mud stood next to the tree, watching the creature bound off too quickly for the dog to catch.

"Well," Corvaire said. "Solves that mystery. At least we don't have another platoon behind us."

"No, just one in front," Ceres said. "And they're about to make their way into the trees."

Chapter Twenty-One

The ten warriors took slow steps into the shaded trees, leering deeper into the woods. The tallest one at the head of the pack ducked under low hanging branches as he made his way through. Stone clutched onto the grip of his sword tightly, as Corvaire told him to wait with a slow move of his hand. The tall Runtue man scanned the deep forest with keen eyes, as the pack made their way almost silently into the trees—stalking their prey like a panther would his next meal—eager to sink its teeth and claws into its soft flesh.

They must be looking for me. Why would they come this far into the forest just to flush out a group of travelers? It's me. I've put my friends in grave danger.

He looked over at his friends and saw the same look he'd seen in Adler and Ceres' eyes too many times in such a short span. It was the panicked look of not knowing if you were going to be alive in the next few minutes, or if those were going to be their last moments ever. But they looked ready. Their faces remained as calm as he'd seen, and they'd already gone to war before. Even against such hardened soldiers that were coming after them—they looked ready to spring at a second's notice—as soon as Corvaire gave them their cue, or necessity reared up.

Stone's boots dug into the damp ground, and his muscles tensed as a bead of sweat dropped from his chin. The leaves from the tree before him rustled in the light wind, and it scratched against his cheek. He knelt motionlessly, eager to pounce, but stared at the tall man as he waved for his men to crawl deeper into the wood. He heard the slow pull of an arrow into a bow as Ceres pointed it down to the ground at her side.

Corvaire's head hung as Stone thought he was preparing a spell, and Mud let out a low growl.

They weren't far off then as they inched their way closer and closer, some with long, curved swords drawn, others with their hands surprising empty.

Here we go. This is where we go to war with Arken's men. This is the place where we stand our ground. This is where…

An arrow whistled through the air, and then another, and another. Two of the Runtue behind the tall one spun quickly, knocking the arrows away with quick slashes of their swords. Stone looked over at Ceres to see her arrow still pulled back in the bow. She returned a confused look with a shrug of her shoulders.

Corvaire was scanning the area through the trees to see who was doing the firing, but he didn't seem to know from where the arrows had come.

The Runtue moved like a well-orchestrated unit, without panic and like they rehearsed it a hundred times. They scattered into the trees, nearly disappearing, like hardened assassins they turned to shadows. The arrows continued to whistle in, many of which sunk into the thick trees, and others landed softly in the grass. Stone could hardly make out the Runtue from the trees as he scanned the area.

Stone felt a hand on his back, startling him, as he almost fully unsheathed his sword.

"It's time to be off," Corvaire said. "And quickly."

"We shouldn't stay and fight?"

"We shouldn't stay and die!" Corvaire said, pulling him by the sleeve.

"Who's firing?" Stone asked.

"Doesn't matter," Corvaire said. "And I'm not sticking around here to find out."

"But what if they need our help?" Adler asked, still kneeling low.

"They attacked a group of Runtue soldiers. If they're brave enough to do that, then they'd better be strong enough to back up that courage or stupidity. Come now. Who knows how long of a break this will give us?"

Stone walked after Corvaire, and Mud trailed along next to him. All the while he looked back over his shoulder to see who might be sending those arrows threading their way through the trees.

But then, the Runtue emerged from the shadows in the forest and were sprinting out of the trees as loud horse neighs rung out from the road upon the plains. The arrows had gone from hurtling in the forest to striking into the thick hides of the rider's horses—which cried out in pain. Even Corvaire stopped to watch the attack.

"Foolish," Corvaire whispered. "But effective."

"That's going to curdle their blood," Adler said.

The Runtue ran out with their swords drawn, and that was when Stone finally saw who was leading the attack. Flying in with their own swords drawn were soldiers in full armor, and they wore the colors of crimson and yellow.

"They're soldiers from Verren," Adler said. "What are they doing up here? Where did they come from?"

"I bet they were hunting down the Runtue," Stone said.

"Don't think so," Corvaire said. "Kellen said they were too far away. They didn't know they were this close. I think... I think they were looking for us."

"Us?" Stone asked, with his eyebrows sprung up.

"They were following us," Corvaire said. "Maybe King Roderix wanted the new Wild Majestic for himself, or maybe he wanted us brought back to the castle. Either way, I doubt the soldiers were planning on running into these riders."

The two groups of soldiers collided in swift combat, with the Runtue soldiers letting out loud battle cries as their swords clashed. Stone then saw the soldiers that weren't holding swords quickly let small objects fly from their hands, sending those being struck by those objects flying back as if they'd had a javelin thrown through their chest.

"What are those things?" Ceres asked.

"I—I don't know," Corvaire said. "But the soldiers of Verren are falling quickly. We need to make our way out of here. Now!"

Stone couldn't deny that they should leave while they had their chance, but it was hard to look away from the way the Runtue riders moved in combat. They were precise, organized, and brutal. He'd never seen someone fight so smoothly. It was as if they were born and bred to fight. He couldn't help but wonder how he'd fair in one on one combat with one of them with a sword. He didn't know, and he told himself he'd rather not know. He followed Corvaire deeper into the forest.

As they moved farther away from the battle, the loud shrieks of men were cast out into the trees. Stone turned, just barely able to see through the growing thickness of the trees, another soldier of Verren struck in the chest by one of the objects being thrown by the Runtue. He fell back, clutching his chest and letting out a guttural cry in pain.

I'm not sure I want to know what they're throwing back there. And I don't see a single Runtue missing from the battle, but there are many soldiers of Verren down. It's a massacre.

Another ten minutes later and the cries and moans were so faint they were barely audible, and they continued pressing on deeper and deeper. None of them spoke as they wove their way through the trees, occasionally getting caught up on thick-barbed bushes or trees. They all knew that once the Runtue had killed the last of the soldiers they could easily still make their way into the forest, and find them for a battle that they all knew they possibly wouldn't survive.

So, even though they knew the new mother was north, they had to hide in the forest until they thought it would be safe to get out and make their way again to find her.

Time trailed on, and the blue sky overhead darkened through the perforated forest ceiling. They didn't stop to take a break or stop to eat. But every once in a while, Corvaire would stop to scan the area behind them, and once he felt secure they weren't being trailed, they continued on again. It went on like that for several hours, before Adler eventually sat on a fallen tree and dropped his pack to the grass.

Corvaire looked back to protest, but must have seen the wary looks on their faces, as he let out a low grunt and watched them all sit. Stone quickly let out a yawn, and Ceres followed with her own.

The twilight hours were nearing, and a cool breeze blew through the forest, sending the beads of sweat on Stone's brow cold.

"Will we be able to rest the night?" Ceres asked Corvaire, who was looking back to the trees once again.

"I—I don't know," he said. "I don't know our foe well enough to know if they're following us."

"Is it possible they were hunting the soldiers of Verren?" Adler asked. "And not us?"

"I don't know," Corvaire said. "But one thing I do know, is

that the Runtue know how to fight. Did you see the way they moved? Their speed? Their ferocity? They fight like men who've been jailed their whole lives and are now free with a wicked vengeance on the blades of their swords."

"Women too," Ceres said, after taking a bite of a sweet roll she'd pulled from her pouch.

"What's that?" Corvaire asked.

"They weren't all men," she said, still chewing. "There were two women in the Runtue."

"There were?" Stone asked.

"You didn't see them?" she asked. "You know, the ones who had breasts?"

"I didn't notice," Stone said bashfully.

"You boys don't notice much, do you?"

"Don't know if I want to fight a woman," Adler said. "In the guild, we're told that the only way a woman can be a target, is if she's been proven beyond reasonable doubt that she committed a planned murder."

"Looks like those women Runtue have had plenty of experience with murder," Ceres said. "You gonna have problems defending yer' life against those killers? They'd strike you down in a moment if they had the chance. So, do me a favor, will ya? Stop saying such dimwitted things. Better yet—just don't open yer' mouth at all."

"I was just making a point," Adler said. "I—"

"I think we get it, you two," Stone said, and he noticed that Ceres had a chill creep through her as he lifted her cloak over her head. "You think we'll be able to get a fire going tonight?"

Corvaire shook his head.

"Damn," Adler said. "Another cold night. I sure am going to miss that bed back in Verren. Who knows the next time we'll have a bed like that?"

"We'll just try to stay low and out of the wind," Stone said. "And try to get some sleep. I'll stay first on watch if you want."

"I'll stay up with you," Corvaire said. "I'm not eager to fall asleep while they're still somewhere out there."

"Maybe they went off back out into the plains?" Adler asked, laying his blanket out onto the grass, and laying back on it.

"Perhaps," Corvaire said.

"I don't think they liked their horses being attacked," Adler said. "Maybe they're staying with them to get them healing."

"Yes," Corvaire said. "That's possible too. But I worry they're not the types to give up easily—if at all…"

So they rested. For hours Stone sat by Corvaire, and Corvaire told him stories about old fables he'd learned as a child: one about a pesky hedgehog who ate so much he grew as large as a dog Mud's size, but burst from eating so much, and another about a bolt of lightning that struck a wizard, and upon striking him, gained his knowledge and became a dazzling wizard itself.

Corvaire smoked from his pipe much of those hours, and Stone even tried a puff off it, but nearly toppled off his seat from coughing so hard. Adler snored softly behind them, and Ceres slept soundly with her golden hair falling out of the front of her hood.

Stone thought about that sweet moment where she kissed his cheek without a word. He decided he was going to ask her about it at some point.

Corvaire was halfway through another one of his stories when he stopped. It took Stone a moment to notice, but when he did, he caught Corvaire glaring off into the trees. He pulled the pipe away from his mouth slowly.

"What is it?" Stone asked. "Do you see something?"

"There," Corvaire said, pointing out in front of them. "You see it?"

Stone peered through the trees but didn't see anything.

Mud ran up next to Stone, looking out into the forest with his tail up.

"Wake up," Stone said to the others, who slowly stirred awake.

Corvaire stood, not taking his gaze off what he saw, but Stone couldn't see.

"What is it?" Ceres said, wiping the sleep away from her eyes.

"There's a light," Corvaire said. And just as he said that Stone saw what he was talking about.

It was a pale, glowing white light with a blue hue around it.

"What is it?" Stone asked, as the light slowly got brighter and larger.

"Don't know," Corvaire said. "But it's coming right at us."

They were all up then, standing in a line, watching the light, which was at their eye level dart from side to side as it got closer.

"Is that—?" Ceres asked.

"Ghost?" Stone asked.

PART V
THE SILENT DEATH

Chapter Twenty-Two

The glow from the fairy's wings reflected off the trees wet with moisture and the damp puddle in front of them. The pale bodied Ghost fluttered her turquoise-blue wings like a hummingbird would, and her long—for her short stature—violet hair flowed elegantly down her nude body.

Stone knew better than to think the fairy's infrequent arrivals were anything but an omen that something bad was coming—unless they followed the small creature's direction, and they found that in the manner of Ghost waving her arms for them to follow her. They didn't hesitate.

They all gathered their things and made their way to follow her. Ghost had come from the direction they'd come from—but then—she was leading them north. They didn't know how far the forest led on in that direction, and they knew that traveling through the thick wood impeded their movement, but they knew they didn't want to run into the riders again. And they knew that they trusted Ghost to lead them away from trouble, so they followed.

The fairy bobbed in and out of trees, almost playfully

traversing her way in front of them—or perhaps it was impatiently. She didn't speak their tongue, but Stone wondered perhaps if she wanted to communicate with them in a manner other than simply ushering them on.

"What do you think it is?" Ceres asked, trudging through the dark forest after the fairy brimming with an angelic glow.

"She's usually leading us away from something," Stone said. "Maybe there's something after us again?"

"It's different this time," Adler added. "We've got a real destination this time. Maybe she's just leading us to the new mother?"

They walked on for another stretch that felt like a half hour to Stone, and since he'd found no sleep since he was on first watch with Corvaire before the unexpected creature came to them. He found himself yawning frequently, and wiping his eyes with the backs of his fists to try to stay awake.

"Here," Adler said to him, holding out a small brick of chocolate. "It'll wake you up, maybe just a smidge, but it might help all the same."

Stone took it reluctantly with a slow movement of his hand to lift it from his friend's hand.

"Are you sure?"

Adler nodded. "We'll get more in the next city we stroll into. Try it."

He didn't know if it worked to keep him awake, but he couldn't deny that the sweet and salty flavors after spending a damp night in the woods warmed his soul.

Mud scampered along next to him as they walked slowly through the darkness.

Ghost turned around—facing them in the pale moon light—and urged them to hurry with rushed movements of her arms and wide eyes. They picked up their pace.

"I wish she could speak," Adler said. "I trust her, I just don't know what the rush is about this time. If she could just tell us Arken's men are on our trail, then—I don't know—I'd probably be torn up from running through the woods blindly. But this… I don't know. We have no horses, and no grand weapons. Ceres, you don't have magic enough to stop them. If they are behind us, I don't really know what we'd do to stop them."

"Stop." Ceres turned around as her hair flew from over her shoulder to her chest. "We've already discussed this. They attack; we fight. That's it."

"I know," he said. "But I'm just stating the obvious. They attack; we are surely dead unless something happens totally unexpectedly."

"You mean," she said with a sly tone, "as if a platoon of soldiers showed up from out o' nowhere to save our scrawny asses?"

He thought for a long moment, scratching his chin. "Why, yes. I suppose it'd have to be something like that—yes."

"Shh, you two," Corvaire said. "Keep it down. We don't know what's out there."

Stone watched the two of them as they both shut their mouths, but both rigid as if they wanted to continue their squabble. Then he watched as Ghost turned and beckoned them to follow quicker with her fingers gesturing.

"Corvaire," Stone asked. "Do you know what she is? Do you have an idea of where she came from?"

"I'm afraid I don't."

"None at all?" Stone asked. "She was the one who led Ceres to help me escape from my underground prison. Is she all benevolent? Always doing things when we need her most? Or is she working on the behest of another?"

"I have thought about it at great length," he said. "While I meditate, I've hoped that the answer would come to me. But just like the creature that leaps in the shadows, peering at us with those dead eyes, I fear there are things moving in these lands that are beyond my knowledge. There are forces out there that are playing their hands after living in the veiled shadows. The true powers want what is to come."

"And what is that?" Stone asked.

Corvaire looked back at him, with a heavy glare of having lived many winters. All of the sudden, Stone saw him not as the keen, strong fighter, or the man from a sacred lineage of famed soldiers. He didn't see him as the man who'd saved their lives by using magic Stone never could have imagined existed. No. He then saw him in the light of a wise man, who'd live a life almost no one in the Worforgon could dream of. And with thin wrinkles around his eyes, and no sign of a smile, he simply said, "True power."

"What's that?" Adler said, from behind them.

Stone turned and saw Ceres staring in the same direction as him.

"You saw it?" Adler asked her.

"Yup." She pulled an arrow from her quiver, and loosed it out into the darkness, and Stone couldn't believe the same shadowy creature leaped a few trees over.

Mud growled.

"Easy boy," Stone said.

"You should just let him after the thing again," Adler said.

Ghost grabbed Corvaire's sleeve, and tried to pull them forward.

"Will you just kill the damn thing?" Adler asked Corvaire. "Put it to rest already. Another bolt of lightning! This time straight on!"

"No," Corvaire said. "There's no storm. If the riders understand anything about the magic here. They may understand exactly what it was. And it would lead them straight to us."

"So," Adler said. "No one's got any idea of how we're going to get this thing to stop lurking after us?"

"I have the feeling that it and the Runtue don't have anything to do with each other," Stone said. "So it may be best to worry about those ten men that are trying to kill us first, versus some creature that's too scared to rear up its head."

"True," Adler said. "But I hate being followed and spied on. Call me paranoid, but I'd rather put that thing in its place."

"C'mon," Ceres said. "Ghost wants us to go, and go we should."

They continued on another long stretch of forest—weaving through the thick foliage and massively round-trunked trees. Ghost flew like a hummingbird through it, lighting the way. Stone looked back over his shoulder many times, but didn't see the shadowy creature again. Perhaps it got scared and wondered off, or it just fell deeper into the shadows.

They heard a crashing sound behind them though, and each of them spun around—this time with their swords drawn, dimly lit in the glow of the fairy's blue wings.

"What is it?" Ceres whispered. "Is it the creature again?"

"Don't think so," Adler said. "That thing doesn't make much noise when it's moving. It's nearly silent. Whatever is coming at us is clumsy . . . or just doesn't care if we know."

They waited anxiously for whatever was coming at them in the darkness. Whatever it was, it knocked bushes out of the way, had heavy footsteps on the fallen leaves, and was heaving in deep breaths.

Ghost flew in front of them to look out into the forest. She turned back to them and waved her arms for them to stand down. Stone was confused, but as soon as the person coming at them came into light, he knew that it wasn't one of the Runtue. It was a woman, and she wore the colors of Verren.

"I've found you," she said, sucking in air and clutching her ribs with a blood-stained hand. "I've found you."

Ceres went to run to the woman, but Corvaire restrained

her by stepping in front of her with his hand out. "One moment," he said. "What're you doing here?"

"I was in the battle," she heaved. "It was a massacre. We didn't stand a chance against them. But we had no choice . . ."

"What are you talking about?" Corvaire asked. "You attacked them from our vantage point."

"They were going to find you," she said.

Find us? What's she going on about? And did she run all the way out into the dark forest just to find us?

"Yes." Her eyes were distant as she collapsed against a tree next to her. The blond hair that was sweat-laden against her head was thick with debris and blood, and her hands were shaking from either weariness or shock.

Ceres brushed past Corvaire's hand, leaving him with a ruffled composure. "Where are you injured?" She pulled back her armor to inspect her ribs.

"Son of whore!" she screamed out in pain as Ceres pulled her hands back quickly. "Careful there, Ceres."

"You know my name?" Ceres stood up with a concerned look.

"Yes, yes," she said. "I know all of you. Maybe not the dog, though. We were sent out to find you."

"King Roderix sent you?" Stone asked. "Or was it the chancellor?"

"It was the king's orders. He wanted us to escort you back to the kingdom."

"Why?" Stone asked. "Why would he force us back there?"

"I'm . . . I'm just a soldier," she said. "But he said to use force if needed."

"Talk about a son of a whore," Adler said.

"I warn you," she said. "Do not talk about my king in that

manner. I may be down, but I can still cut your lying tongue from your mouth."

"Why are you here?" Corvaire asked in a low, serious tone.

"To warn you," she said, coughing and blood spattered on her hand she used to cover her mouth.

"Warn us about what?" Stone asked. "The riders?"

"Yes," she said. "We were only there to find you and bring you back. We had no idea they were this far into the mainland."

"Were they looking for us?" Ceres asked.

"Don't know," she said. "But it seems they do now."

"What do you mean, exactly?" Corvaire asked.

"We were coming up on you in the woods, but then we saw them Neferian riders getting closer and closer to ya. We figured an ambush would be the best course, so we flanked from both sides." Her eyes went wide and distant again. "Never seen anyone or anything fight like that."

"What were the things they were flinging from their hands?" Corvaire asked.

"Some sort of metal weapon, but they were coated in some sort of dark magic, they were. Killed my men before they even had a chance to get out of the way. Those bloody bastards! They'll pay for what they did . . ."

Ceres lowered her head, and then looked back up at Stone with a sadness on her face.

"Are they all dead?" she asked.

The soldier cried.

"I'm so sorry," Ceres said.

"The weapons they threw," said Corvaire. "You said they were metal with black magic? How did you know they were magical?"

The woman brushed away her tears, trying to collect her thoughts. She winced in pain, gripping her side.

"They had a sparkle to them, like a flickering candle, but not with bright light, more like black sparks."

"Black sparks?" he said, almost to himself.

"What can I do for you?" Ceres asked. "What can I do to help you?"

"My side keeps bleeding," she said. "I've been trying to stop it since I fled, but I fear I've lost a lot of it."

"Why come all this way?" Stone asked. "Why not go back to Verren to get help? To tell them?"

She looked up at him with a serious, stern face. "Because that's why I came. *You* need to go to Verren. *You* need their protection. And *you* need to tell them about the riders. They must know. The king must know!"

"I—I can't," Stone said. "We have another mission. One that is much more important. I'm sorry. But we can't return to Verren just yet."

"You must!" the soldier said, trying to get back to her feet as Ceres inspected the wound. But she collapsed back onto the ground with a groan, and then another nasty cough.

"We cannot," Corvaire said. "You should've gone back yourself. There's nothing back that way for us now. You should've . . ."

"The riders," she said, interrupting him, "the riders, some of them came into the woods. You're not safe here. You have to get back to the city. They're coming. They're coming after you . . ."

Chapter Twenty-Three

"How do you know this?" Corvaire asked. "Answer me, please."

The soldier's face contorted in pain, lulling from side to side as Ceres pressed a cloth up to her ribs, but looked pale and worried.

"I saw them," she said. "Six of them stayed back with their horses. We even killed one of them, but the other four. They went deep into the woods. I think they found your tracks. They're looking for you, and let me just tell you that you don't have a beggar's chance against them. They'll kill ya, they'll kill ya all before you even have a chance to draw your swords."

"Well, thanks for the encouragement," Adler said snidely.

"This is no joke, Adler," she said. "They are going to find you. That's why you must circle back through the western edge of the wood and head back to the safety of the city. You're not safe out here, and there's nowhere to hide."

Her wide eyes narrowed and focused in on Ghost. "Is that? It can't be . . . Is that a fairy?"

"Yes, she's our friend," Ceres said. "And that's why we're not too worried about those Runtue at this moment. She'd have noticed them by now. She got more than just women's intuition."

"Never knew they were real," the soldier said. "But didn't know dragons were either." She tried to laugh but ended up coughing in a worse manner than before, and more blood flew from her lips.

"We've got to get you up," Ceres said, moving to hoist her. The soldier tried to get to her feet again but winced in agonizing pain—falling back down again.

"I just need to rest her a little bit longer . . ."

"We can't stay here," Corvaire said. "We can help you walk, but we must be moving again if what you say is true."

"Just a little bit longer," the soldier said as her voice trailed off. "Just a little longer. I'm so tired . . ."

"You have to stay awake." Ceres shook her shoulder.

The woman then turned to her. "This is as good a time as any to die, right?"

"You're not dying," Ceres said. "We've got to get you up."

"Funny thing," the soldier said, "I always thought life would flash before your eyes when ya die. But all I can think about right now is my son. Who's going to read to him at night?"

Her voice was faint, and her head collapsed to her shoulder as Ceres pulled away.

"We should get moving," Corvaire said, as Ghost floated just before him.

"Should we say something?" Adler asked. "I feel like we should say something."

"Say something if you will," Corvaire said. "But let's be moving on. I don't like what she was saying about that dark magic."

"Do you know what you're gonna say?" Ceres asked.

"I—I don't know," he said. "All I know is what the guild

says when people pass on. But that's not appropriate for this. It's only for those in the guild."

"You want to make something up?" Stone asked.

"Fine," Adler said, while Corvaire turned his back impatiently. "May your soul pass into the Golden Realm with haste and love." He was unsure what to say after that.

"That was nice," Stone said. "Short and simple."

"I feel like I should say more," Adler said.

"That was just fine," Corvaire said. "Let's be back northbound. There's still far to go."

Ceres rummaged through the soldier's belongings with an astonishing swiftness.

"I suppose we got over the whole, 'not taking from dead people issue,'" Adler said.

"You're incorrigible." She sighed.

"Hurry," Corvaire said, and they all quickly followed him, who followed Ghost.

As they pressed on through the night, and with the knowledge that there indeed were Runtue in the forest, they grew tired. It was that sort of tired where your feet ache, your legs feel tight, and your eyes are difficult to keep open. Stone even found himself feeling upset at little things—such as stepping on a stick wrong and its poking him in the side of the leg. He even stumbled a couple of times. He knew that he needed rest, but with the sun coming up in only a couple of hours, he didn't know when that time would come.

When are we going to feel safe enough to be able to rest our heads? Do the Runtue sleep? They're people after all . . . aren't they?

The following hours were the worst of the night. Adler groaned and Ceres fell behind a couple of times—hungry and exhausted.

"We must press on," Corvaire urged them. "We need to find a place to rest that's not out in the open like this. Ghost will take us there. We just need to keep putting one foot in front of the other."

"I don't know if I can," Ceres said. "I need a break. Only a couple of minutes."

"The sun is about to rise," he said, facing east and the lightening sky. "We should move. Maybe in the sunlight we'll find a place to rest."

"Where?" Adler asked. "Where are you leading us?" He was pointing at Ghost, whose lips didn't move, and she ushered them to keep following her.

"We can't fly," Ceres said her. "We need rest. Can you take us somewhere safe? I don't know how much longer I can keep doing this without sleep."

Ghost zipped over to her in the air, and pulled on her sleeve for her to get moving again. Ceres didn't fight though. She trusted her fully.

"All right, all right," she said with another sigh. "I'll keep on."

Ghost flew to the front, and each of them walked after. With each passing minute the sky grew brighter through the thick leaves overhead.

To their left, Stone caught a glimpse of a fawn grazing in the grass, and once he saw them, she froze. Her dark eyes stared at them, motionlessly as blades of grass stuck out of her mouth. After a moment though, she resumed chewing, as she didn't seem to perceive danger as they walked by.

Mud stared at her though, seemingly wanting to inspect her. But Stone calmed him, stroking the back of his neck.

Then, the fawn's gaze shot south, behind them. Stone noticed and quickly turned to look, but saw nothing, and by the time he looked back at the fawn . . . it was gone.

"Did you see that?" he asked his friends.

"What?" Adler asked wearily. "The deer?"

"Yeah."

"I saw it, yeah," Adler said, watching his footsteps.

"But it looked away, and then it was gone," said Stone.

"They'll do that," Adler said.

"Ghost," Stone said. "Do you see anything? Do you see anything back there?" He pointed behind them. The fairy seemed to understand and flew next to his shoulder—scanning the woods behind them. She appeared to not notice anything, but Stone could tell Mud was uneasy as the fur on his back stood up, and he patted his paws on the ground anxiously. "I think something is out there."

Corvaire went back and stood with them.

"What is it?" Ceres asked.

That's when Ghost gasped, and motioned for them to get down, which they quickly did.

"What's out there?" Ceres whispered.

"That fawn," Stone said. "She saw something and then ran off."

"I bet it's that shadow creature again," said Adler, slightly louder than Ceres' whisper.

"Shh," she said.

"I told ya we shoulda' killed that thing."

"Quiet down," Corvaire said.

Stone realized that Mud was nowhere in sight.

Where'd he go off to? We need him to keep quiet. What a bad time to go out for a run . . .

Then, he caught sight of him, actually, more like sound of him. He heard the dog running through the brush to the east.

"What's that damned dog doing?" Adler asked.

"He's causing a distraction." Corvaire smiled.

Through the dark trees with a slight hue of light kissing each, Stone saw something move. It was as silent as an owl swooping down to the grass to grasp an unsuspecting mouse in its talons. It was definitely a man, as its head and shoulders were visible as it moved through the forest after the dog who was scampering off. And then he saw another person trail behind.

"It's them," Ceres said with dread on the tip of her tongue.

"We need to get out of here," Stone said.

"Wait," Corvaire said, also seeing the four Runtue glide through the forest. "Mud's leading them off our trail."

"What if they catch him?" Stone asked. "What will he do all alone against them?"

"He'll be all right," Adler said. "He's as swift as they come, and damn smart for a street dog."

The Runtue disappeared from view again, back out into the dark forest, and the sounds of Mud's paws faded away to nothing. Ghost rose from the ground, with her wings fluttering, and she led them away, back north again. Their fatigue was replaced by worry, so their feet moved swiftly through the forest.

"Is it a good thing that there are only four of them?" Adler asked. "That does increase our odds."

"They killed a whole squadron of soldiers without losing one," Stone said. "Better if we just try to avoid the fight altogether, eh?"

"The sun's rising," Ceres said. "We're not going to have the night's shade to hide in any longer. I'm worried, Stone."

"Me too," he said. "But we've got to trust in Ghost. She's gotten us out of these sorts of situations before."

"Like this?" Ceres asked.

Stone groaned. *No. Not like this. This is different. I don't know if we'll even be able to defend ourselves against these invaders.*

It was then that the pale bodied nude fairy with the long, wavy violet hair pointed to something up ahead. Stone saw what she was pointing out, but didn't understand why.

"Is that a cliff?" he asked.

It appeared to be a steep drop off where there were no trees on the other side. It was fifty yards up, so each of them ran. They got there quickly and they found that, yes, it was a cliff they were perched upon. First Stone looked out at the valley below and the long stretch of beautiful plains of rolling grass, but then he looked down at the bottom of the valley and his heart brimmed with excitement, and Ceres clutched onto his arm as she jumped up and down.

"It's them," she said, with her voice cheery and elated. "Ghost brought them back to us."

"I don't believe it," Adler said, flabbergasted. "I don't believe it."

"Believe it," Stone said. "It's them."

"Never doubted you," Corvaire said to Ghost. "And I never will."

At the bottom of the ravine, grazing on tall springs of green grass were four horses—*their* horses: Angelix, Hedron, Grave and another strong, brown one they didn't recognize.

"What are we waiting for?" Adler asked, and they made their way to the edge of the cliff and scooted down it.

"Where's Mud?" Stone asked. "I still haven't seen him. We can't leave without him."

"He'll find us," Adler said.

"How? How will he find us?"

"He's clever. He will."

"No. We can't leave without him," Stone said as they neared the bottom of the cliff, and each of the horses then looked up at them, neighing loudly.

Once they got to the bottom, they each ran up to the horses.

"They still have our saddles," Ceres said. "Amazing."

"Indeed," Corvaire said. "Amazing indeed. Hurry now. Saddle up." He got onto the brown horse's back quickly.

"We can't leave Mud," Stone said as the others got onto their horses.

"We need to leave, now," Ceres said. "Don't make me push you up onto Grave's back."

He heard a high-pitched humming sound, and he didn't even have time to look at where the sound was coming from. In front of him, Ghost flapped her wings wildly, narrowly evading what looked like a small metal disk that flew past. He noticed a slight, dark twinkle on it.

Oh no. They're here . . .

Fear locked tightly into his chest as another of the metal disks flew at Ghost, which she just dodged by flying straight down.

"Get out of here, Ghost," Ceres said, and with a flash the fairy darted off out into the tall grass of the plains and disappeared.

"Time to go," Corvaire said. "Get mounted, Stone. We've stayed here too long." And he was off with a kick of his heels onto the horse's sides. Stone leaped onto his horse and went off after him.

Three of the Runtue slid down the cliff with thick dust flying up behind them. Atop the cliff was a single Runtue in the gold and black paint, readying to throw another pair of the disks.

From the ground beneath him, a swarm of insects rose, buzzing all around him. They appeared from that distance to be a cloud of flying locusts. The rider had to bat the bugs away from his face, falling back into the forest.

Stone saw Corvaire riding but turned back and with his hand out up to the rider.

Another spell . . . We're safe from that one, but for how long. We've got to get away from them!

"Ride!" Corvaire yelled out. "Ride like your lives depend on it!"

Chapter Twenty-Four

Stone's hair whipped behind him and the wind bit at his weary eyes as they rode. The horse hooves battered the ground as they stomped their way north through the roadless grass. So much dread ran through him seeing the Runtue finally catching up to them—and now he was on his own strong steed riding quickly away from them.

Thank you, Ghost. You've done it again . . .

"Where is she?" Ceres asked. "Where'd Ghost go off to?"

"She may have flown back off to wherever she goes," Adler said. "But many thanks to her!"

"How did she find our horses?" Stone asked. "How would she have known where to find them and how to bring them to us? Or us to them?"

"I bet she speaks horse," Adler quipped.

Stone saw they were far off from the canyon and the Runtue. Corvaire seemed to notice that too, and slowed his horse to a trot. The others did the same.

"Any sign of them?" Adler asked, turning back around on his horse.

"Don't see them," Corvaire said. "And I don't think they

brought their horses through the forest. I'd say they probably had to go back and fetch the others and get their horses. That may have given us some time."

"Some time to do what?" Stone asked.

"We need to find a direction," he said as he pulled back on the reins and his new horse neighed. "We can't just blindly keep heading north. Ceres, I need you to try again. Can you do that?"

"I can try," she said.

"You can do this," Stone said, bobbing his head, trying to reassure her.

The four of them sat atop their horses in a circle, watching Ceres as she closed her eyes once again and sat silently, but drawing deep breaths and exhaling slowly.

"I can feel it in me, somewhere deep. It's as if it's in a place I never felt before—like somewhere I didn't know existed until now. But it doesn't feel like it's a part of me. It feels more like it's been placed inside of me. But it don't feel wrong, it feels kinda warm, as if there's a warm egg sitting in me' stomach."

"Focus on that," Corvaire said. "There's nothing out there but that feeling. Feel it. Breathe it. Be it."

"There's something else, though," she said, squinting her closed eyes. "Something new. It feels . . . It feels like . . . somethings trying to drive it out of me. Like a hawk's claws is trying to rip it out."

"What do you mean?" Corvaire asked, leaning toward her. "Tell me about it."

"Wait . . . it's not as if it's trying to pull it out of me. No . . . now it feels like its pulling me with it." She opened her eyes as they glistened in the rays of the rising sun. She clicked her heels on Angelix's sides, and the horse walked forward.

"You feeling something?" Stone asked as the other horses followed behind her. She was heading north.

"Yes, it feels more rested in me the more we move in this direction."

"That must be it," Stone said to Corvaire.

"It's difficult to hold onto it though," Ceres said. "I can already feel it fading."

"We don't need much," said Corvaire. "Just ride a little bit and tell us which direction makes the pulling feeling lighter."

She clicked again and the horse trotted farther toward the north, and after a few trots, she pulled the reins slightly to the left.

"There," she said softly.

She sent her horse off to a gallop then.

"Feel good?" Corvaire asked as the three of them galloped after her.

"Yes," she said. "I think that feels all right."

"That'll be good enough for now," he said. "You can relax. We know which direction to go in now. Well done."

"Just northwest," Adler said. "Toward those mountains far up ahead."

"I can try it again later," she said. "Perhaps when I'm more rested."

"I fear rest isn't going to be in our immediate future," Stone said.

"We won't be able to ride forever without resting," Adler said. "We just need to find somewhere safe to have some walls around us—and an army wouldn't hurt if those riders came stalking after us. Let's see . . . what's in that direction?"

"No cities with walls," Corvaire said. "The coast is . . . I'd say five or six hundred miles away. If that's where she is . . ."

"With these horses we may get fifty miles a day," Adler said. "They're strong for sure. But that's still gonna take us ten days to reach the coast."

"If that's where we're going," Stone said. "Remember, she could be closer."

"But there's no real cities up there," Adler said. "Just small villages that don't even fit on most maps."

"That's enough for me," Stone said. "I doubt all the Old Mothers were born on beds lined with silk sheets."

"How are we going to outrun those riders?" Ceres asked. "Once they regroup, they'll know we're heading this way. We maybe have a day on them?"

"Maybe," Corvaire said. "But, we can hope that their horses are just that . . . horses. They'll need to rest, drink and eat. So if we keep good pace we should get there before them. We're not loaded down with heavy armor either. We have a chance of getting there before they get to us."

"What then?" Adler asked. "What do we do when we find her? The riders are hunting us—their hunting you, Stone."

"As I said, we need to get her to Endo Valaire, whatever it takes."

They slowed the horses to a walk again, and after a while Stone felt a heavy veil of weariness fall over him. He even drifted off to the point where he startled himself awake after he nearly fell off his horse.

"Stone," Ceres said, riding up to his side. "Stay awake now. We'll find a place to rest soon. Corvaire's sure to be getting hungry too."

"I hope so," he said. He looked up with tired eyes at her. Her blond hair bounced on the back of her neck as the horse carried her forward in the brilliant sunlight. Her green eyes were kind and caring as she stared back into his.

"What?" she asked, pulling back with a raised eyebrow. "Why're you looking at me like that?"

"Ceres," he said shyly. "Do you remember the other night? The night we were forced to flee Verren?"

"Yeah," she said. "What about it?"

He slowed his horse to give more distance between them and Adler who was up ahead.

He cleared his throat. "Do you remember what happened before you felt what you felt in that tavern?"

"Yeah," she said with a scrunched nose. "We were drinking like fish in that old bar with those locals."

"Do you remember pulling me outside during all that?" he asked.

She pulled her reins and her horse came to a stop. So did his. "Ah, aren't you cute?"

What? What's she mean, cute?

"You talkin' about that little peck on the cheek?"

He didn't know what to say. He was so taken aback by the blunt way she said that.

"Listen, Stone, I know you're only a few weeks old." She laughed, and leaned toward him. "But don't read too deep into it. I was as wet as a pickled herring with not a crumb in me' tum. I pecked ya because I care for ya, and appreciate ya. We've been through a lot together already the three of us."

Stone opened his mouth to speak but no words came out. She smiled, winked, and kicked Angelix back up to ride behind the others.

"Don't expect another one anytime soon," she chided as she rode off.

Clever, Stone . . . real clever. Why'd you have to bring it up?

He rode slowly behind her with his head slunk down.

Hours passed until Stone found he could hardly sit up on his horse. It wasn't twilight yet, but it was approaching come the next few hours. Corvaire had been leading them up to a blunt-topped rock that was erected out of the ground at the top of a hill.

He dismounted by a stream at the bottom of it, and each of them did the same as the horses drank the cool, clear water.

Looking up at the tan, chalky-looking rock it was probably twenty feet high, Stone guessed.

"This will be where we rest for the night," Corvaire said. "Ceres, why don't you come with me and we'll try to find an easy way up it. Adler, food? Stone, wood?"

Both of them nodded.

"We're making a fire tonight?" Ceres said in surprise.

"They know where we are," he said. "The key is that they're far behind us. Even if their horses can ride all night, they'll still need to rest at some point. Tonight will be our long night, while we're farthest ahead. The next nights won't be like this."

"Aren't you worried?" Ceres asked him.

"I am," he said. "But I'm also not riding off blindly without leaving some little trickery to aid us on our path unabated."

A grin crept across her face. "What did you do?"

"It's not what I did. It's what you're going to do."

"Me?"

"You're turning out to be quite the powerful sorceress," he said. "At least that you've got potential."

"I do?"

"Come, I'll show you when we get up there."

They made their way up the hill and to the top of the rock easily with a section of it laden with deep folds in it that made it a quick climb. Stone brought up his first bundle briskly, and was curious what the two of them were doing, looking out to the south as the prairie wind whipped past and the sun kissed the land to their right.

He went over and stood next to them without a word.

"What do I do?" she asked.

"Take this." He held his fist out over her hand.

She opened her hand and down came a fistful of grass blades.

"Do you know what we're going to do with this?" he asked.

She shook her head.

"Stone?" he asked.

"Huh-uh."

"We're going to cover our tracks."

"We're . . . I'm . . ." she said. "I'm going to un-trample the grass we came along on?"

Corvaire nodded.

"How much of it?" Ceres asked.

"As much as you can," he said.

"What if I can't?"

"Then you can't."

She scratched her head with pursed lips.

"What do I do? What do I say?"

"You know what to do. And the words are *Terras Aliaxis Gronum*."

She clasped the grass in both her hands and said the words.

"You can do it," Stone said.

Ceres spread her legs apart wide, in a powerful stance as the wind howled, the eagles crowed overhead, and the fields on the plains waved in ripples.

Stone could see their tracks they'd made winding through the valley down from the south, and if he could see them from the dying light, then the hunters on horseback surely would be able to follow them.

The wind grew, as Ceres recited the words. "*Terras Aliaxis Gronum.*"

Stone also saw Adler out in the distance to the west, his legs hidden in tall grass, as he watched from below.

She repeated the words slowly and deliberately, focusing in on her Elessior. Stone couldn't believe how different she looked then. She looked like a true, focused and powerful enchantress—and in such a short period of time.

She raised her arms up and yelled out, "*Terras Aliaxis Gronum!*"

Stone's jaw dropped as he watched from on high, as the trampled grass below shifted and swayed. For as far as he could see, the line they'd taken disappeared as the tall grass rose from the dirt ground up to a swaying hip-height again.

"Magnificently done," Corvaire said, with a rare laugh. "The Old Mothers would be quite proud of you. Quite proud."

She had a spectacular grin on her face as she lowered her arms, put both fists on her hips and nodded proudly.

Chapter Twenty-Five

A low-burning fire warmed them on the backside of a hip-high wall on the edge of the tall rock. Dark clouds drifted lazily over them as sparkling stars slowly appeared in clusters. Wind howled hollowly over the rolling plains, and insects chirped harmoniously from the tall grass.

"I'll take first watch," Stone said, trying to keep his eyes open.

"No, you won't," Corvaire said. "Get yourself some rest, before you topple over."

"I'll stay up and help keep you awake," he said. "You've got to be at the edge of sleep too."

"I'll be fine," Corvaire said, nestling into the backside of the wall and turning his head to gaze down at the long southern plains as the grass swayed in the breeze and rabbits scampered through them. "I mean it. Get some rest. You'll need it for tomorrow."

The horses neighed below before they went into a deep sleep themselves.

Stone sat across the fire from Ceres, and Adler was already

fast asleep after they ate the three pheasants he was skilled enough to skewer with arrows. As Corvaire pulled up a blanket over his chest, staring up at the sky, Ceres waved Stone over to sit next to her, and behind the wall that broke the chill wind.

He went over and sat next to her, pulling his blanket up over his shoulders. She glared into the fire; as did he.

"There's a certain beauty to it," she said. "There's really nothing like it. You can see the beauty in a sunrise, or that sea view from the top of the mountain on Endo, but there's something about staring into a fire that captures ya. Like when you stare into it, everything else kinda drifts away." She looked up at him. "Do ya know what I mean?"

"I know exactly what you mean."

There were a few minutes of calm silence as the insects continued to chirp in a flowing rhythm.

"You ever wish we never had to go through this?" she asked, her words were lined with an aura of sadness. "Like, if you had the choice. Would you really choose to be here, doing all of this, in the middle of everything that's going on around us?"

He thought about that for a long moment. "How many really get to choose where they are in life?"

"I know, but, I'm just sayin', if you could *choose*. Would you choose this?"

"There are things I'd choose, yes." He scratched his chest. "I wouldn't want the responsibility that's on me for all of this, but things like that you don't really get to choose, I suppose. And I wish Mud was back here with me."

"I'd tell ya where I'd rather be," she said. "I'd be sitting on the front porch of me' old house next to me' mum. My father would be smoking his pipe, fishing down by the stream, and me' cat would be purring in me' hands. I can smell the elderberry pie in the oven, baking away. The sky is a brilliant blue that's like nothin' else, and I wouldn't have a care in the world."

"That sounds brilliant," he said. "Wish I could've known your folks. I bet they were splendid people."

"Aye," she said with her eyes glowing orange from the firelight.

"I bet they'd be proud of you," Stone said. "You're turning out pretty well I'd say."

"Pretty well?" Ceres frowned and playful grin.

"I mean it," he said. "Ever since I've known you since you dug me out of the ground, I've seen you do some pretty incredible feats. Like tonight. That didn't take you long at all to get that spell to work. It's inspiring. I hope to have some magic someday, myself."

"You will," she said, looking back at the fire. "We just need to find her, and then we should be able to get you practicing pretty quickly I'd wager."

"One thing I've been thinking about—worrying about. The Indiema. Do I have one?"

"I—I don't know. I'd think you'd have one. I mean, it wasn't like you were born in the dirt like that. You must've come from a father and mother just like every other person with two legs."

"Sometimes I just don't know . . ." he said.

"But you saw yer' mum," Ceres put her hand on his.

"That might've been just a dream. It might not have been real."

"It's as real as it felt to ya'."

"It felt real," he said. "It felt very real."

She pulled her hand away and slapped her thigh. "Well then, there ya' go. You'll see her again in another dream. I promise. But for right now, you look like you've got one eye half shut and the other not long after. Get some sleep. You've earned it."

Stone tried to fight it. He tried to stay awake, but there's just some times when there's no use fighting it. He laid on his side and put his sack under his head.

"You going off to sleep too?" he murmured. But he didn't hear the answer, as he was fast asleep before she even had the time to respond.

THE FOLLOWING MORNING, Adler woke them just before first light, as Corvaire had at some point switched with him for lookout. Stone felt like he'd been asleep for all of twenty minutes, but it had been all night. And there'd been no sign of the riders.

They packed their bags quickly, ate a few bites of dried fruit they'd brought with them, and were mounted back on the horses. The four horses trotted off back northbound toward the mountains in the distance. They didn't talk much as they rode.

A fresh morning dew clung to the grass as the horses glided through, and roosters crowed from somewhere to the east. For much of the day, Ceres rode up next to Corvaire at the lead—asking him questions about her magic, and Stone rode with Adler.

Adler talked about his time in the Assassin's Guild, but oddly enough didn't mention his mentor much. He spoke more about the technique he'd learned from different guilds, and what was the proper etiquette to use when meeting those of varying skill sets.

That day went on as the horses trotted on, and Corvaire had guessed they had gone at least the forty miles they'd hoped, possibly more. Ceres cast her spell again, and they made shelter in a patch of trees nestled up against a ridge on the south side. That night, Adler found them a pair of small pigs, and the eating was good—as was the sleep, after Stone took first watch.

The next few days rolled on as they rode atop their great steeds. Light rain trickled down from the heavens on the third day, but mostly it was warm weather and clear skies. That wasn't to say there wasn't a stark amount of nervousness brimming in them. They still worried about how the Runtue riders had traversed such a long distance from when Kellen had told them they were spotted in the eastern lands to find them in the forest just days ago.

The night after they slept upon the tall rock and Ceres said she'd spotted the leaping shadow creature in the dark of night, but that it scattered off as soon as she roused the others. That was growing to be a troubling concern to them—but not as much as the Runtue—so they agreed that they'd deal with the mystery of the creature after they'd gotten the new mother up to the safety of Endo.

On the fifth day, they arrived at a river that, at its narrowest they found, was thirty yards across. The water was a deep blue which made it difficult to gauge its depth. But they found that it was shallow enough for them each to walk across, even if it was deep enough to nearly reach their chests. Ceres was light enough to ride Angelix as it crossed. The water was a rigid, sharp cold.

Once on the other side they found themselves sopping wet, and dumping water from their boots as the bottom of the river was full of sharp rocks. It was nearly twilight by the time they'd gotten across and found a suitable enough place to camp for the night. And Stone knew he needed a fire to warm away the chills that crept under his skin.

It wasn't the most preferable place to camp—on the outskirts of a thin thicket of small trees—nearly out in the open on the plains. But the mountains they'd been riding toward had been getting much closer day after day.

Stone offered to take first watch, and the others hung their clothes by the fire and did their best to drift off to sleep. He sat with his legs crossed facing the southern horizon as the stars collected once again above. A brilliantly lit full, white moon beamed down, casting a shadow behind him.

He whistled a tune to himself that he'd remembered from the tavern back in Atlius all that time ago. Next to him lay one of the bows with a full quiver of arrows. The shadow creature never got close enough to them for an easy shot, but if it did, they'd all be sure to sleep just a little bit better without that thing stalking them from the shadows.

At one point in the night an owl draped in shadow flew down like a shadow itself into the grass and emerged with a long-tailed rodent. Stone marveled at such a wide-winged bird swooping in so silently. But as the owl arched back up into the sky with the rat squirming and squeaking, a rustling appeared in the grass down by the river's edge.

Stone picked up the bow and placed the quiver on his back.

He knelt and strung an arrow into the bowstring.

If it's the creature, I'm going to fire true.

But something was different that time.

It seems to not be scampering off this time. It's . . . it's heading right for us . . .

Not only that, but it was running at them at a quick speed.

Stone aimed the arrow at where it was in the grass, and as his heart thumped in his chest, he awaited for the moment the beast would emerge from the grass, just twenty-five yards down a dirt-covered bank.

He steadied his hand, gazing down the shaft of the arrow. Ready for a boar, or even a wildcat to come bursting through—his sword was a quick grab at his hip. The commotion seemed to garner enough attention that Corvaire roused from his sleep.

"What the—?" he began.

Then, the animal burst through the grass at a startling speed. Stone's eyes widened as he gripped the arrow tighter in his hand, letting the bowstring relax gently, and dropped it to the ground. He threw both his arms out wide to his sides and let the dog with the black fur and white spot over his eye plow into him—sending him falling onto his back as Mud licked his cheek.

"Where have you been?" Stone laughed as he tried to push the dogs licking face from his. Soon they were all awake and smiling to see their returned friend.

But Mud didn't stay on top of Stone long. He leaped back off him and stood with his front paws out wide, and was *barking* at him.

"Hey," Stone said. "Don't bark at me. Are you that mad?" Adler and Ceres laughed from where they lay. But the dog didn't let up, and they quickly stopped laughing.

"What's wrong, Mud?" Ceres asked, sitting up farther.

Mud then spun around and was barking south, to the other side of the river.

"You don't mean—?" Stone said slowly.

Corvaire rushed to Stone's side and looked out past the river. The other two were quickly on their feet.

"Corvaire?" Ceres asked. "You see anything?"

Stone was looking too, and didn't seem to see anything, even in the glowing moonlight.

"There!" Corvaire pointed out up to a high hill far past the river. "You see that?"

To Stone, it just looked like another shadow from the blowing grass from that distance, but then after focusing harder, he saw the shadow was moving closer to them.

"To the horses," Corvaire said.

"Is it them?" Ceres said. "Have they found us?"

"Get to the horses!"

They ran to the horses, mounting them quickly.

"We can't outrun them for days," Adler said. "Not with this far to go. We should stay and fight."

Corvaire glared at him with his dark hair whipping behind him as he prepared to mount his horse with one boot in its stirrup. "We stay here . . . and we won't live to see tomorrow."

Chapter Twenty-Six

The cool night wind flew past them as their steeds laid heavy hooves upon the plains as they tread through the darkness. Long shadows trailed behind them as they rode toward the brightly-glowing moon.

Stone lurched around on his horse, but saw nothing behind them as they traveled north. There were many miles between them and where'd they'd seen the riders on the other side of the river, but he remembered how they looked like when he first saw them when they were in the forest.

The Runtue glided effortlessly, and nearly silently, down the hills. He didn't know if there was some sort of magic in those steeds or not—but he didn't want to find out. So they kept on riding.

"Where do we go?" Ceres asked loudly as the wind rushed past them, and a hawk flew overhead with a squirming snake in its talons.

"There's got to be somewhere we can hide," Stone said. "They're too swift to outrun."

Corvaire didn't answer, but kicking the sides of his horse, he looked around nervously.

"We're going to have to stand our ground," Adler said. "We can't outrun them like Stone said. We're gonna have to fight."

"Ten to one," Corvaire said. "Ten hardened soldiers that wiped out a trained squadron of soldiers from one of the greatest cities in all the Worforgon. They didn't lose a single soldier. What chance do you think the four of us have against them?"

"We have magic," Adler said.

"And you think they don't?" Corvaire quipped.

Adler whipped the reins harder then.

Mud panted as he ran next to Stone, who was mounted upon Grave's back as he neighed as Stone whipped his own reins. Then, Stone saw Mud's long shadow disappear next to him, which was quickly replaced by the dog's loud barking behind him, which grew faintly quickly.

He looked back to see the dog with his front paws spread wide, his head lowered, and the fur on his back straightened as he barked. Far past him on the hill on the horizon to the south were the distant silhouettes of the riders—all ten of them—and they were riding straight after them.

"Mud!" Stone pulled back on the reins.

"What're ya doin'?" Ceres called out, halting Angelix's run.

Adler stopped and turned to watch. Corvaire also slowed to look back in anger with his brow furrowed.

"Forget about him," Adler yelled back to Stone. "He'll take care of himself!"

The dog barked madly like a hungry hellhound let loose upon its attacker.

"Adler's right," Stone said. "How long can we outrun them?"

Corvaire rode over quickly to his side.

"It doesn't matter," he said calmly to Stone. "You are

astonishing with a blade, Stone. Sure, I've got my magic. But what about your friends?"

Stone raised an eyebrow at him.

"Adler's talented. But you saw how those riders fight. Adler could maybe take *one*, but *two . . . three*? And how long would Ceres be able to perch on the outskirts of the battle shooting arrows into the fray? Are you planning to kill all ten on your own?"

Stone's brimming fire waned inside him, and logic crept back into his rage-filled mind.

"The dog has proven he can take care of himself," Corvaire said. "He may even be trying to get them off our tracks again. Come now, Stone, ride—ride!"

The two were back off into the plains then, with Ceres and Adler just behind.

Mud's barking was mute and distant as Stone turned back to see the riders encroaching upon them gradually.

There were still many hours left of night as they rode under the bright light of the beaming moon and the starlit sky.

How long can we ride like this? What's going on in Corvaire's mind right now? Does he have a plan? Or is this the plan?

Stone could no longer hear the dog's barking, nor could he hear the patter of the unnaturally soft hooves with which the Runtue horses rode. The ten of them were behind them still, riding at them in a long line with all ten visible—and Mud was nowhere to be seen. Stone felt his stomach up in his chest. He worried not only for his dog, but for what Corvaire had said only moments earlier.

Ride! Just keep riding, maybe they'll get tired and have to rest behind us . . . maybe . . .

"There!" Corvaire yanked on the reins to his right. The others followed behind. He didn't point but they were heading then toward a steep-sided butte surrounded by a ring of short-looking trees.

None of them asked why they were going there—they all knew—that's where they were going to stage their defense against the warriors of Arken.

The dark-tan butte was only a twenty-minute ride away by the time Mud came running along back at Stone's side, which gave him an overwhelming relief, and let him breathe easily again, but still—the Runtue were gaining on them with each gallop.

Once they rode in through the trees, they found that they were thick with thorns that pricked their skin and tugged at their clothes. They ducked their heads and rode carefully through the thick limbs—eventually making their way to the wall of the butte, which went up a good fifteen feet on its lowest side.

"The horses won't be able to get up there," Ceres said with wide eyes. "They'll be killed down here all alone."

"There might be a path up on the other side," Adler said.

"No time for that," Corvaire said. "They're going to have to ride off on their own. The riders won't care about them. They're after us. They're after Stone. Climb!"

They dismounted and after Ceres gave her horse a soft kiss, they each went to the stone wall and started to climb.

It was a fairly easy climb for Stone and the others as there were spots with several inch-wide cracks and pits. They were soon standing upon the preface of the butte's edge, looking down as the ten riders stopped at the edge of the tree line and looked into the deep thicket, speaking to one another in soft voices.

"Maybe that'll keep them," Adler said. "At least until daylight."

"Wouldn't be too sure about that," Corvaire said. "I'm thinking they're more checking to see if there's a spell cast upon it."

"Is there?" Ceres asked.

"Not yet," he answered.

"Whose doin' the casting?" she asked.

"Both of us," he said.

"Tell me what I need to do," she said in a firm voice.

Stone's heart beat wildly, and he could feel his heartbeat in his hand which held his sword's grip tightly.

"You ever see Marilyn use a spell that created vines that came out of the ground?" he asked. They each nodded. "That was Vines that Hold. You're going to use that to keep them in place. And then I'm going to send down lightning like they've never seen before."

Stone had tingles running up and down his back.

He did have a plan all along. And not a bad one! He's going to kill them with his lightning spell!

"How do I do it?" Ceres asked.

"You're going to have to reach deep down for this, Ceres. It's not an easy spell, and there are many of them. Take up ten blades of the longest grass you can find and clutch them in your hands. Hurry."

She went and plucked them from as closely to the ground as she could and rushed back over, just in time for them to all see the riders dismount and slowly embark into the trees—disappearing into its shadow.

"Okay," she said with a deep breath.

"*Vinitulas Windum Granum*," he said. "Go on, hurry now. Dig deep. Bring your emotions into this one."

"You can do it," Stone said.

She said the words with open eyes darting around, scanning for them in the darkness—repeating the words. The riders were stealthy, but they could all see the tops of the trees bustle as one of them surely got snagged up on the sharp thorns.

"There!" Adler said, motioning to a tree that swayed mightily from one of the Runtue.

"*Illietomus Creschiendo*!" Corvaire yelled out, sending a

blinding bolt of lightning down onto that tree from the clear sky. It sent a roaring, nearly deafening crack that burst the tree into flames. It was immediately accompanied by a boom of thunder.

Each of them covered their ears from the explosion, just as Mud scampered up the backside of the butte.

"Again," he said to Ceres. "Cast again."

"I don't know if I got it," she said.

"It doesn't matter if you know," he said. "Just keep casting. Hurry!"

"*Vinitulas Windum Granum*," she said again, clutching the blades of grass tighter as they draped out of both sides of her clenched fists.

Another tree swayed like a fish line being tugged by a hooked fish.

"There," Stone said, pointing out.

"I see it," Corvaire said. "*Illietomus Creschiendo*!"

Another brilliant burst of searing lightning he cast down upon the tree. It exploded into an eruption of white-hot light and flying splinters.

"There!" Adler pointed once the light faded, and Corvaire sent another lightning strike down onto that spot.

Stone was exhilarated by the spectacle, and for the first time, had the feeling that they may get out of the attack alive. But that's when his hopes diminished in the form of eight Runtue running into the sides of the base of the butte, each of them spread out along its long side.

"Corvaire?" Adler asked in worry.

They all knew the warriors would easily be able to scale its side.

"*Vinitulas Windum Granum*," Ceres repeated quickly.

"Draw your bow," Corvaire said to her. "The spell isn't working. It's time we fight."

It was then that Stone noticed Corvaire's breaths were labored.

He's getting tired from that many spells. I'm going to have to take the lead in this fight. I'm going to have to stop them all.

Five of the soldiers climbed the wall, getting to their feet quickly, each of their eyes were reddened and ready for blood behind their gold and black painted faces.

Ceres sent an arrow flying, but with a flash of his hand, one of the Runtue sent out a small metal disk from his hand with a shadowy tail, it hit the arrow midflight with a ping that snapped the arrow into pieces.

She strung another arrow, as the other three Runtue climbed up. Six of them had their swords drawn and with wide stances. The other two held empty hands over pouches on their hips.

"Hold," Corvaire said to Ceres. He, Stone and Adler each held their swords in their hands.

The four of them faced the eight Runtue on the top of the butte as a strong wind rushed over the tall rock and the air was empty of any animal or insect sounds. They were all silent, waiting and anxious for what was about to happen.

"Runtue riders," Stone said. "We mean you no harm unless you mean to harm us and any innocent people of these lands. I'm sure there's a way we can end this without any of your deaths."

"Yesss—" one of the Runtue said with a slight hiss. A woman with two empty hands and a thin, wicked smile across her face. Her eyes narrowed in on Stone. "There isss a way we can end thisss."

"And what's that?" Adler snapped at her.

"You—SSStone. You come with us. You help usss find the Majessstic Wild, and we'll let your friendsss go away to live their ssshort lives free."

"No way," Ceres yelled. "He's not going anywhere without us."

The Runtue woman's smile snapped away to a sneer. "It mattersss not to usss. Our king caresss not for any of you. He wantsss the boy alive for himssself. And he wants the Majessstic too. So we kill you, and take SSStone—yesss we will."

"Over my corpse you will," Corvaire said, pointing out with his long sword at her.

The other Runtue shifted quickly to defend the woman at their center.

"Fine by me, man of the Darakon," she said. "I'm going to enjoy this."

As both sides prepared to rush in for battle, the wind picked up again. Their long shadows emphasized their strong stances and their sharp swords. The growing tension built in a deafening silence, and Stone eyed his attackers intensely.

"Ready?" Corvaire asked. "Aim for the neck and under the arm. Ceres, shoot at the ones with swords. I'm going to try to take out the others first." He was whispering as quietly as he could. "Gotta kill those ones first that are throwing those disks. Then we can focus in on the others."

Stone's arms throbbed with adrenaline and his head was pounding. He was eager to rush into battle—he was eager to defend his friends.

The Runtue's boots shifted, as they prepared to rush out. The ones without swords readied their hands by moving their fingers in a fanning wave above the pouches.

"Ready?" Corvaire yelled out. But then Stone noticed the woman's eyes move to the side, as if focusing on something else. Her head turned back to the forest, as did the other Runtue's.

"What's happening?" Stone asked in surprise. But he then heard something snap in the forest below.

"Don't know," Corvaire said. "But now's our chance. Attack!"

They rushed toward the Runtue, who had their backs turned to them, as Ceres let an arrow fly. The woman snapped around and sent a shadow disk at the arrow, snapping it harmlessly away. And as they ran forward, the Runtue backed away from the butte's cliff to a defensive, V position, causing Corvaire to pause again, holding them back.

"What the devil is going on here?" he said.

It was then that he got his answer as a dozen men and woman climbed up the cliff silently, creeping up to its top, each with long cloaks that nearly perfectly matched the shade of the dark-tan rock. More than a dozen more climbed up after them.

"What is going on?" Ceres asked. "Who are they?"

Each of the men and women in cloaks spread out smoothly to surround the Runtue on the edge of the cliff. They let their hoods down and Stone saw they were all like them, and not painted like their enemies.

"I don't believe it," Adler gasped. "It's actually them . . ."

"It's actually who?" Stone asked.

Adler turned with a face brimming with excitement and a wink. "It's the Masters of the Assassins Guild. It's the Silent Death. They've come to fight with us."

Chapter Twenty-Seven

"We're not fighting *with* you," one of the Silent Death said to Adler. "We're fighting *for* you. Now ride away from this place and find the new Wild Majestic. Now!"

In the ranks of the group of assassins, Stone found Lucik Haverfold was the one telling them to run off. She was the leader of the guild in Verren, with the burn mark on the side of her face and her long gray hair falling down her back.

"We aren't leaving you here," Adler said as the tension was growing between the assassins and the Runtue as they yelled back and forth. "You came here to fight, and so did we."

"She is more important than any of us," Lucik said with a rushing urgency for Adler and them to be off with a wave of her sword. "Go find her, and quickly, before Arken does. He can't get his hands on her. He just can't."

"Go," said another assassin, as the Runtue sneered at the larger group cornering them on the edge of the butte. Stone took a moment of gazing into her light blue eyes, trying to remember where he'd seen her before.

"Hydrangea," Adler said as she also was flicking her head

to the side, motioning for them to go. Her long, brown hair blew in the night wind.

She's the one from the guild in Salsonere who we met before . . . How'd they all get here so fast to save us . . . were they following us?

"It may be time for us to go." Corvaire nodded to the two women, as they both turned their sights upon the invading riders.

"We can't," Adler said. "I'm one of them."

"You'll have to pick then," Corvaire admitted. "Stay with them, or come with us. They're right. The new mother takes precedence, she may be the turning of the tides in this war. Not us. Not the assassins. Come now, we must go and gather the horses, now!"

He ran over, with Ceres following him, leaving Adler and Stone to think through the choice that was given. Mud barked madly at the men and women in the gold and black makeup and thick armor.

"We should go," Stone said. "Ceres is going to need our help out there."

"No, we need to fight with the Silent Death. It would be a great honor for me, and then after we kill the riders, we can all go together."

"If we survive," Stone said. "If any of us live . . ."

"They'll live," Adler said. "They're the best warriors in the . . ."

The Runtue erupted into a loud war cry and let out a flurry of the metal disks, flying into the assassins where they were waiting for their own moment to strike. The Runtue ran forward at the others, with sharp swords in hand, eager to draw first blood.

They flew into the ranks of the Silent Death like a crashing wave onto a blunt stone, and metal clashed with metal as the two forces met in battle. The disks struck one of the assassins, sending him reeling to the ground with a twisted face of excruciating pain.

"We have to go." Stone pulled on Adler's sleeve.

"No, go on without me." He brushed Stone's hand away and walked toward the skirmish with sword in hand.

"We need you," Stone said. "Ceres needs you. She needs us."

Adler paused as the fighting intensified with flashing swords in the bright moonlight. The assassins moved with an artistic style of combat that made them look more like deadly dancers than soldiers. They dipped their heads under swift sword swipes and their footwork made them spin in circles around the slower, heavier soldiers of Arken. But the power in their attacks of the Runtue was immediately evident, as a crushing blow cracked the rock of the butte in one blow.

"Come, now," Stone said to him. "They can fight this fight. This is our one chance to escape, and the assassins—your people—asked you to flee. Now come. We're losing time."

Adler sighed, shaking his sword angrily. "Fine."

Stone ran over to climb down to join the others, and Adler followed reluctantly. Just before he started to climb down, he saw two of the assassins fall to the ground dead, one from a flying disk and one from a Runtue's sword. But he didn't see any of them injured.

Damn these bastards are hard to kill.

Mud ran over to Stone who picked him up and carried him down. Corvaire took the dog down from Stone's arm and placed him on the ground. Adler was soon down after.

"You there," said an elderly voice over from within the trees.

Corvaire spun to look in the direction. "Who's there? Show yourself."

The sounds of battle raged over them with the constant

clanging of metal cracking onto metal and the all too familiar grunts of men fighting for their lives.

An old man stepped out into the moonlight, he was holding something in his arms and hands—something heavy, Stone could tell.

"Hold it right there," Corvaire said.

"Master Conrad." Adler ran over.

"Who is it?" Stone asked.

"Master Conrad Galveston of the guild. He's the guild master!"

"Take these," Conrad said, with his beady, dark eyes showing little emotion. His silver hair was short and wavy, and he held an aura of old wisdom and confidence in him. "Your horses are out past the trees next to ours. You must go now. Seek out the Wild Majestic. Use your magic, Ceres. Now go, and may haste be on your side."

"We will," Ceres said while Stone gathered the items from his arms that were draped in a thick, green tapestry. They were long and sturdy from what he felt.

"May Crysinthian look over you in your journey." Conrad waved for them to be on their way. "Go. Ride!"

They ran through the thorny thicket and emerged back on the other side of the trees where a great gathering of horses waited for their masters. They found their own horses waiting just on the outside of them.

"What are they?" Adler asked Stone, who was tying the tapestry to his horse.

"No time," Corvaire said. "Off at once. Let's go."

Each of them mounted and rode north once again, as Stone careened his head back and watched the shadowy figures on the butte fight in a vicious battle, where to be honest to himself—didn't know who was going to survive.

Chapter Twenty-Eight

With the thumping of the Masummand Steel swords against the strong thighs of their horses, a strong wash of sunlight warmed them—brushing the afternoon rain away. Stone watched his friends as their downtrodden woes were temporarily relieved.

The horses' hooves stamped on the road as they trotted farther and farther north—still with Ceres feeling the new mother pulling her closer with each passing step.

"Sun feels good," Ceres said simply.

To the west, far off in the vast plains, the final tips of the Worgons were cascading back to the ground, ending the mighty range's reach. To the east, a wide river flowed back inland, and before them a great empty unknown, where eventually the great saltwater of the Sonter lingered.

"You know any of the villages up there?" Stone asked Adler. "You know where she might be?"

He looked over at Ceres, "Oh, what's the name o' that one town up on the coast?" She shrugged.

"It's from that old song," he said, scratching his temple.

"How's it go? . . .*By the old town mist, to the crowded ships, and the bottles strewn a-way-hee* . . . *to the* . . . Oh, what's it again?"

Corvaire chimed in, ". . .*to the old hag's lamp, and the thieve's camp, it's at Thistleton we stay-hee.*"

"Thistleton!" Adler said. "That's it. It's near the coast, ain't it?"

"Aye," Ceres said. "I think I've heard of it."

"The song's about pirates and where they rest their heads on their adventures," Adler said.

"I believe it's a song about their conquests," Corvaire added. "It's about where they loot and plunder, and then they stay after they've robbed the place blind."

"Oh," Adler said, cocking his head back. "I hadn't heard it since I was a child, I don't think. Kids don't think of pirates that way, I don't think."

"That's an old one," Corvaire said. "My father used to sing that to me when I was a lad."

"Hard to think of you ever being a boy," Adler quipped.

Corvaire feigned a rare smirk. "I was a boy, just like every other man. That's how life works."

"How old are you?" Ceres asked. "Where were you born?"

"How old do you think I am?" he asked her with that same smile.

"Hmm . . ." she said with pursed lips, and her fingers on her chin. "Thirty-eight!"

He snickered.

"Thirty-two," Adler said.

"Fifty-five," he said. "I think . . ."

"No," Ceres said. "You haven't got a gray hair on your head.

"People in my family tend to live longer lives than most. Marilyn and I were born on the island of Androgia, to the southeast."

"How long do you live?" Stone asked.

"My father lived to be one hundred thirty, my mother one hundred and fifty-two."

"What?" Adler snickered, as if he were jesting. But Corvaire's smirk faded to a serious face. "You're serious, aren't ya'?"

Corvaire nodded.

"That's incredible," Ceres said. "How's that possible?"

"Don't know," Corvaire said. "But it gives me time to learn important things others don't have the ability to."

"Learn things such as . . .?" Ceres asked, prying more from him.

"I gathered a cache of information from the great texts in the darker parts of the old kingdoms. I studied from great swordsmen from coast to coast. I learned from the Majestic Wilds themselves."

"And you've still got another hundred years to learn, or more!" Adler said.

"Not if things keep playing out the way they are," Corvaire said, in a sort of half-joke that Stone recognized.

"I've never heard of Androgia before," Adler said. "At least I don't think I have."

"Not much there," Corvaire said. "Well . . . I should say to most there isn't. But to me, it was home. Still is." Corvaire's black hair waved behind him in the warm light of the golden sun. The dark stubble on his tan skin accentuated his lined dimples and his hazel eyes stared out into the plains before them. "The Obsidian Sea is dark and murky to most, but to us —it was our own beautiful paradise. The Forest of Ure gave us all we needed to live off of. And I can still remember the smell of the forest and sea air in the morning as my father lit the kettle."

There was a calmness in the air then, where each of them felt a warmth and security they hadn't felt since being in their shanty house back in Verren.

The horses panicked. There were loud neighs and each of them stopped in a harsh uproar—flinging the startled Adler clear off Hedron. Stone managed to stay atop Grave's back; clutching onto his sturdy neck. He pulled the brand-new, forged sword from its sheath with that clear ringing echo.

What's there? Who's out there that would startle the horses like this? Why can't I see anything?

The horses continued to cry loudly, spinning in circles, frantic about whatever was causing this.

The world swirled in black wisps of smoke, and his friends faded into the darkness. His heart raced, and he gripped his sword tightly.

Stone leaped down from his horse and strode out in front of it with his sword reflecting a hazy red hue. He took a deep breath, struggling to calm his nerves.

"Arken," he said in a low tone.

"Stone," the Dark King replied, with his thick leathery cape framing his wide body.

"You've come for a fight?" Stone said.

"You look weak," the king said in a grizzly voice. "You look tired. It wouldn't be much of a fight."

Stone looked for an opening for an attack that might catch the king off guard, but there was something strange about Arken that he couldn't quite catch.

"You seek what I seek," Arken said slowly.

The Dark King's one eye twinkled with its ebony luster. He removed his iron horned helmet, exposing his slick black hair and scars on his ashen skin.

He held his helmet in his gauntlet at his side, and it was then that Stone noticed his cape wasn't flapping at all in the breeze, no matter how heavy it was.

"I should kill you right here and now," Stone growled.

Arken laughed a singular laugh as spit flung from his lips.

"Not so weak, I gather," he said.

"What do you want?"

"The Majestic Wild," Arken said in a low tone. "Same as you."

"You can't have her. She needs us and we need her. Stay away."

"She's the one with the gift to find her— your friend Ceres," Arken said, glowering at Stone. "Do tell me, what do you know of her? She's the one who can end this war and give my people the peace they've yearned for, and deserved for far too long."

"I'll tell ya nothin' of her! You monster! You're not really here, are you?" Stone said. "This is some sort of dark spell of yours. You can't even come face me yourself, coward!"

Arken's one eye glared heavily at him. "Call me what you want, but a coward I'm not. Call me evil, call me a monster. But I'm no coward."

Stone could feel he was telling the truth.

There's some other reason he's not here to face me . . . I wonder what that could be . . .

"Where are you? Really?" Stone asked.

"The real question is, where are *you*?" Arken responded, drawing out the words in a sinister tone.

He doesn't know where I am? How is he doing this then?

"You can't have her," Stone said, sheathing his sword.

"I want the girl. I want all the Majestic Wilds. They're going to help me fulfill the promise that Vere, Gardin, and Seretha made to me all those ages ago."

"You want us to help you find her?" Stone demanded. "You killed the Old Mothers with your rotten beast, and now you ask for our help?"

"I don't ask," the Dark King said. "I demand."

"Why would we do anything you demand?" Stone said. "You're a fool if you think—"

"I'll give you all what you truly want most, if you help me

find the ones I seek. If you help me find the new Majestic Wild, I can bring back for you what you and your friends want most. I'm the only one who can give you what you all dream about at night, what you wish to the stars, what causes that broken feeling deep down in your hearts when you're alone."

"What are you speaking of?" Stone asked flatly. "I have no reason to trust you, and I grow tired of this."

"I can bring your parents back to you," he said.

"You lie," Stone growled, clenching his teeth and squeezing his fist.

"I speak no lies," Arken said. "If you help me find the young women who will be blessed—and cursed—with their knowledge and powers, then I'll bring your families back to you."

Stone's head whirled at those words. He felt an anger ping in his chest, and a sorrow swell in his stomach. "Don't you dare," Stone rasped through clenched teeth. "Don't you even dare."

"Yes," Arken said with a higher pitch, and a black drool creeping out of his mouth. "You had a mother and father, just like all the others. But the difference between you and your friends is . . . You're going to love this . . ." He smiled widely, with his yellow teeth sharpening out of his mouth. "Your father . . . he's not dead."

"You lie," Stone snarled.

"You have until the next moon's light to decide," Arken said. "I'll even let you live. Because I know the pain of losing everything, that if you help me get back what was taken from me, then I'll let you live free lives."

"You son of a bitch!" Stone lashed forward with his sword locked over his shoulder.

He sent his sword cutting through Arken between the neck and shoulder, and wisps of smoke rose from the cut. Stone's face was only inches from Arken's—looking into that one dark, hollow eye.

"One day," Arken whispered. "Choose wisely . . ."

With a warm gust of wind, Arken vanished in a scattering of dark smoke.

Stone's chest was heaving, and tears welled in his eyes.

It can't be true . . . It can't . . . but if he is telling the truth . . . then I have a real family somewhere out there? And I have to find them . . . I must *find him.*

Chapter Twenty-Nine

The world spun, and Stone's head whirled as the black mists faded and reality crept back. He clutched his head in one hand and was dizzy.

"What happened?" Corvaire asked, snapping Stone back to where he was.

"It was him," Stone said, shaking his head slowly.

"Arken?" Ceres asked with her fingers spread out wide.

Stone nodded.

"How?" Adler asked.

Corvaire grumbled, taking slow strides away.

"He.. he wants the Majestic Wild we seek," Stone said.

"What? He can't… what right does he have?" Ceres shot off. "There's no way…"

"He wanted to trade," Stone said, still shaking the cobwebs away.

"Trade?" Ceres said. "Trade what? What would he have to offer us that would even make us think about siding with him and his murdering dragons?"

Stone glared at her, sighing. "He offered what we want

most. He offered… to bring back the ones we love. The ones who died."

"What?" Adler breathed with wide eyes.

"No! No! There ain't no fuckin' way I'm agreeing to that creep's demands." Ceres' hands balled up into fists.

"That bullshit ain't gonna fool me either," Adler said with reddening eyes full of rage. "He can go suck on a cow pie!"

Is it true?

"No one can bring the dead back," she said. "And even if they could, we all know they wouldn't be the same."

"How's he even know that much about us?" Adler asked. "How could he even know?"

Can I have a . . . a father?

"He's just pulling at your heartstrings," Corvaire said. "There is no truth to it. Don't believe a lying word that hound says."

But what if he is telling the truth?

Mud barked in the background at the spot Arken's image had appeared.

"What if he's tellin' the truth, though," Ceres said, letting her fingers uncurl. "What if there is a chance?"

"No way, no how," Adler steamed. "Huh-uh. It's not possible . . . right?"

I'm not going to give into his demands. But . . . is there a chance to bring their families back to them?

"Corvaire?" Ceres asked—and all of their eyes were drawn to him.

"No."

"There's no chance he could be telling the truth?" Ceres asked.

"It's not that simple," Corvaire said. "Nothing like bringing back the dead is ever simple, or ever has worked out the way he's said. Do not fall for his trap. He only seeks the power of the woman we are after. That's all he cares about. There's nothing more that matters to him than that."

"You said bringing back the dead isn't simple," Adler said. "But you didn't say it was impossible."

"Can you do it?" Ceres asked.

"We really need to be moving on," Corvaire said. "I know you miss your families. And I miss Marilyn and my parents. But there's no sense in dwelling on nonsensical bringing your loved one's back talk."

"But . . . it is possible, then?" Ceres asked with narrow eyes.

Does Corvaire know something he's not letting on?

Corvaire sighed. "I never said it wasn't outside of the realm of possibility. There've been legends about it. Hell! Look at your friend standing next to you here. But I'll say the prophecy that Seretha and the others followed led to Stone—the single person that was thought to have been dead, but now walked the grasses of the Worforgon again."

"What legends?" Adler asked, acting as if everything else he'd said didn't matter.

"There were those," Corvaire sighed again. "Necromancers . . . legends told of."

They were all fixated upon his next words.

"We should be on our way," Corvaire said. "We've no idea if they're on their way behind us."

"This is important to us," Ceres said, "please."

Corvaire looked back down south down the road, but after seeing nothing, said, "They were like gods to men back then."

"There were other gods?" Adler asked. "Other than Crysinthian?"

"Crysinthian wasn't always the one god."

What? There used to be other gods? How much does Corvaire really know that he hasn't told us? Or hasn't had the time to tell us?

"Keep in mind this was ages ago. This was before Arken was even a mere man."

"So—what of these older *gods*?" Ceres asked.

"I don't know anything for sure," Corvaire said. "This is all legend. But there were those with the powers to resurrect the dead. But they couldn't just do it, the same way we learn to use our magic . . . It was a power bestowed upon them."

Each of them eagerly awaited more from him as the prairie was as still as a cavern's stagnant air—as if Crysinthian himself were listening in.

"The old ones who could regather the deceased were not given the gift or born with it. It was a found treasure. But it was also a found curse."

Again, deafening silence from them and the dead breeze.

"There were artifacts back then, things that the old ones hounded over—went mad over—killed one another over. Wars were fought, won and lost over. They were the most prized possessions a man could possess. They were told to give unlimited power, and unlimited loss . . ."

It sounds like he's telling an old fable . . . something a grandfather would tell his young grandchild, but I've never known him to lie. And I can see it in his eyes: he believes what he's saying.

"Go on," Ceres said. "We're listening."

"There are things we speak about now, such as the Majestic Wilds, or the Old Mothers, but these are new things. The kingdoms, the way the lands are, these are all new things in the grand scheme of time. Did you know, for instance, that there are other lands out there? Across the seas that are so treacherous and manic."

"I've heard of those lands," Adler said. "That's where the dragons are flying from to war with the Neferian."

"Yes," Corvaire said. "But there was a time the seas weren't so violent, and people could sail across their shining waters. Those were times before people discovered . . . the weapons that turned them to gods . . ."

Stone looked around and saw the bewildering, enchanting

lights in the eyes of his friends, just like a grandchild listening to his grandfather tell him an old tale.

"Go on," Stone said. "We're listening."

"Again," he said, "these are all things I've heard that my father told me passed down from generations, but . . . there were beings that existed ages ago, long before the time of the Majestic Wilds. They lived alongside monsters like the old giants that were the sizes of mountains, serpents that were so large and powerful they lived in the entirety of a sea. These old beings were no match for the powers that existed in the olden times . . ."

"What were they?" Ceres asked.

"Why . . . they were just like you and me."

"They lived here?" she asked.

"They lived everywhere."

"Where did they come from?" Adler asked.

"That's a question you'd have to ask Crysinthian himself."

"Go on with the story," Stone said as at last a calm breeze strolled in.

"Those like us were dying by the drove by those monsters, and they were in desperate numbers, and one day . . . as if strolling out of the Golden Realm itself, a man walked out of the Sacred Sea and walked night and day up to the king of the time. He walked over mountain and bog, stream and shore, and lake and forest to reach him. And once there, past all the king's men and women; he walked up to the king and whispered in his ear: *under stone, under rock, under grass and under hill, you will find your salvation. Life long, you'll grasp, and the power of eternity you'll wield."*

"Power of eternity?" Stone asked.

"I don't know the exact wording," Corvaire said. "My father told me and Marilyn this tale long ago, but I believe this is the gist of it. I don't know what he meant by the power of eternity. If I did, I'd be more descriptive."

"So, what's this got to do with Arken?" Adler asked, swinging his arms.

"The only person who was ever told to raise the dead," Corvaire said, "was that king whose ear was whispered into by that man from the sea."

"Hmpf," Adler said. "An ol' matron's tale."

"Yes, perhaps," Corvaire said with a wave of his hand. "Absolutely. But with Arken's mention of this, it begs me to remember the past. It is possible that to have survived as long as he has, and to be as powerful as he is now . . . maybe he found something wherever he was banished to. For what he was remembered as in the past—he was honorable, proud, and above all . . . had integrity."

"Is this the same Arken we are talking about that burned Seretha, Gardin and Vere alive in front of us?" Adler sneered. "In front of our own eyes?"

"I'm speaking of the man he once was," Corvaire said. "I know not the man who rides atop the backs of those dark dragons."

"So," Stone said. "You're implying Arken found some old power by an old race of man?"

"That is what I'm implying, yes."

"So," Ceres said slowly. "There is a chance Arken was telling the truth about what he spoke. There's a chance?"

"There's not a chance enough for us to trust him," Stone said. "Not a chance enough for us to give him the girl we're trying to save."

"I'm not saying that," she said, whipping her head toward him with her golden hair flicking over her shoulder. "I'd never trust him. I'm just asking."

Stone stood back in silence.

"If he's able to bring back the dead," Corvaire said, "which is almost completely unlikely, then that adds another deeper mystery to what's going on right now."

Then, Mud barked back down the southern path of the road, and each of them turned to face whatever threat came their way.

On the road, down at a far distance away, a plume of high-rising dust hovered above it—exactly what a horse riding at full speed would look like.

Once the rider appeared, and each of them slowly let their weapons fall loosely back to their sides, Stone finally broke the silence as the two women on horseback approached.

"How did Arken do that? Appear in front of me? But . . . he didn't seem to know where I was?"

"I'm afraid to say that's a mystery for another day," Corvaire said, scratching his thigh.

Each of them seemed to not have a thought about how that could've happened.

How could he reach me like that? And could he do it again? I hope not . . .

The riders who approached were welcome faces to see, for sure. They saw them hop down from their steeds as soon as they came up to them.

The two of them were from the Assassin's Guild: Hydrangea and Lucik each let their boots touch the dirt and came up to Stone first.

He looked at both of them with the soot and blood marking their faces, and each of them had that battle-trodden, weary look in their eyes.

"Where are the others? Are you all right?" Stone asked, softly gripping their shoulders.

"Many are lost," Hydrangea said with hardened, glaring eyes. "But we took some of them bastards with us."

"How many?" Corvaire asked. "How many of you and them are left?"

"Most are lost," Lucik said with an almost unnoticeable quiver in her lip. "On both sides."

"Are they on their way here?" Ceres asked.

"No," Lucik said. "Their horses were slaughtered by Conrad. There were a few that were left, but they'd be far behind."

"Thank you." Stone bowed his head. "You saved us."

"We know what lies at stake for all of us," she said. "You need to find that woman, and soon, before anyone else. The kings and queens know of her birth, but you must get to her first."

"Then let us ride," Corvaire said, and they were all back upon their horses quickly, and Mud was eager to run.

"We ride for the coast," Stone said. "And no matter what stands in our way. We'll find her before he or they do, and we're not going to succumb to the fear and temptation he tempts us to fall into. Let us find this mystic and find what we need in this life . . . on our own . . . together."

PART VI

ICE AND FLAME

Chapter Thirty

Four days later.

Their horse's hooves trudged through thick mud and clacked upon the large, flat stones that paved the way forward. Heavy rain poured down on their already soggy hoods as the rain looked like a solid sheet of water over the town before them.

Dim lights illuminated the small, clay homes that scattered the already scattered town. A hunched woman walked slowly through the roads, carrying what appeared to be a crying babe. At the center of the town was a single two-story building erected of wood, with many rooms and a large bell hanging at its top with a spiked roof above it.

They'd left the tall grasses of the prairies two days ago and had been riding through rocky terrain with short grasses and high, rocky outcrops and low valleys. The sun had been hidden for nearly a day and a half by thick clouds, and Stone wished nothing more than to remove his soaking wet socks and dry his feet by a blazing fire.

Their spirits were high approaching the town, as Ceres had used her magic to sense that the girl indeed was close by, but they felt downtrodden by lack of sleep and the stark pressure of wondering—would they get to her in time?

"We're here," Stone said, wiping his brow, and putting his flat hand over his brow to gaze out at the town.

Normally someone would be there to greet visitors, and do an off-handed inspection of them, but even in this late afternoon, there was no one there, so the six of them—and the dog twice his weight then—strolled casually into the town.

"Where is everyone?" Adler asked, spitting on the wet, muddy road.

"They're in the homes," Corvaire said. "As any of us would be. These folks aren't used to trouble, or strangers like us."

"Is that a good thing?" Ceres asked, with beads of water dripping from the front of her hood.

"It is a good tiding," Corvaire said. "It means that we're the first ones here."

"Once we meet with her," Lucik said. "We need to get her out of here as quickly as possible though, as more are sure to come."

"And Arken shouldn't be far after us," Hydrangea said with a strong voice. She looked at Lucik. "And what if the woman doesn't come willingly?"

"She will," Lucik said, with a calm face. "We'll let her know what is at stake. She will come of her own free will."

"I'm not so sure about that," Hydrangea said. "Who'd want to leave a place like this? Imagine if your life could be as simple as this? And a pack of people like us come along and tell you to leave the only home you've ever known . . ."

"She'll know she's different," Corvaire interrupted. "She's

going to have the eternal wisdom pressing upon her whether she knows what it is or not."

They strode into town in the near twilight hours as each of them looked into the warm-looking homes with thin tapestries waving in their windows as the subtle sounds of the seas coupled with the salty-smelling sea waters brimming in their nostrils.

"Should you try now?" Stone asked, with his whole body soaking, the spot between his ass cheeks nearly on fire from the saddle. His mind raced now they'd gotten that far.

Ceres turned to look at him with her lush green eyes shimmering like emeralds under her low hanging hood. "I can."

She closed her eyes after a deep breath, scanning the area. Stone looked at her for a long moment, thinking of the times they'd spent together along their brief travels together.

It felt like a lifetime with her, but we've only been together a few months now. I don't know if even I remembered my past, if I'd have felt as indentured to someone. That's not the right word. I mean I feel like I owe her my life. Adler too. And Marilyn and Corvaire. Whatever life this is, I owe it all to her.

It didn't take her long, as she'd been practicing frequently over the last few days, and her eyes opened as she was looking out toward the far side of the town straight ahead.

They continued their gallop past an old man with a sun-worn wrinkled face who gazed up at them as if they'd come from another land: Essill to the north perhaps.

"She may be just up here," Ceres said. "The connection is strong—very strong. I feel like she's tugging at my heart. Pulling at my soul to come find her."

They galloped through the overcast town with the dying light of the sun fading behind the thick clouds. The rain continued to pour heavily upon their heads. Mud shook off the rain with a quick shake.

They were near the two-story wooden structure and finally

a woman came out to meet them. She had a large leaf pulled up over her head. "What do you want?" she demanded with an annoyance for having to be out in the rain in her dry, wide dress. "We ain't got no inn here. Strange time of night to be passin' through like this."

"We're looking for someone," Adler said. "It's of an urgent nature."

"Doubt it's that urgent it can't wait til' morning," she said. "You'd be best to find some shelter til' this darned storm blows o'er."

"This is as urgent as you can imagine," Stone said, leaning down to look into the woman's eyes.

"Nothin's that urgent you can't wait til' someone's had a good night's sleep and a warm morning sun to—"

"This is more important than sleep," Adler said. "Haven't you heard of the dragons invading these lands? Haven't you heard of the Neferian and their riders?"

"Oh," she said with a sighing wave. "That's the matter of kings and scholars. That ain't no concern of us here. Now, why don't you go find a dry spot to hunker down? There's a good patch of tall elms o'er there . . ."

"Ma'am," Ceres said. "We came from afar to get to here. I reckon if ya' don't help us find the one we're a lookin' fer', then you're gonna have a lot more wicked business in here than just a few folks on horses." She glared at the woman deeply. "Help us, please. For this is not a threat, but your lives will never be the same if ya' don't aid us. We will leave if ya' do, and you won't have to witness what I foresee comin' here."

"That sounds an awful lot like a threat dearie," the woman said. "I'm likely to round up the chancellor."

"It's a matter of life and death," Stone said. "We are not here to cause you harm, but harm is coming for you here. We are looking for a girl. Someone who may have . . . *changed* . . . in the last few weeks. You see, we're going to help her. And you can trust me when I say that. There are people coming for her, that's why this is so urgent. Will you help us?"

The woman's left eye squinted, and she tried to look away but gave a glaring eye at Stone.

"We've got no one here like that," she sneered. "Best be on your way." She turned to walk away.

"She'd be born the twenty-eighth of Juenar," Stone said.

The woman snapped her head back.

"She'd appear to be perhaps twenty-five," he said. "My friend, Ceres, has told us that she's got long, brown hair, warm, hazel eyes, and a rosy complexion. You know who I speak of don't you?"

"I don't know no one of the sorts," she said, turning back around, back toward the wooden building with the many candles burning warmly from its insides.

"She's going to die," Ceres said. "She may be as innocent as a spring tulip, but there's people coming for her. People as evil as you can't imagine." She leaped down from Angelix, with her boot clumping in the mud. "I'm telling you the truth. She has to leave this town. Something has happened to her. It's something wonderful, and something that's gonna make her make people want to take her and change her." She was inches from the old woman's face then. "I promise ya', we are here to help her. We're gonna protect her. 'Cause see, she's meant to change everything. She's gonna hold the knowledge of the world, and she's gonna have to decide what to do with it to not only help us here, but all of us . . . all over."

"How do I know you're telling the truth?" the woman spat. "You don't look like kind folks to me. There ain't no girl like that here!"

Each of them looked at each other in worry, each wondering what there was next to do.

"You know," Ceres said, getting back up upon her horse. "I

can find her whether you want me to or not. I've got magic that can do that for me."

"You lie."

"I'll put a curse on this whole town," she said, waving her hands in front of the woman. "I'll turn ya all into frogs; horny toads if that's what it'll take!"

"You wouldn't dare," the woman said. "We don't deserve that. Things like that are left to wizardly folk." She quieted down, leaning in and whispering, "if I really help ya', you'll help Gracelyn, right? You'd help her, wouldn't ya?"

"Yes," Stone said. "We promise."

The woman looked all four directions, scanning if anyone was looking at them in the pouring rain.

"Follow me," she whispered in a raspy voice.

Each of them followed her eagerly, northbound up the road. They passed by a slender steeped church, a home that had a roof burned away long ago, and a pair of cats that meowed longingly for something—presumably food.

The heavy raindrops fell into large droplets on the tops of their hoods as their soaking boots trampled on the rocky road behind the woman. Stone was preparing himself for the unexpected, after all, Arken had only given them a few days to decide—and turn down—his proposal.

He still didn't know if the Dark King was following them and knew where they were or not. He hoped and prayed that he didn't. They needed to find this girl, he supposed Gracelyn was her name, and get her up to the high peaks of Endo Valaire before Arken could find her.

"She's just up here," the woman said in a weary, still reluctant voice.

They followed eagerly behind her, where an elderly couple walked out of a front, red-painted door to a small, single-level thatched-roof home. They were holding each other as they stood under the front awning that only stretched three feet out.

They both glared at the woman that was leading them to the home, and then they glared up at Stone and his friends with wet eyes.

They've both been crying . . .

"Who are these folks?" the man asked, in a gruff voice that made it seem as if he'd gone too many days without sleep.

"They say they can help her," the woman said in the pounding rain.

"Why've you come?" the man asked. "This here's a personal matter."

"We've come," Ceres said, "because something's happened to your . . . *daughter*? We know what it is, and we can help her. But we don't have much time on our side."

"What're you goin' on about?" he groaned. "She's just goin' through a tough time. She don't need no one helping her, except her family! Now be on your way, before I fetch me' sword."

The woman standing next to him, put her hand on his chest to stay him.

"Let's hear what they have ta' say," she said up to him. "There's more goin' on with her than just a normal change in a girl her age."

Corvaire took a step toward them, flapping his tunic's tails to cover his sword hilt.

"Your daughter has caught the eye of Crysinthian himself. She's becoming something that will change all these lands. It's no curse though, it's the most wonderful power imaginable. She'll live many times your lives, growing to become the wisest and venerable of all that walk here. But someone that powerful always garners the attention of those who crave power over all else. That's why we need to take her to her city."

"What's he saying?" the man said to his wife and the woman who'd led them there.

"I think he's sayin' she's turned into a witch or somethin' of the sort," the woman said at his side.

The man's glare turned sour, and he pushed his wife's hand away, as if to go and grab his sword.

"She ain't no witch!"

"Well . . ." Adler began but Stone cut him off with a punch in the arm.

"We're not saying that," Stone said. "But doesn't mean she's not going to become powerful. Where we're taking her, you can come visit. I will show you the way, but it won't be until things simmer."

"We can't visit her until you say so?" the mother asked.

"She's going to play a role in the wars happening now," Stone said. "The Neferian, the warring kings . . . she's going to help get these lands back to the way they were supposed to be . . . at peace."

"Gracelyn don't have the power to do that . . ." the woman said who'd led them there. "You're wrong about her. She ain't no more special than any other girl here. She's just sick."

"I think you're missing one point we're trying to make here," Adler said with both his arms outstretched. "They're coming after her. The kings, *all of them*, are coming to get her when they find her. And when they come, they won't be asking!"

"He speaks the truth," Lucik added. "This girl here before you, her name is Ceres. She's got the gift to seek out what your daughter has become. But she's not the only one with this gift. Others are coming . . . They're on their way now. You must trust them."

"We've got to think about this," the woman said, next the door, who began sobbing again. "We can't let her go with no one—not now, not yet."

"You must decide," Corvaire said. "I'm sorry. But you must let her come with us, tonight."

"It's all right," came a sweet, calm voice from the creaked open, red door behind the couple. The tall girl walked between her mother and father, looking deep into their eyes. "I know him. I don't know him, but I do . . . it's all right."

Her mother continued to sob, pressing her head into the girl's shoulder.

The girl standing before them had near-black hair that flowed wildly behind her shoulders, her skin was smooth and tan with slightly rosy cheeks and her eyes were that burning hazel the woman mentioned.

"Gracelyn?" Stone asked. "You know our friend, Corvaire?"

"Yes," she said. "He's from the line of Darakon, correct?"

Corvaire bowed.

"They're correct in what they said," Gracelyn said to her mother and father. "What they speak is the truth. I need to go with them. They can help me. And they'll keep me free. I can't go with any others, and I can't stay here."

"But . . ." her mother wept.

"We'll see each other again," Gracelyn said softly.

"Are you sure? Do you promise?" her mother asked, pulling her head up from her daughter's shoulder to look into her eyes.

"I don't know," she said. "But I feel that we will. This shouldn't be the end. It should be the beginning."

Chapter Thirty-One

"Goodbye, my sweet, sweet daughter. You take care of her now," her mother said to them.

"You take care of her like she says," the father said. "Or you're gonna' have the Dark Realm's wrath to pay from me."

"We will," Stone said. "As long as we draw breath, she'll be safe with us."

"Goodbye," Gracelyn said to her parents as they embraced one last time. And after, in the still-pouring rain, and with lightning striking to the west, and booming thunder following, the young woman pulled her cloak up over her head, and stepped out into the storm. "I'm ready."

"Let's make haste," Corvaire said. They'd been pulling the horses up behind them, and he led her to a horse Lucik, and Hydrangea had brought with them. "Gracelyn." He bowed. "Would you please?"

She placed her boot in the stirrup and mounted. While atop the horse she stared deeply into Stone's eyes, and he found he couldn't look away from the knowing hazel eyes. "I know you too," she said. "There's something about you. I feel as if I've known you my whole life."

"I DON'T THINK that's possible," Stone said. "I haven't been around very long."

"There's more to you than you know," she said. "I believe I can help you with that."

Stone's heart thumped in his chest.

She . . . she knows about me? Does she know about my father? Can she feel he's still alive? Can she help me find my family?

"Miss Gracelyn," Corvaire said. "There's much to tell you, but we have to get you away from this town—right away."

There was another stark crack of lightning off in the sky.

Each of them mounted their horses.

"Do we warn her about Arken?" Adler whispered over to Stone. "Arken wants his answer tonight."

"I don't know," Stone said. "We'll tell her later when we're out of the town and safely away."

Corvaire kicked his horse with his heals and they were off down the road after Gracelyn blew kisses to her sobbing parents, left framed in the open door to their home. Stone truly didn't know if they'd see their daughter again, but he hoped they would. There was nothing worse than losing your family, he thought.

It didn't take long for them to reach the outskirts of the small town, and as they wound west, the great, dark waters of the Sonter Sea flowed on endlessly with crashing waves in the storm.

They rode at a faster speed at a trot, galloping through the sandy grass toward the western edge of the Worforgon. They'd have to wrap around the Worgons and ride down the coast to get back to the mountain that housed the city of Endo Valaire. They had well over a week to travel that distance, and out in the open, Stone worried about her safety, glancing all around as they rode.

But after a half hour of riding in the wet night, Corvaire's horse neighed loudly, rearing up on its hind legs and causing the caravan to crash to a halt.

Gracelyn looked nervously back at Stone, who'd been riding right behind her horse.

Corvaire tried to calm his horse as it walked off the path they'd been on, and Stone could see the silhouette of a man with two large horns curling up from his helmet. He immediately recognized who was in front of them on the road.

Stone leaped down from his horse, calmly petting Grave's neck. Walking past Gracelyn, he said, "Stay up on your horse. No matter what you do, don't get off her, and stay behind Corvaire and the others. I don't want him to scare you."

"I'm not scared of him," Gracelyn said in a strong voice that surprised Stone. "I want to speak with Arken."

She dismounted, and Stone felt as if he should stop her, but didn't know if he could with how confidently she walked up to the Dark King. Each of them got down and walked toward the tall king standing alone in the road. Mud scampered up to Stone's side, growling lowly at Arken.

"So . . ." Arken said in a low, grumbling tone. "This is the new Majestic Wild. What's your name?"

"Gracelyn Meadowlark," she said.

"That's a nice name," he said with a wry smile. "It's nice to finally lay my eye upon you. I can't wait for us to meet in person. You know destiny is calling you. It's screaming for you. You just have to come follow me, and I will show you your path."

"No," she said. "That's all I have to say to you. Come now." She motioned for the others to follow her back up on their horses. "He can do nothing while in that form to us. Let's be back on our way."

Arken's smile twisted down. "Stone, Ceres, Adler. What say you to my offer? I can help you get everything you've ever wanted in this life, or I can take away everything that is left. What say you? You will only receive this offer once. Be reunited with the ones you love? Or have your miserable lives ended? Those are the two offerings I behest. Which do you choose?"

Stone looked at his friends, while Mud barked madly at the Dark King. Each of them nodded with stern, determined looks on their faces.

"We chose neither," Stone said with his hands balled up into fists.

"So, death?" Arken growled.

"We're going to help Gracelyn become the most powerful Wild Majestic of all. She's going to help us to defeat you."

"Defeat me?" Arken laughed a wretched, foul laugh. "You're going to do what time itself couldn't? I'm more than man, now. Know this. If you go to war with me, then you are going to war with the gods themselves."

"Man or god," Stone said. "You're going to flee or die here. Those are your two offerings I bestow on you!"

A crack of lightning shot out over the Sonter then, followed quickly by another.

Arken's nostrils flared as an anger brimmed within him and his face twisted.

"I'm not the type to play childish games with, boy," he sneered. "I'll kill you and take the girl."

"You're going to have to kill each of us first," Stone said. "That's what family does. We protect one another."

"I don't care about your sentimentality," Arken said.

"You don't have the power to do anything to us," Stone said. "You don't even know where we are, do you?"

Arken's downturned frown, crept up to another eerie smile. "I may not . . . But they do . . ."

"They?" Stone said, pulling back in confusion.

From behind him was the sudden explosion of a fiery roar, followed by the trickling away sound of shattering, thick glass. White fire burned high in the stormy sky, followed by another roar just to the side of the first, and another plume of hot fire lit the clouds.

"There's two of them . . ." Adler said in a shaky voice.

In the white-fire lit clouds Stone could see them, two Neferian . . . Past the whirling wind from the sea, Mud's fervent barking up at them, and the crashing lightning, he could make out the two riders atop the dark dragons.

"Ride!" Corvaire yelled.

They were quickly back upon their horses as Arken's shrill laugh wove through the rain, and Stone's last glimpse of him was as he was pointing up to the sky with his massive dark gray sword's blade dully reflecting the light of the two Neferian's night dragonfires.

Then the Dark King vanished again, only leaving a wafting dust in the ocean wind. They rode straight through them back onto the path, riding as quickly as the horses could carry them.

"We'll have to find shelter," Corvaire yelled out in the howling wind and pummeling rain.

"Where are we going to find shelter out here?" Hydrangea asked, with her long brown hair damply whipping behind her.

Corvaire didn't answer, only desperately looking around, but the mountains were far off to the south, and there was nothing visible on the horizon that might protect them from the swift dark dragons.

"I wish Grimdore was here," Ceres said.

"Who is Grimdore?" Gracelyn asked

"She's the dragon that saved us from Arken, last we were in Endo, but she's been resting in the sea. As far as we know, she's the only dragon that's survived a fight with one o' them."

"And she's farther down south," Adler added. "Closer to Endo."

The pair of Neferians let out another blast of explosive fire high up in the air as they swooped down."

"We can't outride them," Lucik said, with the long burn mark on her face shown in the light of the dragon's fire. "Corvaire, you'll need to stand ground for us. Use your magic to slow them."

"Won't work long enough," he said. "Even if I survive, you won't be able to ride away from them. I can slow them for a time, but we've got to find another way."

"The other way may have arrived," Hydrangea said, turning her head back, staring up at the sky.

Stone turned to see what she was looking at, and behind the two Neferian with their wings out wide to their sides, in a steep descent, a pair of other winged beasts followed.

"The dragons!" Ceres said. "The good dragons have come to help us!"

A blasting lightning bolt ripped through the clouds behind them, revealing the silhouettes of the two ensuing dragons—visibly smaller than that of the monstrous Neferian.

"They're going to die," Corvaire said. "But they might give us a chance of getting away. Pray to Crysinthian those dragons have the strength and ferocity to cause some damage to the two of them."

"We should split up," Lucik said. "Us two and Corvaire will stay back and help the dragons while you four ride for the mountains. You may find shelter enough to hide."

"No," Stone said. "We're sticking together. We're not going to separate. We're stronger together."

"None of our lives matter," Hydrangea said. "Except yours and hers. You both have to survive."

From the lightning-lit sky behind them the two Neferian turned and flapped their wings strongly, hovering, waiting for the two dragons to come at them.

They watched as the two dragons collided into them at a

menacing speed, narrowly flying out of the path of the two plumes of white dragon fire.

Sending the two Neferian back, Stone's hopes rose that perhaps those two dragons could be the ones finally strong enough to kill one of the dark dragons for the first time.

High in the air, fighting in the murky, dark clouds, the dragons and the Neferian roared out so loudly they were surely heard for fifty miles in each direction. They flapped their mighty wings, snapping their jaws with sharp teeth, biting down onto one another as they toppled lower and lower in the sky.

The two dragons clawed at the dark dragons' necks and wings—ripping, tearing, slashing wherever they could. Stone was always amazed at the pure, feral ferocity of dragons.

After minutes of grueling fighting in the air, nearly falling all the way to the shores of the Sonter, one of the Neferian sunk its long mouth onto the neck of one of the dragons, and as it twisted and jerked while the dragon screeched out in pain, the Neferian ripped its head from its neck.

The Neferian's head rose, letting its long neck streak up toward the sky, and with a snap of its jaws it sent the smaller dragon's head rolling down the inside of its neck.

"No," Ceres cried. "Not another one."

The pair of Neferian attacked the sole dragon left, with one biting onto one of its wings, while it tried manically to fly away, but the other dark dragon bit onto one of its hind legs, pulling it back down as the dragon frantically tried to free itself from the two, more powerful, dark dragons' grips.

"Keep riding!" Corvaire said, pulling up on his reins and halting his horse.

"Corvaire!" Stone yelled out.

"Keep riding," Lucik said. "Keep going."

Corvaire raised his hand out toward the two dark dragons, about to rip the smaller dragon apart.

"*Excindier*!"

A single bolt of lightning roared down from the heavens, surging into the lower Neferian, causing it to screech out in pain, nearly knocking the rider from its back, but he somehow managed to send his dangling feet back into their stirrups.

"Yes!" Stone yelled out in glee. "Do it again. You hurt it!"

"*Excindier!*"

Another bright bolt of hot lightning shot into the same dragon, sending it out roaring again. This time the other Neferian rose back higher up into the sky.

Corvaire's shoulders were heaving up and down while he sat upon the horse.

"*Excindier!*" he said again, but that time his breath was labored.

The third bolt ravaged the same dark dragon, this time sending it toppling downward through the air while thrashing and screeching out, crashing onto the bank below them.

The other Neferian's dark mad eyes shot to Corvaire, and flapped its might wings, sending it flying at an astonishing speed toward him.

"Again," Stone said to him, while his horse had stopped and the others rode on. "Do it again."

"Excindier," he said with heavy breaths.

The lightning bolt surged down from the sky, and the Neferian turned its right wing upward, letting the bolt narrowly miss it, as it struck the beach with an explosion and boom of rippling thunder.

"Again, do it again!" Stone said.

"Stone," Ceres called out. "Come. Come with us."

"He needs me," Stone said.

"We need you," she said. "Come with us, now."

He needs me. That dark dragon is coming right for him. I'm sorry, Ceres. I know I told you we'd stick together, but I can't let him die like this. I can't let another one of my friends die.

He kicked his heels in their stirrups on Grave's side, and the horse fearlessly ran toward the oncoming dark dragon with its maw opened wide, and white fire brimming from the inside. Mud ran with the horse at startling speed.

"Stone," Ceres cried out. "Don't do it."

Stone pulled his new Masummand sword from its scabbard.

"Come on, you bastard," Stone growled as the sea wind and rain bit at his face, salty seawater brimmed in his nostrils and he gritted his teeth. "Let's see what you're worth against my sword!"

Corvaire sent another bolt through the air, which the flying Neferian, once again, just evaded, still flying at the man. The second Neferian and rider were regaining their senses and had both their sets of eyes focused on Corvaire.

Stone was nearly fifty feet away from his friend, and the swooping Neferian was farther off, but coming in at a frightening speed, ready at any moment to send its sizzling fire down on them. Stone could see the small dragon had turned back around and was flying at the first Neferian, but it was still far off, and not as swift as the dark one.

Corvaire readied himself to cast the spell again, and Stone rode madly at the Neferian with his bright sword glowing in the moonlight. But that's when he heard from behind . . .

"Gracelyn . . . what are you doing?"

Chapter Thirty-Two

Adler yelled out again after Gracelyn, who was atop her horse running quickly after Stone.

What is she thinking? She can't risk herself for this.

"Turn back!" Stone yelled in the storm. "Turn back!"

A rushing wind blew in and Stone's long black hair whipped in front of his face.

She wasn't listening to any of them calling out her name. Gracelyn rode as fast as she could at them.

Stone stopped his horse and faced her, unsure of what to do.

"*Excindier!*"

Stone heard the crackling lightning back where the dragons were and turned to find the Neferian still cruising at frightening speed at Corvaire, and the second flying low in the air behind it. Behind them both fell the smaller dragon after, which Stone could see then was a crimson red with black horns all the way down its back.

He looked quickly back at Gracelyn whose eyes were squinted and had her teeth exposed, showing her determination catching up with Stone.

"Turn back around," Stone tried again, but she didn't listen, but whipped the reins harder.

What's she doing? Can I stop her? Can I convince her to turn back?

But who am I kidding? The dark dragons are coming for us whether we want them to or not. We have to fight. It's our only chance.

"Excindier!"

This time Corvaire had focused his magic on the injured Neferian behind the first, striking it in the back and coursing the electricity through its body, sending it crashing down head and neck first into the coastline yet again with a boom that shook the ground at all of their feet.

Turning back, Stone saw Adler was running out after Gracelyn, with his sword fixed firmly in his hand.

If today is our day to die, I may as well meet it head on.

Stone flicked the reins and rode off back toward Corvaire. Mud ran right next to him. He hadn't realized the speed with which Gracelyn's horse ran, and she quickly appeared next to him.

"What are you thinking?" he asked.

"Corvaire cannot fall," she said. "At least not yet. I can't let him succumb to the Runtue."

"You can't fight that Neferian! You don't even have a sword!"

"Who needs a sword," she said with her eyes gleaming white from the reflection of the dragon fire brimming in the Neferian's mouth. He turned back and saw the Neferian was going to cast its fire upon Corvaire.

"Ride," Stone yelled to him. "Ride to us!"

Corvaire pulled the horse back and it ran back toward them.

"He's not going to make it . . ." Stone said.

"He doesn't need to," Gracelyn said, raising her bare arms up, letting her tan skin glisten in the light of the fire.

"What—?" Stone gasped.

A biting chill rose through him.

"*Thyfonus Bitternex Onum*!" she yelled out into the rain.

A shear wind bit into Stone's back, nearly freezing his wet cloak's tails. It rushed past him in a motion parallel with the ground. It picked up in speed immensely, knocking Corvaire clear off his horse, knocking it onto its side. The wind rose, and as the dark dragon unleashed it brilliantly bright and hot dragonfire, the wind blasted into it with a thunderous fury.

The dark dragon winced in pain, as if it had flown into the sharp rock of a mountainside. The Runtue rider was hurtled backward off the beast, and the dragonfire was extinguished in a powerful hiss.

Stone's bottom jaw dropped open as Adler rode up to his side.

"How in the—" Adler said in shock.

Gracelyn lowered her arms just in time for the Neferian to fall crashing down to the ground with a thunderous boom. The Runtue fell far off behind it, and Stone hoped it had killed the rider.

The small dragon also felt the cold blast of wind that Gracelyn had conjured and both of its wings froze as it hurtled toward the ground. Stone clicked the reins and rode after Corvaire, with his sword still in hand. Adler and Mud were on either side of him.

Corvaire got up to his feet as the lead Neferian shook its head to regain its strength. The small red dragon eventually got its wings flapping again, managing to avoid plummeting all the way to the ground. It arched in the air and glided onto the back of the Neferian, biting and clawing wildly at the giant beast.

The Neferian fought to knock the red dragon off its back as the second Neferian was back into the air, and flying toward both of them.

It was a bitter gnashing of sharp claws ripping at tough dragonscales.

Stone got to Corvaire and leaped down to his side.

"Is he okay?" Adler asked from atop Hedron.

"He's weak," Stone said. "We need to get him back to the others."

"No," Corvaire coughed, pulling his sword out, and pointing it into the ground to help himself up. "We stand our ground. We can't outrun them any longer."

Stone also helped him to his feet as Corvaire's horse rode off. Stone saw that Ceres, Lucik and Hydrangea were riding to them as well, beyond Gracelyn, who was watching the red dragon and the Neferian battle.

"What's next?" Stone asked Corvaire. "What do we do?"

"We'll go after him," he said, looking past the fighting dragons to the dark figure just getting up to his feet in the distance.

The Runtue rider?

"He's smaller," Corvaire said with a grin, "and there's only one of him. And three of us."

"C'mon," Stone said, hoisting Corvaire up onto Grave's back, and Stone mounted Hedron behind Adler. "Ride!"

They rode quickly at the Runtue as the dragons fought wildly in their skirmish. The Runtue saw them approaching and pulled two swords—one in each hand. Stone could see he had the same black and gold paint on his face as the others, although it was streaking down in the rain.

The Runtue rider took slow, yet fumbled strides at them as they rode. He tossed his torn tunic to the ground after it blew wildly behind him. His two swords gleamed from the white fires of the dragon battle to his right as he held them out low.

Stone heard Gracelyn say the words behind them again, and this time, each of them dismounted and clung low to the ground as a roaring wave of frosty air swept over the land.

Stone could see his breath in front of his face, but the true intense cold was blasted upon the dragons, who writhed in pain, flapping their freezing wings to get away, which caused huge sheets of ice to break off them.

The smaller red dragon with the black spikes on its back huddled behind the large black Neferian as the second—which had nearly been close enough to attack the small dragon—was blown back with so much force, its wings froze and it fell back the ground with such an impact it toppled end over end, sending the other Runtue rider flying off its back.

"There you go, Gracelyn," Stone said.

I've never seen the Neferian take such a beating. I've never seen them take hardly any damage.

"Get them!" Adler said. "Send them back, crying off to the Dark Realm!"

Corvaire and them got back to their feet as the wind died off again, and they ran at the Runtue rider with their swords ready to tear into him, as he slowly strode forward.

While they were nearly upon him, the small dragon swooped back down onto the half-frozen first Neferian as it fought to break free from the frost that had formed on its back, neck and long arms with its wings caked in the thick, blue ice. The small dragon tore into the beast with a newfound fury, this time biting so viciously into its neck that thick dragonblood ran down its teeth.

Stone and the Runtue clashed into one another first, and Stone found his sword moved just as easily as it had the last time he'd been in battle. Adler was soon behind him, running to the backside of the Runtue, as they both slashed and hacked at the burly—yet agile—rider.

Corvaire, still heaving deep breaths, ran in just in time for the second Runtue to rush in, as they locked swords with a loud *clang*.

The Runtue with the two swords let out a deep groan with

each slash of his swords, as Stone and Adler parried carefully with the large man.

Corvaire moved well for being in his current state, but Stone could see he wasn't his normal self.

"Go," he said to Adler. "I can handle this one. Go help him."

Adler reluctantly ran over to the other skirmish and brought the full attention of the Runtue—who was smaller, but quicker—than the first onto him. Letting Corvaire regain his breathing.

The sword in Stone's hand, as he felt the way it struck the other unknown metal of the Runtue blade felt like a dream. It slid through the air like a bird, upon impact it was as sturdy as an ox, and the grip didn't vibrate in the least from blows. He saw a quick opening, and slashed down at the rider's calf, just on the backside of its thick armor, and the Masummand blade sliced not only the skin, but the armor as well. Stone couldn't believe it that anything could cut through that thick of armor.

The large Neferian broke the sheets of ice upon it with a powerful shiver that made the enormous, long muscles in its back bulge and glisten as the rain continued to pour down. The second Neferian, once again, got back to its feet and was running toward the small dragon that was still biting and clawing the large, black one.

Lucik and Hydrangea stayed back with their swords drawn with Gracelyn, but Ceres, who'd grown impatient, was riding her steed toward her friends in their fight.

As the rider fought Stone with his two swords, he lurched back in pain as Mud bit into his calf with the deep cut and was pulling him back. The rider nearly sliced the dog's ear off—or worse—but Mud leaped back just before one of his swords had arced its way to him.

It was a chaotic whirl of madness as the battle raged in the bitter storm. The two Neferian were now attacking the one small dragon with their towering statures and more powerful jaws and larger, sharper teeth. Stone was holding his own against the two-bladed rider, and with the sneaky attacks of Mud, it was feeling more and more like his position was improving over the fierce fighter. It was Adler and Corvaire he was worrying about.

Adler's movements were slowing, and Corvaire was gasping for breath as they both fought the wild Runtue, whose eyes were reddened in his blood rage. Ceres was halfway to them then, when they all heard the screeching from the small dragon.

Stone looked over in horror as the two Neferian had the dragon in each of their clasped teeth. One had its tail in its maw, and the other had a hold on its chest—and they were both pulling . . .

The small dragon bit as wildly as it could onto one of their heads, but the might of the two black Neferians was too great for it, and as Stone's stomach churned and his heart ached at the sight, the two dark dragons tore the small, red dragon in half, with it splitting at the torso in a gruesome mess.

One of them gulped down the top half, lifting its head up to let it slide down its gullet, and the other bit the tail clean off and ate that too.

Dread filled Stone then, as he knew there was nothing standing in the way of the two Neferian's sights upon them—nothing, except the powerful magic of Gracelyn, which she was readying with streaks of bright blue swirling around her hands as she twirled them up over her head—readying another spell, and Stone felt it couldn't come soon enough as the two Neferian's fully opened mouths glowed a bright white.

Chapter Thirty-Three

Blazing hot fires churned in the dark dragon's mouth, stained with the blood of the two dragons that had come to save Stone and the others. Smoldering smoke bellowed out the sides of their mouths opened wide—and even the two dragon riders had stopped fighting, staring up at the two dragonfires about to be unleashed upon them.

The Neferian's eyes were wild, hungered, and ravaged with a feral anger beholden to no other beast. They'd been injured far more than Stone had ever seen, and they were angry—they were out for blood.

The sky turned white then, as the dragons roared, bursting the white-hot dragons' flames down on them. It was as pure a white as Stone had ever seen, and for a moment he thought it was the grip of the Golden Realm welcoming him.

That hot white turned to a cool blue, as Stone looked up to see the foggy view of the two dragons pouring down their fires, but an icy blue aura shooting in from the side.

He looked over to see Gracelyn pouring an enormous magical blast of freezing cold in between them and the dragons. Gracelyn's eyes were lit in the same blue, and her arms trembled as she held them out.

The two Neferian belted their fires down harder upon the magic as the near-deafening roar of their fires colliding with her magic had each of them ducking down with their hands covering their ears. Stone's head buzzed, and he saw Ceres fall off her horse as Angelix herself fell to the ground, staggering and running off. It was as if the Dark and Golden Realm's themselves were at war in the moment that seemed to go on for a grueling eternity.

But just as quickly as it began, the roaring disappeared, and the dark dragons both pulled back to regain their breaths, and Gracelyn collapsed, with Lucik barely able to catch her.

"Gracelyn!" Stone yelled, but feeling the oncoming attack of the Runtue behind him, he spun, ricocheting the rider's first attack, then parrying his second, and thrusting his sword into his chest, through his thick armor quicker than Stone even planned it. It was as if his arm and sword had taken over his body. The Runtue's berserking eyes glazed over, and both pupils shook as he fell to his knees. As Stone pulled the sword from his chest the smaller of the Neferian roared as if it had been stabbed itself.

The dark dragon ran at them, with its long arms and claws digging into the wet ground. It snarled and hissed bitterly, snapping its jaws as it bounded forth.

Stone looked to Gracelyn, who was still struggling to get back to her feet. He clasped his sword in both hands, readying himself to test his new steel upon dragonscale.

"Come on, now," he growled. "Let's see what you're made of . . ."

As it ran, thin strands of white clung to its legs and tail, eventually shooting up to its neck from thin cracks forming in the ground. The dark dragon slowed as it bit at the sticky webbing, clinging to it in thick strands.

Stone recognized the spell, and looked to Corvaire, still on a knee with heavy beads of sweet running down his brow.

He's casting his Webs that Wind spell again. Now's my chance . . .

Seeing Adler in battle with the other Runtue rider, Ceres back to her feet, fixing an arrow in her bow, and Mud snapping his jaws at him—Stone ran at the Neferian.

The dark dragon towered high over him, screeching and roaring in its madness.

"No," Corvaire yelled. "What are you doing Stone? Don't try it!"

But Stone didn't listen. He knew that was the only chance they had to defeat the dragons, survive, and get Gracelyn to safety.

This is for them. This is for my family!

He ran next to the dragon, as it tried to pull its head free from the webbing to devour him, he thrust his sword in between two large, thick black scales in its front hand. The Masummand sword slid through easily, as the dragon pulled back— letting out a fiery blast of anger.

Stone was so focused upon the first dragon that he didn't notice the second, larger dragon had reared up from behind the first, and its blazing red eyes were fixed murderously on him.

Corvaire seemed to be trying to move his spell to the second dragon, but instead he yelled, "Damn! Blast it all! Stone, run, run!"

I'm not running. There's nowhere to run. I'm standing my ground!

The large black dragon with thousands of spiny gray-white spikes snarled, letting its nostril flare as smoke poured out of them.

Stone stood there, with his sword, dripping with dragonblood swaying between the two of them.

"What are you waiting for?" he yelled up to the giant

monster whose head loomed thirty feet above him. "Come on! Show me what makes you so tough!"

"Stone, no!" he heard Ceres cry out.

Then he felt a crippling pain in his left side, and the next thing he knew the dragon before him was gone, and he was toppling end over end, rolling across the wet ground. He felt a sharp pain in his back as his tumble stopped as he landed against a blunt boulder.

"Argh!!" he cried out. He felt for his sword, but it was nowhere around him, and he looked out to see the Neferian that was caught in the webs had broken loose and thrashed him in the side with a flick of its arm. It snarled savagely at him with wild eyes, and both of the dark dragons were slinking toward him.

He felt his side, and his hand was wet with his own blood and he knew he'd broken ribs. Trying to stand, he fell back down quickly wincing from the pain.

Get up. You've got to get to your feet. You can't die like this.

He looked to Corvaire, who was nearly keeled over, heaving deep breaths with wide eyes staring at the two beasts lurching at Stone. Ceres shot arrows at them, but to no avail, and she was still screaming for him to run. Stone's eyesight blurred and his head fogged. He looked and saw Adler fighting with every last ounce of strength, but the wild Runtue was pushing him back, getting the upper hand. He heard a faint barking, and saw Mud's raised tail in between him and the two dragons.

"Good boy," Stone murmured. "You're a great best friend to have, Mud. Good boy . . ."

Stone was at the brink of unconsciousness when he was startled awake by what he expected to be the final blast of dragonfire that would burn his flesh from bone. But instead he heard a voice call out like a goddess herself had descended upon the lands.

"*Thyfonus Bitternex Onum!*" the woman's voiced echoed throughout the surrounding storm. It rippled in his head as the two dragons were a mere dozen feet from him, eyeing the madly barking dog, about to swipe him up in either of their mouths.

Both of their heads snapped west, and a bright blue haze blinded Stone, causing him to real his head back, covering his eyes. He felt Mud leap into his lap, causing him to cry out in pain. Then he felt the cold. It was the coldest he'd ever felt in his life, like being thrown naked into a frozen lake. Every ounce of his body felt as though he was going to die from the biting cold.

Mud shook in his arms as Stone still couldn't open his eyes as he felt his eyelids frozen to his wet eyes.

He managed to mouth the words, "If this is how we go, I'm glad I'm with you."

Mud cried in his arms, as Stone held the dog in tightly to his chest, and all pain subsided.

This is it. This is how I die. At least I did my best to protect them. To protect Ceres, to protect the new mother—Gracelyn. At least I died trying . . .

After what felt like waking up after a nap that was twelve hours but probably only twenty minutes, he felt a hand stirring his shoulder. He managed to open his eyes as his entire body was suffering from the poking pins. He winced again, and found himself looking into a pair of vivid, mossy green eyes that were kind and caring.

"Let's get you up," she said with her golden hair framed by a clear blue aura. He blinked hard, and brought his hands up to wipe his eyes, and Mud nuzzled into him.

"Ceres," he said with a smile.

"C'mon ya oaf. I told you to run. What were ya' thinkin'? That's your problem! You're never thinkin'. You're just another dumb boy is all!"

Stone couldn't believe his eyes when they finally focused on what was behind her. Only feet away, were the two massive, terrifying heads of the two Neferian, both gazing to the west with mouths wide open, and their long sharp teeth menacing from their mouths and their slender tongues curling out of the mouths motionlessly.

The two dark dragons were murky reflections behind ten feet of solid ice. Even their wild eyes were fixed in place.

"Are they . . ." he said. "Are they dead?"

"No," Corvaire said, staggering up to him. "I don't think they're dead. But I bet they're not too happy to be in there."

Stone stood with Ceres' help and looked over to see Adler kneeling with his sword tip in the ground, leaning on its hilt, taking deep labored breaths, and feigning a smile at Stone. The Runtue had been stricken in the ice too and was mid-swing with his sword—like an ancient statue carved long ago.

Past him he saw Lucik and Hydrangea hefting a weak Gracelyn up onto a horse.

"Gracelyn," Stone said weakly, "is she okay?"

"I don't know," Ceres said. "But we've got to get goin'. Can you walk? We need to get far away from here."

"I—I think I can," Stone said, holding his ribs and watching Mud limp next to him.

"We all made it," he said with a faint smile at Ceres and Corvaire.

Corvaire nodded. "Let's get you healed up back in Endo. You did well, Stone, I'm proud of you."

They managed to find their scattered horses and get back atop them, riding back off along the shoreline back south. The two dragons behind were cast in the thick sheets of ice that bound them, and Stone hoped it would hold them forever.

"Arken isn't going to be happy about this," Adler said.

"Good," Stone said, petting Grave on the side of the neck. "Maybe he'll stay away now."

"He'll probably double his efforts to find us now," Adler said, and looking back at the frozen dragons, "it shouldn't be too long before he knows where we were. He may even guess we're on our way back to Endo."

"He does think Endo is destroyed," Ceres said. "So perhaps not."

Stone caught a glimpse of Gracelyn who'd stirred up to an upright position on her horse, and her hazel eyes were looking at him as her long dark hair draped down her back as the horse galloped on.

"Gracelyn," he said. "How did you do that? How did you cast such powerful magic?"

"I—I don't know," she said. "It just came to me in the moment."

"Are—are the dragons dead?" Adler asked her.

"I don't believe so," she said, looking back at the frozen monsters. "I feel that they are in a deep slumber. The cold has eased their minds, and they are in a sort of hibernation, like the great bear."

"Let's hope they stay that way until we reach the mountain," Corvaire said.

"Let us make haste," Lucik said. "For we've won the battle, but we are far from winning the war."

Chapter Thirty-Four

The following day in the light of the overcast sky, his bones ached, his ribs burned, and his head was splintered. He awoke hazily from his head resting on Grave's neck, and the horse happily neighed as he lifted his head. Even his fingers felt sore and aged.

He sat up, stretching out his back and shoulder blades. Running his fingers through his black hair on the sides of his head, he pulled it back and tied it with a piece of twine from his pocket.

"I did what I could to heal you while you were out," Ceres said. "I used a spell, I hope ya' don't mind. But you're pretty banged up. Gonna need rest more than anything . . ."

He looked around and saw Corvaire slouched over his horse, and Gracelyn's head bounced lazily as she drifted in and out. Adler sat tall on Hedron, as did Ceres atop Angelix. Lucik was at the lead of the pack and Hydrangea at the rear.

The waters of the Sonter sparkled in the faint sunlight casting through the thick, gray clouds above. The tips of the Worgons were growing up ahead, and they were in a wide stretch of valley with scattered tall oak trees. The tree limbs swayed in the breeze overhead as they were underneath one of them. He could smell the sap running down its long trunk, paired with the wetness of the grass at their horse's hooves.

Mud ran over and relieved himself on the large tree, with his gaze darting around for squirrels—or dragons—surely.

"I think I feel a bit better," Stone said to Ceres. "Thank you."

"I can't believe you were daft enough to run up to that dragon," she replied, shaking her head. "You're as dumb as your dog!"

"I'd like to think I'm as brave as him," Stone laughed.

"You two are an inseparable pair," Adler chimed in.

"My sword," Stone said. "It was able to pierce their armor. The Neferian can be hurt."

"You didn't do as much damage as you think," Adler said. "That shiny sword of yours is sharp, but it's tiny against those things. I wouldn't do that again if I were you. Best to let the sorcerers and dragons fight those things off, while you run."

"We can't always keep running," he said.

"Until we know how to kill them, we are," Adler said, nodding as if he expected to reach Stone.

"My head feels as it I've got daggers rolling around inside it," Stone said, clutching it with both hands.

"Let me try," Ceres said, and holding out hand toward him, she whispered, "*Allias Metomorphus Allilé.*"

Stone felt nothing at first except the pain, but then a warm light washed into his head, like a warm idea or an inspiration happening. He smiled. After a few seconds he could still feel the pain, but he was relieved by how much it had diminished.

"Thanks, Ceres. Now I can't wait until we can get some real rest and get a fire to dry these clothes that've been clinging to us."

"I could use a bite of warm food too," Adler said. "Hell, I could eat your dog my stomach's growlin' so."

"Don't you even jest about that," Stone said, acting as if to pull his sword from his hip.

"You know I'd wallop you in a duel," Adler joked, putting his fingers around his sword's hilt.

"Will you boys never grow up?" Ceres laughed. "Besides, you both know I'd best you. Even at the same time!"

Stone and Adler both sighed, then all three of them joined together in laughter.

❧

THAT NIGHT, under a brilliant starlight sky, and after the clouds had parted and blew inland, they made a bright fire on the beach, watching the waves roll in and out in a daze.

Hydrangea had gone off hunting hours earlier and had returned with a doe, pierced through the heart with an arrow. It then roasted on hot rocks next to the fire as she sprinkled salt over the crisp meat.

Stone had to wipe his mouth several times from the drool flowing from it. A warm wind blew past, flickering the fire. He was sitting on a dead piece of white driftwood between Ceres and Gracelyn. In the hours they'd been on the beach waiting for Hydrangea to return, Corvaire, Gracelyn and Ceres had been able to meditate—recuperating their Indiema. Each of them looked refreshed.

Gracelyn had been mostly silent, but each of them had many questions for her, but they figured they would keep the conversation light-hearted, and wait for her to warm up to them.

There was one thing primarily still on Stone's mind though, one thing that took over his entire being at the thought of it: *was Arken telling me the truth? Is my father still alive out there?*

"How do you feel?" Lucik finally broke the silence to

Gracelyn, whose untied long black, course hair wafted in front of her face.

Gracelyn took a long moment to respond.

"I believe I am well." Her eyes and thoughts seemed distant.

"Do you want to talk?" Ceres asked. "It's all right if you don't."

"No, its fine," she replied, dazedly staring into the fire. "There's just been a lot of things filling my head lately. It's been difficult processing it all."

"How did you know how to use that spell?" Corvaire asked. "Wind that Freeze is a spell that only the wisest of the Mystics could cast like that."

"I—I don't know, I'm afraid," she said. "It's as if I'd been casting it for decades. It felt like I was just waving my arms around, but the words came out as if I was in a dream, unable to control myself."

They all sat there while Lucik cut strips of meat from the venison, placing them on a platter, handing it to Adler to taste and pass around.

"Can I ask you a question," Stone asked shyly.

"Why yes," she said, moving her gaze from the fire to him. Her eyes were enchanting as they sparkled from the flames.

"You seem to have some knowledge of things now, so . . . Arken appeared before us to offer us what we wanted most in exchange for us helping him find you."

"Yes," she said. "I can feel that . . ."

"He told me that I still have a father . . . that he is still alive . . . Can you sense that? Can you tell me if he was telling me the truth or not?"

"Hmm . . ." she thought, squinting her eyes, gazing back to the fire. "I cannot tell if you have a father or not. I'm sorry. But I can safely say that Arken was not known for being a man of lies when he was alive. Now . . . I cannot say—"

"What about the Neferian?" Adler asked. "Do you know if there is a way to kill them?"

"No," she responded quickly. "I do not know that either. I'm sorry to say."

"What about Arken?" Lucik asked. "What can you tell us about him that we may not know? Is there a way to defeat him?"

The meat had made its way around to Stone and he laid the warm, salty strips in his mouth, nearly swallowing them whole he was so famished. He passed them to Gracelyn who ate them gently.

"Arken is still a mystery to me, but one thing that perturbs, me and may be a clue as to something to find out about him. I'm unsure why he's able to appear in front of us—or perhaps just Stone—but he cannot sense where we are, or even seem to see our surroundings. Strange spell that one is . . . I will have to meditate on that later . . ."

"What about the warring kings?" Hydrangea asked. "Is there anything you can tell us about them that we don't know? Are they planning another attack? Is there any way to get them to pledge a truce to help us defeat Arken?"

Gracelyn swallowed her food with a pleasing sigh and smile, with her tan cheeks getting their rosy color back. "I have a feeling something else is happening deeper in the shadows than we know . . ."

"What do you mean?" Corvaire asked.

"The warring kings are blinded by their hate for one another," she said. "But there is another that is growing in power while they thirst after one another's blood and lands."

". . .The Vile King," Stone said. "We've heard of him, in the south. Is that who you speak of?"

"I know him as Salus Greyhorn. But yes, he is growing his powers in secret. He seeks to take the kingdoms in this war, while all eyes are to the sky or to the two kingdoms of Verren and Dranne."

"We will have to remember that," Stone said, petting Mud who snored next to him.

"Do you know about the old Majestic Wilds?" Corvaire asked. "The ones who Arken killed and gave birth to the new you?"

"I don't believe so," she said. "There was one moment though, little more than a week ago, where I was soundly asleep in my bed and woke up in a panic as if I'd had a horrible nightmare. But it was as if the nightmare couldn't be woken from. Everywhere I looked I could sense people's pain, and their anger—their fears and their hopes. I could sense it through walls as they slept or walked the streets. My hands felt as if they'd been set alight by fire and my head ached as if it were about to burst. I cried for days from the pain and my mother and father didn't know what to do to console me. Nothing helped, there was no relief from the overwhelming sensations and pain. Not until . . . the night you all showed up on my doorstep. Then there was a strange calm that came to me, as if I all of the sudden, I knew exactly what was happening to me, and I was able to accept it for what it was . . ."

"And what was that?" Adler leaned in.

"Fate."

Each of them seemed entranced by her answer, and how elegant and perfect it seemed.

"Can I ask you another question?" Adler asked, and she nodded. "Do you know what the leaping creature in the shadow is that's been following us? It's near driven me mad at night."

"Hmm, I don't believe I know."

"What about a naked fairy with purple hair that comes and

leads us from place to place. Do you know anything about her, about where she comes from?"

Gracelyn shook her head and shrugged.

"There is another thing we were thinking of too—" Ceres said. "We've been trying to determine Stone's magic set here, we didn't exactly know which one he is . . . but we narrowed it down . . . so maybe if you could use your magic on him, we could—"

"Oh, Stone is Wendren Set," Gracelyn replied, and almost every one of them leaned back in surprise. She seemed to notice that and apologized. "Did that startle you? Sorry."

"How do you know that?" Stone asked, with his mind racing.

If she's right, I can start practicing my magic . . .

"One look at him and I sensed it," she said. "Can't anyone else feel it? It's like its pouring out of him. No? Huh . . ."

"We're not exactly like you," Adler added.

"What am I? Her face was calm, innocent, but endearing as her hair rustled in front of her face.

"You're one of what are known as the Majestic Wilds, or the Old Mothers," Corvaire said. "We searched for you, and we will need to find the other two of you when they awaken. Together you will help save us from all this conflict—all this war . . ."

"Stone," Ceres whispered to him. "You're Wendren Set. You're the same set as the mothers. You could be able to conjure that same spell as her someday."

He was brimming with eagerness to practice in the following days.

"If only Marilyn was here to hear it," Stone said. "She'd be so amazed with your progress, I bet."

"Marilyn?" Gracelyn asked.

"It's Corvaire's sister," Ceres said. "She passed away saving our lives in Atlius."

"Oh yes, Marilyn," Gracelyn said. "She's of the Darakon line too . . . amazing how long your family lives. You both could live to be over one hundred easily."

There was a long silence, and Ceres clasped onto Stone's arm as she perked up in her seat.

"Gracelyn," Corvaire said slowly. "What did you just say?"

"Your family has the gift of longevity. Oh, and you were mistaken when you said she passed. She's still very much alive."

Ceres and Stone both burst up to their feet.

"Marilyn's alive?" they both said at the same time.

"Yes," she said, looking up at both of them in surprise. "Not a good life she's living in that dungeon of hers, but she's still well and breathing. I can feel it."

"Dungeon?" Corvaire asked, getting to his feet. "My sister is in a dungeon?"

"Sorry," Adler said to her. "We don't have your abilities and we saw her die. Are you sure about this?"

"Absolutely," she said.

"We have to save her!" Ceres said.

Corvaire hung his head in his hands. "She's a prisoner? How has this happened?"

"I loved her too," Adler said. "But we've got to get Gracelyn to Endo first . . . right—? Stone?"

The End

Continued in Book III:
Mages of the Arcane

The Story continues in Mages of the Arcane,

Book III in The Riders of Dark Dragons

In the lands of the Arr to the northeast in the same world, a young girl is kidnapped and trained to become the greatest assassin in all the lands.
Read the Complete Dragon Sands Box Set Now!

All Books Available Now!

Author's Notes

I love writing dragon battles, I'm just gonna throw that out there, ha!

With the connection between our three companions growing solider, they're really starting to find their stride- even with the weight of saving the world on their shoulders.

Stone has become really fun to play with. He's so dedicated to the only ones he really knows, and he even feels love for them. But he sure has seen a lot in his short 'life.'

Ceres is a blast add into the mix, she can be wild and still you get certain sweet points from her. How long has she been out on her own, I wonder?

Adler's growing plot thickens with the Assassin's Guild, which is a growing force in this book, and in future ones.

Gracelyn is an addition I wanted to make to this book to really crank up the stakes- with her strong magic and youthful, small town qualities combining playfully.

I was saddened to see The Wild Majestics die in the first book, and I didn't plan on killing off Marilyn at all, which came as a surprise to me (and my editor, who simply stated, 'Ah, I really liked her!').

But I guess she's still alive!

Taking our heroes deeper into the lands, I wanted to flesh out the environment, and get the leaders of the civil war brought in more.

With the plot thickening, and the stakes getting higher, where will the path of Stone take him? You'll have to find out in the next book, (which I'm still working on the title for, or I would have announced it here.)

Peace friends, C.K. Rieke.

About the Author

Having grown up in the suburbs of Kansas, but never having seen a full tornado or a yellow brick road, he has been told more than his fair share of times while traveling, 'You're not in Kansas anymore.' He just responds, 'Never heard that one,' with a smile.

In the 'burbs' though, he found my passion for reading fantasy stories early. Reading books with elves, orcs and monsters took his young imagination to different worlds he wanted to live in.

Now, he creates his own worlds. Not so much in the elves and orc vein, but more in the heroes versus dragons one- there's a difference, right?

Yes, he grew up with The Lord of the Rings and tons of RA Salvatore books on his shelves, along with some cookbooks, comics, and a lot of video games too.

Other passions of his are coffee, good beer, and hanging around the gym.

To find out more and learn about what he's working on next please visit CKRieke.com.

C.K. Rieke is pronounced C.K. 'Ricky'.

Go to CKRieke.com and sign-up to join the Reader's Group for some free stuff and to get updated on new books!

Printed in Great Britain
by Amazon

23529866R00172